C0-AKC-380

PRAISE FOR CATHY McDAVID AND
THE GATE TO EDEN!

"This book is captivating and totally mesmerizing. The compelling dialogue and intense action drama unfolds making this an extraordinary read. I cannot rave enough about this book! Cathy McDavid pens an outstanding tale that leaves the reader breathless! I could not put this book down. Absolutely great to the last page!"
—Coffee Time Romance

"McDavid's writing stands out...[with] plenty of action and drama....a truly likable and hopeful love story."
—All About Romance

"What a marvelous read....I defy anyone to read this book and stay uninvolved."
—Romance Reviews Today

"The bonds of friendship and love give her story depth, compassion and vibrancy."
—*RT BOOKreviews*

"A great story, *The Gate to Eden* belongs on your book-shelf."
—Roundtable Reviews

"The action-packed story line grips the audience."
—Harriet Klausner

THE PLEDGE

"You're mine," Nick said, his hand fumbling to breech the barrier of her skimpy panties. He gave up and ripped the thin fabric aside. "Don't ever forget that."

"Yes. Oh, yes."

Gillian was hot and wet and so ready for him he thought he'd come right then and there.

"You now know everything there is to know about the creature and my duty to kill him or be killed. There's no going back. If you stay with me tonight, you stay for good. Until the end."

"I'm not going anywhere."

There gazes locked and Nick felt his connection with her grow, solid and sure and unbreakable.

"Good."

Other books by Cathy McDavid:

THE GATE TO EDEN

Night HUNTER

CATHY McDAVID

LOVE SPELL NEW YORK CITY

LOVE SPELL®

July 2007

Published by

Dorchester Publishing Co., Inc.
200 Madison Avenue
New York, NY 10016

ISBN-10: 0-505-52722-7
ISBN-13: 978-0-505-52722-6

The name "Love Spell" and its logo are trademarks of Dorchester Publishing Co., Inc.

Printed in the United States of America.

Visit us on the web at www.dorchesterpub.com.

To Leah Hultenschmidt.
Thanks for giving me the chance
to test my wings with something new.
No pun intended!

Night
HUNTER

PROLOGUE

The portents were small, hardly worth commenting on by the hordes of Diamondback fans converging on Chase Field that warm May evening. A slight rise of temperature. A shift in the breeze. An annoying increase in static electricity. The huge flock of pigeons startled into flight from their roost atop the baseball stadium.

Small signs indeed, but they signaled the beginning of a new cycle.

And once begun, it couldn't be stopped. Not by anyone or anything . . . human or otherwise.

The creature felt a change deep within him and stirred inside the confines of his subterranean cocoon. Without warning, a fiery pain sliced through his entrails, unbearable in its intensity. A scream ripped from his parched throat. Muffled by the thick, protective shell imprisoning him, and layer upon layer of earth, it was heard by no one.

Instinct overruled emotion. He arched his back and pushed with large, powerful feet. Slowly, the surrounding ground began to crumble, then give way. Fresh air rushed in to fill the newly formed cracks and penetrate the cocoon's porous exterior. His nostrils quivered.

For the first time in twenty-five years, the creature breathed.

And smelled.

Hunger consumed him, debilitating him with its voracity and blinding him to all needs save one: He must feed. And soon. Without sustenance, he would quickly die and with him, the future of his entire race.

Calling upon the last of his strength, he made one final, herculean effort. A deafening roar filled his ears. Whether from dirt and rocks falling or the thunderous pounding of his recently reenergized heart, he neither knew nor cared.

His sharp talons pierced the top of the cocoon. In the next instant, the earth above him broke apart. His head emerged through the opening. Shoulders and arms followed. When he could move the upper half of his body freely, the creature hoisted himself from the hole and the leatherlike casing that had housed him for the last quarter century.

Kneeling on all fours, his armor-plated chest rising and falling from his recent exertion, he took a few precious moments to recover from the ordeal of his rebirth and orient himself to his environment.

A city. Yes, he remembered now. Noise. Lights. Automobiles. People. Stench. Memories returned, his own from the year he'd spent in a larvae state before retreating underground, and those implanted in his brain by his parents. He looked around. His compound eyes transmitted a hundred images to his brain, enabling him to see in darkness almost as well as in daylight. Lifting one arm, he flexed his fingers. The six-inch-long, four-jointed digits tingled as blood flowed into veins long ago collapsed from lack of use.

Stiff and sore, he stood awkwardly, holding on to a nearby pillar for support. Grass tickled his scaly skin, reminding him that his mother had selected a place where humans buried their dead for his lengthy hibernation and metamorphosis. She'd evidently chosen well, for he'd awakened whole and mature and undiscovered by potential predators.

Emitting a sound between a squeal and growl, he rotated his shoulders from side to side. Tendons stretched and cartilage shifted. With a loud snap like that of a tree branch breaking, his transparent wings unfolded and expanded to their full fifteen-foot span.

He was ready to hunt.

Disappearing into the encroaching dusk was easy for the creature. His mottled brown coloring provided a natural camouflage, while his wings allowed him to coast noiselessly above the ground.

Within minutes, he scented prey, and the hunger consuming him moved from need to rage. Finding a small stone structure not much taller than himself, he flew to the top, retracted his wings, and huddled behind a sculpted parapet. There, shrouded in darkness, he waited.

His highly developed senses told him what he needed to know. Female. Long past her prime. Small in stature. Feeble. His mind reached out to her, and he learned she'd come to this place to offer tribute to a recently deceased kin.

The creature tensed in anticipation. She'd be easy

to overpower and, though scrawny, would yield enough nourishment to sustain him until the next night when he could feed again.

At last, she came into view, emerging from a small stand of trees. The creature wasted no time, surprise being his greatest weapon. He launched himself from the rooftop, his wings spread wide, and within seconds covered the distance separating him from his prey. She didn't look up until he was directly over her. He could see the confusion on her face as he swooped down and gathered her into his arms. He easily subdued her weak struggle, and carried her back to his temporary hiding place on the roof.

Crouching, he turned her over and laid her across his lap. She still clutched the flowers she'd been holding when he captured her. Fear clouded her eyes, but she didn't shut them. He respected her bravery and decided to honor her with a swift death.

"Are you going to kill me?" she asked in a thin, shaky voice.

He understood her and was pleased that yet another implanted memory had resurfaced. To survive, he would need to speak the language of the humans inhabiting this place.

"Yes, I am." His voice was low and coarse and new to his ears. In his immature larvae state, he'd been unable to vocalize.

"Why?" she asked, tears streaming down her cheeks.

"Because I must feed."

He stroked her wet cheek with one finger, the gesture tender and reverent. Then he lowered his head to sniff and nuzzle her ear. She shuddered in response, her entire body quaking.

"Please," she cried softly.

He obliged her by snapping her neck before biting into her shoulder and tearing out large chunks of her flesh with his needle-sharp teeth. As her life's blood drained onto the rooftop, the creature fed until very little of the old woman remained.

Upon finishing, he rose, unfolded his wings and took flight, careful to keep to the inky shadows cast by the city's skyscrapers. Instinct, old as the beginning of time, drove him. Having fed, he must next find sanctuary. Somewhere he could pass the daylight hours safe from the Huntsman, the human ordained by the Ancients to seek him out and attempt to destroy him in a battle old as the dawn of time.

But before then, the creature must first ensure the continuation of his race. Somewhere in the city, he knew, existed females of his kind. He must find one and mate with her before the Huntsman found him.

The Huntsman came instantly awake and jerked upright in bed. Tossing aside the single blanket covering his naked body, he stood and strode to the window of his third-story apartment.

Come, the Ancients' voices called to him. *Cadamus has roused.*

And the first thing he will do is feed, thought the Huntsman, unlocking the window. It was too late to save tonight's victim, but maybe tomorrow . . .

He no sooner slid the window fully open than thousands of pigeons appeared and soared past, a giant black river gliding through an even blacker night.

"It begins," he whispered to himself.

Cadamus's life would not be a long one, the Huntsman would see to it. But during the creature's short existence, he would embark on a vicious killing spree—just like his predecessor twenty-five years ago.

The Huntsman stood back from the window and shut it, the pigeons having long disappeared. He would sleep no more tonight, and little over the coming weeks.

It was his task, his duty, to destroy Cadamus, destroy him before the creature located a female and reproduced. Since the Huntsman had been a boy of nine, he'd waited and trained for the day the Ancients would call upon him to serve.

And he would not forsake his sacred duty until he succeeded, even if it meant the end of his own existence. For if he failed and the creatures multiplied, the slaughter would be unimaginable.

CHAPTER ONE

"Okay, Celeste. Time to smile pretty for the nice folks watching in TV land."

Nicholaus Blackwater adjusted the lens on his camera, bringing the upper half of TV-7's top-ranked investigative reporter into sharper focus.

" 'Bout time," she grumbled through gritted teeth and positioned the microphone exactly six inches beneath her collagen-enhanced lips.

"Five, four, three, two, one," Nick cued, and zoomed in for a close-up.

"We're just outside the entrance of the Forever in Peace Cemetery where the mutilated remains of an elderly woman were found atop a gardener's house early this morning by a pair of grave diggers."

Celeste's face, the one most watched in the noon and six P.M. time slots, reflected well-practiced hints of shock and concern coupled with the trademark stoicism of any successful TV reporter. Fan mail, both

paper and electronic, poured in daily, most of the
viewers praising her talent for reporting the grisly details of whatever heinous crime she was covering in a
professional, unbiased manner while still conveying
compassion for the victims.

Her reputation, as Nick and everyone else at the
TV-7 News Center knew, was the biggest joke to
come down the pike since Richard Nixon claimed he
wasn't a crook.

Balancing the camera on his shoulder, Nick took a
step backward, then another, as Celeste, whose real
name was Judy Schwichenberg, walked slowly forward, her articulate and evenly modulated voice im-
parting what frustratingly few facts they really had
on the deceased woman.

Keeping her in the left third of the picture, Nick
captured the elaborately crafted wrought-iron gate to
the cemetery in the right two-thirds. Yellow crime
scene tape fluttered in the breeze, holding curious on-
lookers and morbid thrill seekers at a distance.

Suddenly Celeste stopped, looked down, and gave a
shriek of alarm. "God damn it!"

"What's wrong?"

Nick should have turned off the camera but didn't.
He had a drawerful of Celeste outtakes. Once every
few months, when the crew was feeling particularly
snarly toward her, they'd have a late-night private
showing at the station and watch the outtakes. Afterwards, they'd all feel better and less like the pond
scum she was constantly accusing them of being.

"There's fucking dog shit on my fucking four-
hundred-dollar shoes," Celeste screeched. The southern Ohio twang she'd spent years—not to mention
beaucoup bucks—eliminating from her speech had

returned with a vengeance. "Don't they have any groundskeepers at this place?" She glanced around as if one were waiting nearby with a shovel and rake. "What kind of moron takes a dog to a cemetery?" Oblivious of the crowd, she wiped the sole of her shoe on a strip of grass, her lips peeled back in a disgusted grimace. "Oh, ick."

Behind his camera, Nick smiled. Even on his worst days, and today definitely ranked as one of them, Celeste was good for a laugh. "It could have been a stray."

"Screw you."

She'd tried that once already and when Nick turned her down, she'd embarked on a campaign to have him fired. If he hadn't been one of the best news camera operators in the Valley, with the reputation to prove it, he'd have been stuck working at some crummy local cable station for a fraction of his current salary.

Celeste had accepted defeat with minimal belligerence, a rarity for her, and they'd been working together ever since. Despite frequent power struggles, they were a good team, winning a number of awards, local and national.

"Your adoring fans are watching, darling."

Nick's reminder had the desired effect, and Celeste pulled herself together. In the time it took for the red light on his camera to blink once, she stood poised and ready, microphone in place. The whole incident might not have happened except for the bits of grass clinging to her shoe and the slight odor of dog excrement wafting on the breeze.

"And . . . cut," Nick said ninety seconds later when she finished the report. He shut off the camera.

Celeste was instantly on her private cell phone with

her personal assistant, and, by the time they walked the short distance to the news van, she had made two appointments—one with her investment banker and the other with her acupuncturist.

Inside the van, she checked her makeup in a mini lighted mirror while calling Sherri, her administrative assistant at the station, on her business cell phone.

Nick sat in the back of the van at the computer console behind Celeste's seat, adjusting his headset. Hooking his camera up to the transmitter, he sent the footage they'd just shot to the station.

"Heads up, Max," he said into his mouthpiece. "It's coming your way as we speak."

"I got it," Max replied through Nick's earpiece.

"How does it look?"

"Good. Hang tight while I check with the boss. Be right back."

Nick fished a pack of gum from his pocket. Popping a piece in his mouth, he asked Celeste, "Want one?"

She shot him an icy, like-you-don't-know stare. "I have dental implants."

Two minutes later, Bradley McEntee, the assistant news producer at TV-7, came on the wire. "Nick. Get Celeste. I want her included in this."

Nick tossed Celeste the spare headset, earning himself an exaggerated eye roll. She detested wearing anything that mussed her hair.

"Yeah, what is it?" she said once the headset was in place.

"What's with you two? That piece you sent over was pure crapola."

"The police aren't releasing any details." Celeste's soiled shoe held more interest for her than their conversation with Bradley.

"Need I remind you remind our viewership has slipped in the last month. You and Nick get your butts back out there and find something, *anything,* we can scoop KBCB with."

"What have they got?" Nick asked, readying his camera.

"Blood splotches on the outside wall of the gardener's house and Linda Perez's thirty-four-D tits shoved into a size six turtleneck."

Nick's gaze sought Celeste, whose eyes had narrowed to tiny slits.

He had to hand it to Bradley. Their boss knew exactly which of her buttons to push and how hard.

KBCB's recent acquisition had put herself through college by being a regional spokesmodel for a bathing suit manufacturer. Linda's dual degrees and long list of credentials weren't nearly as impressive as her physical attributes. Celeste, still considered tops in the Valley by her peers and fans, had nonetheless begun being compared to the younger, more voluptuous Linda.

It wasn't a comparison Celeste took kindly to.

Ripping off her headset, she tossed it on the floorboard and said to Nick, "Let's go."

"We're on it," Nick told Bradley before removing his own headset and powering down the equipment. Camera in hand, he pushed open the van's side door.

"Follow me," Celeste snapped and set out at a brisk walk.

Nick was only too happy to accommodate her. He'd been wanting a closer look at the murder scene and wondering just how to manage it. Now, because of Bradley, he'd get that closer look under the guise of doing his job.

*   *   *

"Damn rocks," complained Celeste.

Damn your three-inch heels, thought Nick, but wisely kept his mouth shut.

They left the service road and picked their way along the back end of the Forever in Peace Cemetery. Inside the wrought-iron fence bordering the cemetery lay a ten-acre oasis in the desert, resplendent with green grass, sprawling trees, and flowering rose bushes. Outside the fence existed an altogether different world. They trudged across dry, hard ground dotted with small cacti and scraggly weeds. Foxtails and burrs adhered to the bottoms of Nick's jeans like paperclips to a magnet.

Fifty or so yards in the distance, police and other official vehicles surrounded the small gardener's house, obscuring Nick's and Celeste's view.

"Christ, would you look at the cars. We'll never get a decent shot." Celeste grabbed the wrought-iron bars in her fists and pressed her cheeks to the fence, reminding Nick of a child at the zoo hoping for the alligator to stick its head above water.

"Let me try."

Turning on his camera, he panned the area, zooming in as close as possible. Even then, he could see nothing beyond the small fleet of vehicles parked three deep. Just for kicks he took shots of milling police officers and car doors bearing official emblems.

"What've you got?" Celeste asked.

"Zilch."

"Well, shit."

"Wait a second." Nick had spotted a small area of disturbed ground at the base of a tall, leafy oak tree.

There! his mind shouted, his nerves instantly on fire.

Celeste squealed with unrepressed excitement. "What is it?"

"Hold on. Not sure yet," Nick lied.

He actually had a good idea of what the hole in the ground signified, but wanted to see for himself before letting anyone else in on his find, especially Celeste. With luck, the police would be too busy to expand their search of the murder site until tomorrow, giving Nick the chance to come back tonight and investigate—alone.

"Sorry, kiddo." He sighed as if disappointed. "Just a pile of rocks."

"Well, keep looking," Celeste grumbled.

Slowly, Nick moved the camera away from the hole, making wide sweeps back and forth along the manicured lawn. One minute passed. Then two. Celeste's foot started tapping. All at once, something unusual flashed across his line of vision. Sucking in a sharp breath, he inched back along the path his camera had taken until he came upon the object that had caught his attention.

"Son of a bitch," he whispered, fighting to keep his hands steady and the camera from shaking.

"What? What!" Celeste bunched in close to him.

"I think I hit pay dirt." And he had.

"Nick, I'm gonna throttle you if you don't tell me."

Not daring to pull away from the viewfinder and look at her for fear he'd lose sight of his find, he said grimly, "It's a body part."

"Oh, my God!"

He could almost hear her jaw drop.

The camera's soft whir was the only sound to be heard as he filmed the remains of what had once been the elderly woman's forearm.

Under a moving blanket of buzzing flies, bits of stringy tendons clung to a bloody bone stripped clean of flesh. Frail fingers, still intact, one bearing a gold wedding band, clutched a mangled and wilted bouquet of spring flowers. Petals were scattered on the ground around the forearm as if plucked and discarded in a game of he-loves-me-he-loves-me-not.

Nick, his stomach a churning volcano of revulsion, could tolerate no more. He shut off the camera and, leaning a shoulder on the fence, met Celeste's anxious gaze.

"Do you want to see?"

"Of course, you ninny," she snapped and waited impatiently for him to rewind the footage to the beginning.

When she was done watching, she stepped away from the camera, her mouth moving wordlessly, her cheeks a vivid shade of gray beneath her makeup.

"Pretty awful, huh?" Nick asked, his tone kind. He'd been prepared for the gore, at least. Celeste hadn't.

"Yeah," she croaked, pressing a palm to the side of her head and squeezing her eyes shut. "What sort of monster would do such a thing?"

Monster, thought Nick, didn't begin to describe the unholy beast the Ancients called Cadamus and the atrocities he could—and would—commit against his unsuspecting victims.

This poor old woman was only the beginning.

Countless more were destined to die in the weeks to come before Nick located Cadamus and drove the ritual dagger deep into the creature's stone-cold heart.

CHAPTER TWO

Gillian Sayers stared fixedly at the portable TV she'd brought from home, her bouncing right leg hitting the middle drawer of her desk.

"Next up on TV-7 News at Noon," the handsome male coanchor announced from the tiny five-inch screen, "exclusive footage on the elderly woman found dead at a local Phoenix cemetery and what police are calling the most gruesome murder on record in the last twenty-five years. Stay tuned for more on this incredible story."

Twenty-five years, Gillian thought, her heart racing, her head light. Twenty-five long, difficult, and, at times, hopeless years.

Shuffling a stack of test papers she'd yet to grade, she barely listened to a commercial featuring an animated bubble touting a new and improved brand of bathroom cleanser. Since first learning about the elderly woman's murder that morning, her ability to concentrate had dwindled to nonexistent. In truth, she'd been worthless for weeks and constantly on edge, waiting, watching, and listening for any sign of the creature's return.

The dead woman found in the cemetery had to be evidence of it—or so every fiber of Gillian's being told her. The date was exactly as predicted and the similarities to previous murders too astounding to blame coincidence.

Though she was sorry for the victim's family, a small part of her was glad the woman had died. After battling skepticism and mockery for most of her life, Gillian would at last be able to obtain the proof she needed.

How? a voice inside her needled.

She didn't have an answer.

Despite a certain level of expertise in the creature's habits, she doubted she could find it on her own. And even if she did somehow succeed in getting close enough to capture it on film or video, what would stop it from killing her?

She needed help. But who?

Not the authorities.

Been there, done that, she thought. When she was a child, the police had patronized her. After she became an adult, they'd laughed at her theories, calling her a crackpot to her face and worse names behind her back.

The academic world, thank goodness, had treated Gillian more kindly. But then, they didn't know her history. If they did, they, like most everyone else, would ridicule rather than respect her.

A knock on her office door caused her to jerk reflexively. Glancing at the TV and noting that another commercial had just started, she called, "Hello," then groaned softly upon seeing her visitor stroll in and slump into the nearest chair.

"Hey, Professor Sayers."

"Randy." She steeled her resolve. In another thirty seconds or so the news would be back on, and she refused to miss a single second of the broadcast. "I'm sorry, but office hours aren't until three. You'll have to come back."

"Please, Professor Sayers," he cajoled. "I only need a couple minutes."

"You're failing my class, Randy. What can we possibly have to talk about?" Gillian wasn't normally so brusque with her students, but the news had come back on, and the coanchors were discussing the murder. Even listening hard, she could only catch bits and pieces of what they said.

"Is there any, like, extra-credit work I can do?"

"This is college, Randy. Not high school. I'm willing to give you a withdrawal," Gillian said distractedly, her attention on the TV.

"Reporting live from the Forever in Peace Cemetery located in downtown Phoenix," said the female coanchor, "is TV-7's Celeste Todd. Celeste, can you tell us the latest developments in this case?"

The reporter touched the transmitter in her ear and waited a beat before saying, "Well, Rebecca, police are still mystified by the events surrounding the murder."

A red and black banner listing various pertinent information scrolled beneath the reporter while she walked along a wrought-iron fence.

"I read your book, you know."

"What?" Gillian had forgotten about Randy and looked up, surprised to see him still sitting there.

"I read your book," he repeated and nodded at the shelf where her dissertation and two related published works were on display. "You had some cool stuff in there."

Gillian didn't ask him which of her books he was referring to. Only one interested her students and a minuscule fraction of the general public: *Urban Legends—The Psychology Behind These Modern Myths*.

"Thank you," she mumbled, listening to the news and not Randy.

"We understand you have some exclusive footage to show us, Celeste," the male coanchor's voice spoke over a picture of the reporter, now standing in front of the cemetery's main entrance.

Again the reporter waited a beat. "Yes, we do, Doug. This footage was taken just minutes ago. We strongly advise parental discretion, as the images are of a disturbing nature and not suitable for young children."

The scrolling banner echoed the reporter's warning.

Gillian clenched her teeth and held her breath, waiting in both eager and dreaded anticipation for the newscast to continue.

All at once, a bloody severed forearm filled the TV's tiny screen.

Gillian stared, transfixed, her stomach twisting in on itself, the sour taste of bile filling her mouth. She grabbed the front of her desk with both hands to keep from swaying.

Twenty-five years ago, shortly after her seventh birthday, Gillian had seen another severed limb. A foot and partial leg, the flesh gnawed off to the bone, had been lying in the hall outside her parents' bedroom.

It belonged to her mother.

"Professor Sayers. About my grade?"

"What?" Gillian heard what Randy said, but his question bounced off her brain without penetrating.

The news coanchors had moved on to the next breaking story, a four-car collision on the I-17 and Greenway. Gillian inhaled sharply, reminding herself to continue breathing.

"I'm willing to give you a withdrawal. Take it or leave it."

Randy dragged himself out of her office, his hopes for an easy fix to his dilemma dashed.

No sooner did he shut the door behind him than Gillian clasped her shaking hands together and brought them to her chest.

"What now?" she whispered.

Until seeing the elderly woman's forearm on the TV newscast, she'd harbored a tiny seed of doubt behind a thick veneer of confidence. No more and never again.

The creature had returned, Gillian would stake her life on it.

Instead of grading test papers, she booted up her computer and clicked on an icon with the innocuous name of Research Docs. Several clicks later she was reading a scanned copy of an old newspaper article covering her mother's death. She'd memorized the article long ago, but reading it today brought fresh tears to her eyes.

At the time the reporter had penned the article, her father was being held for questioning. Soon after, he was tried and convicted of murdering Gillian's mother.

He wasn't guilty, Gillian knew that for a fact. For she'd seen her mother's killer, might have died along with her mother if not for her father's unexpected appearance at a critical moment. The creature had flown out her parents' bedroom window before the police arrived, leaving her father to take the blame for a crime he didn't commit.

Gillian told the authorities what happened, described the creature in frighteningly accurate detail. No one believed her. Not the police, family, friends, or doctors. They'd patted her on the head and told her how children sometimes make up stories because reality is too awful to accept. In her case, witnessing her father brutally killing her mother.

She'd been waiting twenty-five years for the chance to show them all how wrong they were and to secure her father's release from prison.

One photo, one fifteen-second video, was all she needed. And to get close enough to the creature without becoming its next meal.

Like her mother.

Like that poor old woman last night.

The ringing of her office phone chased away images of severed and mangled limbs from her mind. Wiping her damp eyes, she picked up the handset.

"Professor Sayers speaking."

"Hello," said a female voice. "Is this Dr. Gillian Sayers?"

"It is." Gillian could tell in an instant her caller wasn't anyone on staff or associated with Arizona State University. "Who's calling?"

"Dr. Gillian Sayers, author of *Urban Legends— The Psychology Behind These Modern Myths?*"

"Yes." Gillian tried not to let her growing vexation creep into her tone. "How can I help you?"

"I'm Sherri Hathoway from the TV-7 News Center.

May I ask, Dr. Sayers, have you heard about the woman murdered last night at the Forever in Peace Cemetery? We did a newscast on it a few minutes ago. If you missed it, we'll be repeating it at six o'clock."

Gillian's heart gave a small leap. Could someone else besides her have made the connection?

"I heard about the murder and saw the newscast," she answered cautiously.

"Good." Sherri sounded relieved and happy. "Would you be available for an interview this afternoon? Say, in an hour?"

"An interview?" Gillian's heart gave a second leap, this one into her throat. "What for?"

"Well, ah . . ." Sherri faltered and covered her mouthpiece. Clearly she'd expected Gillian to connect the dots on her own. A moment later she came back on the line. "We'd like to discuss the similarities between this murder and the ones described in your book."

Someone *had* made the connection.

Gillian mentally debated the pros and cons of giving an interview. Would appearing on TV and speaking out about her theories help or hinder her cause? The more people looking for the creature, she reasoned, the better the chance of someone—it didn't necessarily have to be her—finding it and obtaining proof.

But then she'd worked so hard to earn the respect of her colleagues and peers. What if they saw her on TV and thought she was off her rocker? She could lose her credibility.

"Dr. Sayers?"

"Ah, yes. I'm here." Gillian pushed an errant lock of hair from her face. The gesture reminded her of how her father used to tuck her hair behind her ear, when she'd been small. They'd had so little time together.

"About the interview . . ."

Making a snap decision, she said, "An hour is fine. Can you come to my office on campus?"

"Of course!" Sherri gushed. "Celeste Todd, she's the reporter you saw on our noon broadcast, and her camera operator, Nick Blackwater, are on their way."

Gillian jotted down the two names on a notepad. After giving Sherri directions on how to find her office once on campus, she hung up the phone, sat back in her chair, and stared at her computer screen with its blinking cursor.

An interview! Was she crazy?

On impulse, she pulled up her favorite search engine and typed in TV-7 News Center. Dozens of matching Web sites were instantly listed. She went to the official site for the station and, after poking around a bit, found information aplenty on Celeste Todd and Nicholaus Blackwater.

The recipients of multiple awards and accolades, the highly accomplished pair had earned quite a reputation for themselves in the television news industry: Celeste for her investigative reporting, and Nick for his daring exploits in the name of journalism. There was little he wouldn't do, few risks he wouldn't take, to get the shot.

Her interest piqued, she continued searching until she found pictures of Nick. Most were studio head shots of a moderately attractive man with no distinguishable characteristics. Light brown hair of medium length, brown eyes, pleasant features, and a nice, if reserved, smile.

A link highlighted in blue led to another page featuring photographs from a recent awards ceremony where Celeste and Nick were honored for a report they did on gang violence. Gillian studied the photos of Nick accepting his plaque, noting that a tuxedo did amazing things for his looks. Were circumstances different, she'd have appreciated his sexy, lopsided grin and broad shoulders.

Gillian saved the Web page to her list of favorites and closed the Internet, the wheels in her head starting to turn.

She needed footage of the creature to prove her father's innocence. More than that, she needed someone with the balls to rush in there and get the film without regard for danger.

From what she'd just read about Nick Blackwater and his devil-may-care approach to his job, he fit the bill perfectly.

CHAPTER THREE

"Where shall we do this?" Dr. Gillian Sayers eyed Nick's camera as if she half expected it to start shooting a stream of fire at her.

Then again, maybe it was the camera operator she didn't like.

Naw, he decided. It was definitely the camera that made her uneasy. Or, the idea of being interviewed. Him, she found interesting—but not sexy interesting, his bruised male ego reminded him. More like clinical curiosity. Sort of how scientists examine the cancer cells growing on a laboratory rat's tail and ponder the many mysteries.

Given her chosen profession, she probably made a habit of studying people.

"Seated at your desk is fine," Nick told Gillian, already thinking of her on a first-name basis.

No reason he shouldn't. He knew a lot about

Gillian Sayers, PhD, professor of psychology at Arizona State University, thirty-two years old, born and raised smack-dab in the middle of Phoenix. If she ever found out how much and how long he'd researched her, she'd have him arrested for stalking.

Nick perched on the visitor chair in front of her desk, adjusted his camera, and brought her face into focus. Then he zoomed in for a close-up, lingering longer than necessary. She really should sue whoever took the photograph for the back of her book. The grainy black-and-white picture didn't do her justice.

Gillian Sayers was pretty. More than pretty. She was lovely. A tall, willowy blonde, as Charlie, his mentor and teacher, would say. Soft, wavy hair fell to her shoulders. Eyes, dark blue and haunted, looked out from an exquisitely smooth complexion that needed no help whatsoever from Max Factor. Her refined manners went hand in hand with her dignified and conservative style of dress.

Who would guess that beneath such genteel perfection lay a woman with the heart and soul of a tigress?

"Can you move some of the stuff out of the way?" Nick indicated the paper tray, pencil cup, and various other desk accessories cluttering the picture. "Leave that," he said, and she obediently replaced the nameplate she'd picked up. "Good. Makes you appear more credible."

"Do you think I'm not credible?"

The average Joe probably didn't take someone who wrote about winged, flesh-eating creatures seriously. Nick did. He took Gillian very seriously. It was one of the reasons he'd casually dropped her name at the production meeting earlier that day.

"It's not my job to think, Doc."

Their gazes connected, locked, and held fast. Her delicate eyebrows lifted ever so slightly.

Yeah, she definitely found him interesting. And vice versa. If any of his college professors had looked like Gillian Sayers, Nick might've attended class a whole lot more.

Celeste breezed into the office, her plastic smile locked in place. She'd just come from the restroom where she'd wiped the shine from her nose, fluffed the limp from her hair, and yanked the crowbar from her ass. "We ready?"

"Just about," Nick singsonged. "Open the blinds, would you? We could use some more light."

Celeste racheted her plastic smile up a notch. She hated assisting him and made no bones about it. Nick cracked a grin. Whatever hell she'd put him through later for his insubordination was so worth seeing her reduced to performing menial labor.

The blinds swished, rattled, and clacked, absorbing the brunt of Celeste's foul mood. Midafternoon sunlight poured into the office, casting a golden glow on everything it touched, including Gillian.

Nick's breath caught, lodged, and held.

The camera could be a harsh critic. Unkind and unforgiving. Especially in bright light. But it loved Gillian, enhancing her natural beauty rather than magnifying her flaws, of which, from what Nick could see, she had none.

Celeste sat in the visitor chair next to him and fiddled with her wireless microphone. She'd ask the majority of her questions off camera. After the interview, she and Nick would film a segment on the front steps of the building and toss in a few shots from around campus. Back at the station, he and the crew would integrate clips from previous stories and then edit everything together into a mildly informative and definitely sensationalized special-edition piece.

"Shall we begin, Professor Sayers?" Celeste crossed her legs, leaned back, and got into the zone, her features reflecting her changed state of mind.

"Yes, I'm ready."

"Five, four, three, two . . . ," Nick cued and started rolling.

In his viewfinder, Gillian sat at her desk, her folded hands in front of her, her nameplate in the lower right of the picture. The cool, collected demeanor she presented to the camera didn't quite mask her nervousness. A whispery rat-tat-tat from a bouncing leg beneath her desk gave her away.

"We're here with Dr. Sayers, Professor of Psychology at Arizona State University," Celeste said, then went on to discuss Gillian's book, which enjoyed something of a local following among young people. "You have a section, Dr. Sayers," Celeste continued, "about a winged creature that preys on humans. This creature, so the urban legend goes, appears every twenty-five years for only a few weeks, after which it disappears without a trace."

Celeste's normally professional tone contained the barest hint of you-can't-possibly-expect-me-to-believe-this-bullshit.

If only she knew the half of it.

"That's correct, yes." Gillian's leg bounced faster and harder.

"You describe murder victims and scenes which,

on the surface, appear similar in nature to the elderly woman killed last night. Do you think there's a connection?"

"Are you asking me if creatures that prey on human flesh really do exist?"

Nick had to hand it to Gillian. Her deflection was deftly executed.

"Let me rephrase," Celeste said with practiced patience. She didn't like interviewees who gave as good as they got. "How much credence do you put in the urban legends about these winged creatures of the night?"

"Most legends, from Greek mythology to the Lost Dutchman's Mine to Santa Claus, have at least some basis in fact."

"What are the facts regarding these creatures?"

"Not many. Only that there have been at least thirty-two unexplained murders in the past hundred and fifty years, all occurring in downtown Phoenix within a one-mile radius, all involving flesh and organs ripped from the victim's body, and all happening exactly a quarter century apart." Gillian's knee went still, and she stared straight into the camera. "From what I viewed on your newscast earlier today, there is indeed a similarity between the previous unexplained murders and the elderly woman's death."

"Granted, Doctor, a series of unexplained murders are certainly noteworthy, but do you have anything that specifically ties these murders to the creatures?"

Nick muttered an oath under his breath. Celeste was up to something. He quickly switched camera positions and caught her tilting her head in inquiry.

Gillian tilted her head right back at Celeste. "Eyewitness reports, diary entries, stories passed down from one generation to the next, unsubstantiated rumors, and the disjointed ramblings of an old man at the West Valley Mental Health Care Facility."

"Any photographs? Videos? Home movies?"

"No."

"All these years and no one has ever managed to snap so much as a Polaroid of these creatures?"

Gillian's mouth twitched slightly. "Unfortunately not."

"I see," Celeste said, her catlike smile one of satisfaction.

Celeste was obviously attempting to make Gillian appear like a nutty professor rather than a respected, albeit unconventional, academian. Yet one more mark against his coworker.

"There are also references to the creatures in various Native American folklore," Gillian added.

"Are you referring to the Wendigo?"

If Celeste thought to show off, her plan fell flat.

"The creatures of Phoenix urban legends are nothing like the Wendigos. To start with, the Phoenix creatures have the ability to fly, though not to great heights, and are silent predators. The Wendigos of Native American folklore are wingless and reputed to make loud noises, crashing through brush and foliage. Also, Wendigos are forest dwellers. Their habitat stretches across a large number of states. The creatures I refer to in my book are city dwellers, indigenous to downtown Phoenix. A very small area of downtown Phoenix." Gillian pointed a finger in the air as if she just remembered something. "Oh, and they don't appear as characters on any of those vampire-slayer, witch-sisters, or demon-hunter TV shows."

The notoriously unflappable Celeste chewed her bottom lip.

Interviewee one, reporter zero, thought Nick.

Gillian sighed. She'd clearly reached her limit of fun and games for one day. "I didn't make up the urban legends, Ms. Todd. I simply wrote a book on the psychology behind them. And though I don't claim the creatures are real, there are those who would beg to differ."

She's seen one.

The knowledge that Gillian had witnessed a creature firsthand came to Nick with such certainty, his fingers clenched, causing the camera to jiggle.

He should have recognized the haunted look in her eyes. It was the same one he'd seen reflected in the mirror twenty-five years ago when Cadamus's predecessor had killed Nick's family in front of him—and would have killed him, too, if not for a fortunate turn of events.

Suddenly, everything Nick had read or heard about Gillian's childhood took on new meaning, including what her father had told Nick about her. But William Sayers, it now appeared, hadn't been entirely honest when Nick had visited him in Florence Prison.

Why?

While Celeste asked a few closing questions, Nick played out an alternate scenario in his head, one where Gillian's present occupation and keen interest in the urban legends stemmed from her actually seeing the creature kill her mother and not what her father had told her.

It was possible.

No, likely.

And if true, it would fill in a lot of the missing pieces.

"Thank you, Dr. Sayers, for agreeing to see us on

such short notice." Celeste extended her hand across the desk to Gillian, who graciously accepted it.

"When will this be aired?"

"Tonight, I'd say." Celeste turned to Nick for confirmation. "The nine o'clock edition. That is, if we use it."

"We'll use it," Nick said, turning off the camera. And he'd make damn sure they edited the piece in such a way as to compliment Gillian.

When he glanced up, it was to find Gillian staring at him, her lips parted. The hand at her throat slowly uncurled, and her fingers toyed with the intricate gold chain circling her slender neck.

Nick went suddenly still as a surge of desire shot through him, white hot and intense and not entirely unexpected. He'd been aware of Gillian for years. Aware, hell, he'd studied her closely. She was a beautiful woman. It was natural for him to feel an attraction.

But the emotion gripping Nick at that moment went way beyond attraction. On his end, anyway. Whatever Gillian was feeling, she didn't let on.

What he wouldn't give for a chance to shake up the unshakable Dr. Gillian Sayers.

Several wordless seconds ticked by during which Nick's mind wandered and explored the many tantalizing possibilities, all of which involved tangled bedsheets and lots of naked skin.

"You ready?" Celeste stood by the door.

"Ah . . ." Nick nearly bit his tongue in two. "Not quite." Leaving wasn't an option, not while he sported the granddaddy of all hard-ons.

"Nick." Celeste dragged his name out over three syllables and marched toward the door.

"Yeah, coming." He cleared his throat and rose on

embarrassingly unsteady legs. "Thanks, Doc," he croaked and cradled his camera in the crook of his arm.

Busy replacing the desk accessories she'd removed earlier, Gillian lifted her head and gave him a brief nod. "Good-bye, Mr. Blackwater."

Obviously, it hadn't been as good for her as it'd been for him.

Oh, well. Maybe afer he killed Cadamus and things settled down a bit, he could change that.

CHAPTER FOUR

Gillian cruised past the TV-7 station just as a parking space became available. Praising her good fortune, she pulled in, shut off the ignition, fed the meter four quarters, then climbed back in her car to wait for Nick.

Double-checking the car door locks, she slouched deeper into her seat and lowered her cap to cover her face. She wasn't as much afraid of being spotted by Nick as leery of the occasional pedestrian passing by. The station might be located in one of the better downtown neighborhoods, but there were still enough weirdos, gang members, and disreputable characters roaming the streets to give her a case of the willies.

This is no place for a woman alone at night.

The idea that had seemed so good an hour ago now struck her as ludicrous. Nick had no reason to help her. He didn't know her, hadn't met her before today, and she hadn't exactly charmed him during the interview.

However, while he was readying to leave, she'd felt a connection to him she couldn't explain. A very sexually charged connection that she suspected went both ways. It had left her reeling long afterward and prompted her to decide against enlisting his aid in finding the creature. What she needed was a partner, a collaborator, a talented journalist with a penchant for unearthing great stories. Not a marginally cocky, though admittedly good-looking, camera jockey whose brash stare had sent small shivers of awareness dancing along her spine.

Watching the nine P.M. newscast had changed her mind.

Despite Celeste Todd's attempts to discredit Gillian, the segment had been pieced together to present Gillian as a knowledgeable authority on urban legends and Celeste Todd as a professional reporter concerned with uncovering the truth about the old woman's murder. Gillian credited Nick and his editing skills for sparing her reputation.

So, in a roundabout way, he'd already come to her rescue once. He might be willing to help her again.

Immediately after the interview, she'd booted up her home computer and tried to find his address. Forty-five minutes later, she resorted to the phone book and then dialed information. Every avenue she attempted ended with the same disappointing results.

Trying a different route, she'd called the TV-7 station. The night operator told her Nick was still there but unavailable, and forwarded Gillian to his voice mail. She hung up without leaving a message, threw on some old clothes, and jumped in her car. The questions she had for Nick needed to be asked in person.

Now, sitting in her car, waiting for Nick to get off work, Gillian began to rethink her impulsiveness. Her actions smacked too much of a third-rate private investigator trailing an adulterous spouse. Then again, she reminded herself, desperate people such as herself did impulsive things—like approaching a virtual stranger and asking for his help.

Her nagging inner voice shut up the second Nick stepped outside, a spring to his step. He was clearly in a hurry. Gillian fumbled with the key, finally started the car, and shoved the transmission into reverse.

Rather than head to the nearby parking garage, Nick set out on foot in the opposite direction.

"What the . . . ?"

Gillian leapt out of her car, her blood pumping like a freight train, fed the meter a few more quarters, and took off after Nick.

Careful to maintain a discrete distance, she followed him three blocks to a small strip center housing several shops and a sports bar, which, judging by the raucous crowd and blaring wide-screen TVs on every wall, was a favorite with baseball fans.

He didn't go in.

Hugging the side of the building, Nick went around back and climbed a set of stairs to a third-story exterior walkway. Gillian ducked behind a bus stop shelter. From her hiding place, she watched him enter what appeared to be an apartment.

A light came on. Seconds later another light came on in a different room. His bedroom? Gillian glanced at her watch. Ten twenty-three. Late, yes, but he hadn't yet gone to bed. She could still go up there and knock on his door. It seemed absurd to have come all this way, gone through all the trouble of finding him, then chicken out.

Odd, she thought, glancing around and getting her bearings, he didn't live far from her. They'd walked the almost half mile from the TV station to his apartment. Her condo was a half mile north of here. The new high-rise had replaced the low-income housing where Gillian had lived as a child—the same place her mother had been killed.

After her father's sentencing hearing, Gillian entered the foster care system and left the inner city behind, only to return twenty-one years later when she landed a teaching position at Arizona State University. Her colleagues called her crazy for buying a condo so far from campus. They didn't understand Gillian's compulsion to be at the center of the creature's domain, and she had no intention of telling them.

Would Nick understand? Or would he laugh in her face and tell her to start seeing a psychologist rather than be one?

Gut instinct told her he'd at least listen to her.

A young man joined her at the bus stop. His creepy stare was all the incentive Gillian needed. She stuck her hand in her purse, wrapped her fingers around the can of Mace she always carried, and headed toward the strip center. A second look confirmed the young man wasn't following her, and she breathed a tad easier.

At the unexpected sight of Nick coming back down the stairs, she lost her nerve, panicked, and scurried toward the sports bar, blending in with a group of exiting patrons.

"Idiot," she muttered, then called herself a few more choice names when he strolled past the bus stop shelter where only a minute before she'd been standing.

Deciding she was through playing amateur detective for the night, Gillian bumped past a tipsy couple arguing about which one of them was more fit to drive home and struck out again—not after Nick this time, but back to her car.

The same direction Nick was taking on his late-night stroll.

He carried a leather bag over his shoulder, she noticed, and had changed clothes. The baggy jeans and holey T-shirt he wore to the interview had been replaced with not-so-baggy black jeans and a long-sleeved black shirt that molded to muscled shoulders, torso, and arms suitable for the cover of a fitness magazine. There was also something different about the manner in which he carried himself. Still in a hurry, he moved with the grace and agility of a well-trained athlete.

This Nick was completely different from the one who'd come to Gillian's office. Observing his strong, confident strides, her long-dormant appreciation of the opposite sex came instantly awake. As some of her female students would say, Nick Blackwater was a hottie, and Gillian would have to be blind or dead not to respond.

Where did a guy go at ten-thirty at night, dressed like that? A date, she supposed, or one of the many clubs in the area. But there was something more functional about his clothing than dressy. An assignment? They were headed back toward the TV station.

Gillian periodically jogged to keep up with Nick,

though why she bothered escaped her since she'd abandoned the notion of talking to him, at least for tonight.

At the next intersection, he abruptly turned the corner onto First Street. Wherever he was going, Gillian mused, it wasn't the station.

She approached the corner and stood. Continuing straight would take her to her car. In a matter of minutes she could be having her customary cup of herbal tea and grading the last batch of test papers before hitting the sack.

Yet she couldn't force her hand to reach out and press the "walk" button on the lamppost.

Realizing it made little sense, she started down First Street, hot on Nick's heels.

He turned another corner, and Gillian's heart kicked into a higher gear. She knew his destination! The Forever in Peace Cemetery. When he made for the back end of the cemetery and not the front gate, her curiosity rocketed. Nick wasn't on assignment, leastwise not an official one. If he were, he'd have brought his camera.

Gillian quickened her steps only to lose him.

One second he was a hundred feet ahead of her, the next second, he vanished. She broke into a run. Whatever Nick was up to, she wanted to know. At the entrance to a service road behind the cemetery she skidded to a stop.

Nick was nowhere to be seen.

Where had he gone? She stared down the dirt service road, which was tucked between the cemetery and a municipal building the length of a city block. Overhead security lights from the municipal building, while dim, provided sufficient illumination for Gillian to make out a person, even one dressed in black. Had he gone into the cemetery? She regarded the seven-foot wrought-iron fence, the posts of which came to nasty-looking sharp points, and decided he had to be somewhere else.

Go home! her sensible inner voice advised. *A woman was murdered here last night.*

The streets were bad enough. To venture down the cemetery's service road was just inviting a mugger or some other attack. But her greatest threat came from the creature.

This was his hunting ground. Her condo, once the site of her childhood home; Nick's apartment; the TV station; the cemetery—all were situated within the boundaries of the map in Gillian's book.

Coincidence? She doubted it. Just as she doubted the connection she'd experienced with Nick was simple, spontaneous lust.

Steeling her resolve, she advanced a step, then two. The service road loomed ahead, seeming to stretch endlessly. Would venturing down it lead her to danger or the answers she'd been seeking the last twenty-five years?

Taking another step, she slid her hand into her purse, needing both the can of Mace and the small measure of comfort it would provide. Her fingers inadvertently brushed the digital camera she'd recently started carrying.

If she wanted proof of the creature's existence, then, like Dorothy braving the Wicked Witch's castle to steal the broom, Gillian would have to put herself in jeopardy.

Concentrating on her father, on how old and tired he'd looked during her last few visits, she increased her pace, her eyes constantly scanning for Nick . . . or something else.

Shadows, in shades of dark and darker, alternately grew and shrank as Gillian progressed. Ten feet. Twenty feet. Something swished on the ground beside her foot, and she momentarily freaked. The lizard or mouse or whatever it was scurried away, leaving Gillian with her knees knocking, and her chest on the verge of exploding. She felt downright foolish.

If she were this afraid of a tiny animal, how would she react if she saw the creature?

Nearby city noises—a siren wailing, tires squealing, people shouting, and rap music playing from an open window—reminded her that if something bad were to happen, help wasn't far away.

Oh, God! Had she charged her cell phone last night? Gillian ripped it from the carrying case clipped to her belt. Three bars glowed brightly on the display, and her previously knocking knees wobbled with relief.

Pulling herself together, she replaced her phone, removed her camera from her purse, and hung it around her neck. In the damp palm of her right hand she held her can of Mace. How much protection would it afford her if the creature were to suddenly swoop down and overtake her? Some, she hoped.

Probably not as much as the Taser she'd purchased a few weeks ago. But she hadn't brought it with her tonight because she hadn't thought she'd need it.

Gillian continued her journey, reminding herself that cowardliness wouldn't free her father from prison.

Thirty feet. Forty feet. Fifty feet. Still no sign of Nick, and yet, he had to be close by. No one could vanish that completely.

She remained tense and alert, though she became less fearful the longer she went without seeing the creature—and less optimistic she'd obtain her proof. Frustration at losing Nick turned to disappointment. He'd probably used the service road as a shortcut, not gone on a secret news assignment.

This time, when her inner voice advocated going home, she listened. Tomorrow she'd contact Nick through more conventional means, if she were still inclined. Her little adventure tonight had stolen much of the wind from her sails.

A narrow beam of light from inside the cemetery brought her up short. Unlike the stationary ones shining onto various monuments and headstones, it zigzagged.

A flashlight?

Gillian stared, blinked, and stared some more. The light remained, now moving in a circle. Grave robbers? Kids using the cemetery for illicit activities? A homeless person searching for a place to bed down for the night? The police investigating the old woman's murder?

Nick doing his own investigation?

The next instant, the light went out.

Gillian decided not to stick around, and headed back the way she came, glad to be leaving the cemetery behind. She'd accomplished nothing tonight save scaring herself. No discussion with Nick. No encounter with the creature. Not even any research for her next book.

Behind her, a bush rustled. Gillian's steps faltered, and she instinctively turned toward the disturbance. When, after several seconds, nothing more happened, she swung back around.

And came face to face with a tall, dark figure.

Gillian screamed and raised her arm.

Before she could fire the Mace, the can was yanked from her hand and dropped to the ground.

"Careful with that," a man's voice said. "You might hurt someone."

Not pausing to think, she lifted her right leg and kicked her assailant in the shin. Hard.

"Hey!" He didn't so much as flinch.

She kicked him again with such strength her toes cracked.

"Relax, Gillian. It's me."

Me?

The cloud of fear and confusion surrounding her brain began to dissipate.

"Nick?" she asked, her voice pitifully weak.

"Yeah. Are you all right?"

Her? What about him? He should be hobbling around, holding his injured leg.

He cupped her shoulders with his hands, the gesture more comforting than menacing. And impossibly familiar.

"I'm fine." She resisted succumbing to the purely feminine reaction of leaning into him. "What are you—"

"Later." Not giving her time to respond, Nick pulled her along with him back down the service road. "We need to leave now."

Her toe throbbed, and she struggled to keep pace with him. "Slow down!"

He paid her no heed. Only when they reached the street did he stop. By then, Gillian was huffing and puffing as if she'd run a marathon. Nick looked fresh as a daisy. She straightened her rumpled clothing.

"You okay?" he asked, his hand still on her arm.

She didn't attempt to remove herself from his grasp. "Yes."

"It's not safe here." He peered over her head, back the way they came, and tensed, his fingers tightening ever so slightly.

She eyed him curiously. Nick knew something about the old woman's murder, she was sure of it. Something he wasn't telling.

"What were you doing in the cemetery?"

"Checking out the murder scene."

"Oh." So he *had* been on assignment.

"What about you?" His tone held a trace of mirth. "Do you always take late-night walks in cemeteries?"

"I'm . . . ah . . ." She hesitated, the speech she'd mentally prepared on the drive to the station having fled her mind.

Still holding her by the shoulders, he waited for her to answer. She should push him away, she thought, a frown tugging at her mouth. Establish a safety zone between them. Their contact, while not precisely intimate, disrupted her equilibrium and jammed her thought processes.

"Gillian?" he prompted.

She swallowed and blurted the truth. "I came looking for you. I followed you here from your apartment."

If her admission surprised him, he hid it well. "Why?"

"I need your help."

There. She'd said it. And the sky hadn't fallen. Gillian waited for his ridiculing laughter or uncomfortable withdrawal.

All that came was a simple, "I see."

When she would have pulled back, Nick lifted a

hand to cradle the side of her head. He stroked her hair with the tenderness of a lover.

Gillian went still, but more from his next words than his bone-melting caress.

"You've always had my help. You just didn't know it."

From high in the branches of a tall oak tree, Cadamus watched the Huntsman and his mate leave the place where humans buried their dead.

"Fool," Cadamus growled but not with displeasure. His first encounter with his enemy had revealed much, all of it to his liking.

The Huntsman was weak. Careless. Easily distracted and stupid. While he'd been examining the place of Cadamus's rebirth and the pieces of torn cocoon not carried away by dogs, Cadamus crouched among the foliage overhead. Not once had the Huntsman looked up or even cocked an ear.

"*This* is the warrior the Ancients have chosen to fight me?"

Cadamus's blood burned with a fury passed down from countless generations. It commanded him to attack and engage in battle before the Huntsman disappeared from sight. Through sheer force of will Cadamus resisted. Though he felt he could have easily overpowered the so-called human warrior, he couldn't risk it until he'd found a female. He, too, was distracted by the need to procreate. Instantly, Cadamus's loins began to ache.

He'd fed earlier tonight. The young human, his mind in an altered state from smoking a narcotic plant, had been easy to kill. With one hunger sated, the other took precedence and drove Cadamus from his hiding place.

Turning to face the breeze, he scented for a female. With his highly developed olfactory nerves, he could detect the pheromones they emitted from a hundred yards away. To his disgust, only the stench of humans and their foul waste reached his nostrils. No female was nearby, which meant Cadamus must expand his territory beyond the human burial ground and sanctuary he'd discovered in the basement of an abandoned building across the street.

A dangerous but necessary undertaking.

The city had changed greatly during the last quarter century, and the memories implanted in his brain by his parents weren't reliable. Cadamus would have to depend on strength and cunning to survive.

And survive he would.

Before launching himself into flight, he cast a last look at the Huntsman. Wrapping an arm around his mate, the Huntsman drew her to him, protecting her from the loud, smoking machines the humans called automobiles.

Cadamus would have never abandoned the search for his enemy to protect a female, especially one so frail and helpless.

Cadamus reveled in his superiority over the Huntsman, and his confidence soared. This cycle, he would prevail, defeat his enemy, and be revered for eternity as the founder of his race.

"Live, Huntsman," he said and spread his wings to catch a warm current of air. "Live well and to the fullest. For soon you will know what it is to die."

CHAPTER FIVE

"You like cappuccino?"

Nick's smile was warm and friendly and kind of sexy if a woman went for the boy-next-door look. Definitely not the smile of a deranged killer.

So, Gillian told herself, she had nothing to worry about. Right? Deranged killers didn't smile like the boy next door.

"I . . . ah . . . yeah."

"Good. Me, too." He returned to the counter, opened a cupboard, and reached inside. "I only have instant, if that's okay with you."

Little did he know he'd earned major points with her just by having cappuccino, instant or not.

"You're not one of those metrosexuals?" she asked, studying his kitchen and the adjoining living room, both the size of a shoe box and neat as a pin.

"Do I look like a metrosexual?" He filled a neon orange teapot with water and set it on a tiny three-burner stove to boil, then removed a pair of ceramic mugs with delicate Chinese lettering on the sides.

"You didn't this afternoon in my office but now . . ." She shrugged.

In a flash, his smile changed from boy next door to bad boy, and Gillian's heart somersaulted.

"I'm confident enough in my masculinity not to have to flaunt it."

Observing him from beneath lowered lashes, she couldn't disagree. There was, she'd begun to suspect, a whole lot more to Nick Blackwater than met the eye.

Were circumstances different, if the creature were dead and her father a free man, she might be interested in peeling back Nick's many layers one by one. In fact, as she admired the way his shirt stretched across his broad back, she had a sudden and uncharacteristic urge to peel off his clothes as well.

The teapot whistled, and Nick busied himself with preparing their coffees. A minute later, he set a mug in front of her, its frothy contents nearly spilling over the top. "Don't suppose you're ready to tell me what you were doing at the cemetery tonight?"

He dropped into the seat across from her, and the already small dining set shrank to the size of dollhouse furniture. To avoid bumping knees, Nick stretched his right leg out alongside her chair.

Gillian tried not to feel trapped. "Yes, well, I guess you're wondering about that."

"A little."

Tracing the lettering on her mug with a fingernail, she thought fast and hard and opted for a partial truth before coming clean. "I was doing research for my next book."

He sipped his cappuccino and when done, wiped off the residual creamy mustache with the back of his hand. Gillian's guard slipped a notch despite her resolve not to let it.

"Personal or professional research?" he asked.

How much did he really know about her, she wondered, then chided herself. If she planned on enlisting his aid, she'd have to trust him. And who better to trust than a man with pretty mugs and zero fear factor when it came chasing down a story?

"Both. Personal and professional." The cappuccino, while not great, was hot and went down smoothly. She tipped her mug at him in a gesture of appreciation. "Thanks, by the way."

"Do you think the creature killed the old woman? Is that why you were at the cemetery?"

She phrased her reply carefully. "I don't have an opinion on the creature one way or the other."

"Quit with the bullshit, Gillian." Nick's tone and amiable expression didn't match his harsh words.

"I beg your pardon?" She strived to appear affronted.

He didn't fall for her act. "You said you wanted my help."

"Did I?" Taking another sip of cappuccino, she retreated behind her mug.

"Yes, you did. And to get it, you're going to have to level with me."

"I thought I already had your help. 'Always had.'" She peeked at him over the mountain of froth. "What exactly did you mean by that?"

"Let's not get ahead of ourselves." He leaned forward, rested his forearms on the table, and stared straight at her.

Or was it through her? Gillian gripped her mug, and the pesky shiver she thought she'd banished danced through her again.

"Tell me what you know about the creature and what you want with it," Nick said, "then we'll negotiate the terms of my help."

"You talk as if it's real."

"Real is subjective, depending on the per—"

"Now you quit with the bullshit," she said pointedly.

Nick arched his brows, considered her for a moment with that intense stare of his she remembered from her office, then said, "Fair's fair."

Gillian nodded and waited for him to elaborate, her stomach churning. She blamed her queasiness on the strange events of the last two hours. Late-night walks in cemeteries, highly charged encounters with a man she'd just met, and discussing the creature—all tended to wreak havoc on her equanimity.

In retrospect, returning with Nick to his apartment had been a mistake. But she'd been unnerved and he'd been solicitous and anything had sounded better than walking back to her car alone.

Would she ever start looking before she leaped? When he said no more, she rose and contemplated calling a cab on her cell phone. "It's getting late, and I still have papers to grade."

"Wait." Nick put a hand over hers. "Don't go yet."

Soothing warmth seeped into her skin. She wavered, caught him gazing at her, and was held fast by his sinfully dark eyes, which were as full of promise as they were danger.

The longer she stared at him, the less she felt like leaving. Eventually, the need to escape vanished altogether. When she resumed her seat, he leaned back, still scrutinizing her and still holding her hand.

Gillian caught herself conducting a mental inventory of her appearance and put an immediate stop to it. Like she cared what Nick thought of her.

Don't you?

"All right," he said, apparently reaching some sort of decision. "We'll take turns. I'll start, you finish. But be warned, you're not getting out of here until you tell me what it is you want from me. Understood?" He applied a slight pressure to her fingers.

Gillian swallowed. "Understood."

"You're not the only one who's seen the creature."

"I never said I saw it."

He shot her a warning glance. "No bullshit, remember?"

A shudder went through her, one of recognition. "You've seen it, too."

"Twenty-five years ago. When I was a kid."

"Oh, thank God."

Relief rendered Gillian weak, and she buried her face in her hands. Finally, here was someone who had seen the creature and wasn't residing in a mental heath facility or otherwise unbalanced. Nick could speak at her father's next parole hearing. Between his testimony and the video or photos he'd take for her, her father was sure to be released.

This must be what he meant when he said she'd always had his help.

"You okay?"

She lifted her face to him and sighed. "Yes."

Only when Nick reached out and cradled her cheek with his hand did she realize she was crying.

"Sorry." She drew back and averted her head, inadvertently planting her lips squarely in the center of his palm.

At the intimate contact, a jolt of electricity shot through Gillian, and she inadvertently gasped. Nick withdrew his hand, though not quickly and not before she accidentally tasted him with the tip of her tongue.

A wave of heat rolled over her, leaving in its wake a jumble of sensations too confusing to separate, much less understand.

Gillian sat, frozen, flushed with embarrassment, and more turned on than she dare admit. Tucking a stray lock of hair behind her ear, she debated crawling under the table or better yet, bolting for the front door.

What in God's name was happening to her? Ever since she met Nick, it was as if she'd become a different person—she thought differently, acted strangely, and felt a whole new range of emotions foreign to her.

"Gillian."

"I don't make a habit of going home with men I hardly know," she said firmly, lest he jump to the wrong conclusion about what happened. "And I . . . don't . . ."

"French-kiss their palm?" Nick finished for her.

"This isn't funny."

Pressing a hand to her forehead, she sighed. Could anything else go wrong tonight?

"If it helps," Nick said with a chuckle, "I enjoyed it. Though I think I'd enjoy it more if you aimed for my mouth next time."

"Believe me, there won't be a next time." She opened her eyes, only to be confronted with his and the hunger smoldering in their near-black depths.

Apparently she wasn't the only one turned on.

"Any chance we can keep our options open?" he asked.

Something in her expression must have revealed the horror she felt, for he patted her hand and said, "Relax, okay? I was joking. Well, half-joking," he finished on a weak note.

"It's my fault. I haven't been myself the last few weeks."

"Cadamus does that to a person."

"Cadamus?"

Nick drank some more of his cappuccino. "That's the name of this generation's alpha male. The one you and I saw when we were kids was called Radlum."

"The creatures have names?"

Gillian struggled to wrap her mind around the startling information Nick had imparted and subsequent implications. Names implied a sense of self, unique personalities, higher thinking, social structure, and language—all things that put the creatures on a level with man.

Dear God in heaven!

"Don't look so shocked," Nick said. "They're beings. Just not human. I'm unsure about the females, whether they have names or not."

"Females?"

None of her research had ever indicated the creature's sex and whether or not there were more of them on the loose.

"Yeah, three. They're about half the size of Cadamus and extremely reclusive, hiding in back alleys, sewer drains, any place small, dark, and isolated. Which makes them difficult for Cadamus to find, but not impossible. They emit pheromones, similar to a woman's, but stronger. That's how he locates them."

"And once located, he mates with them." Gillian was so preoccupied with Nick's descriptions of the creatures, she forgot about her embarrassment over their semi-kiss.

"Yes. Reproduction is fundamental to every living organism. Cadamus and his kind are no different."

The thought of offspring turned Gillian's stomach to lead.

"On the plus side," Nick continued, "the females don't eat people."

"What do they eat?"

"Dogs and cats mostly. Read the newspapers and watch the news. Petty soon here you're going to hear about a strange increase in missing pets.

"Because the newly hatched female creatures are feeding?" Gillian grimaced.

"Better cats and dogs than all four of them eating people," Nick said. "Dozens will fall victim to Cadamus by the time he dies. At least one person a night."

The researcher in Gillian emerged, allowing her to temporarily set aside her revulsion. She'd frequently speculated on the creature's peculiar cycle and brief appearances. "Why do the creatures have such a short life expectancy?"

"Actually, they live twenty-five years. They're born as larvae. Then, after a year, they bury themselves deep in the ground and undergo a metamorphosis. Twenty-four years later they emerge as mature adults."

"Wait a minute." Gillian sat back and studied him with renewed interest. "How do you know all this?"

She'd been so enthralled with what Nick was saying, it only now occurred to her to ask where he came by his information. He could be a quack; she'd met enough of them while conducting her research. And while Nick appeared mentally stable, looks were often deceiving.

"Then how come no one's ever discovered them as larvae before?" she went on without giving him the chance to answer her first question. "Aren't they rather large?"

"Not as large as you'd think, given their adult size."

"Still . . ."

"They're nocturnal."

"And reclusive."

"Very."

"I assume the larvae are herbivores?"

"You assume correctly."

"Like locusts?" Gillian said, recalling her basic biology class from college.

"There are similarities but also differences. Big ones. Diet, which you already know about, and size. Alpha males stand around five feet tall."

"Is that all? I remember . . . Radlum, did you say? . . . as being gigantic." Had she really just called by name the creature who murdered her mother?

"Their wings are huge, making them appear larger than they are. And you were a child. A very scared child. Your perspective was distorted."

"True." Gillian's voice trailed off as she relived that horrific night in her parents' bedroom.

"Alpha males also have the ability to speak."

Gillian was instantly yanked back to the present. "They talk?"

"English, in fact. As far as I know, the females are mute."

Of everything Nick told her, this was the most

amazing . . . and the scariest. Primitive language she could accept, but English? "How is that possible?"

"The alpha males form a psychic connection with their prey. Also with the females. It's one of the ways they pass information to each other. Another is implanted memories."

"Through suggestion?" Gillian asked.

"More like chemical transfer from parent to offspring. And language isn't all they've gleaned from us. Each new generation uses the information assimilated by the alpha males and adapts accordingly. It's what's enabled them to survive for millennia in a constantly changing environment."

"Survive but not thrive," Gillian speculated out loud. "How come there aren't more of them?"

Nick shook his head. "You and I made a bargain. I've kept my end of it and then some. You haven't."

"Surely if the creatures had lived—"

"Why are you here, Gillian?" His tone reflected the stubborn set of his jaw and prompted her to ponder what had come over him so suddenly.

Since he had, as he'd pointed out, kept his end of the bargain and then some, she swallowed the dozen questions waiting to be asked and mentally changed gears from researcher to subject.

"You're stalling," he said.

"No, I'm not. Really."

Asking for his help had ceased to intimidate her. He shared a common interest in the creatures with her, had obviously studied them in great detail, and would likely pounce on the opportunity to film one— if he wasn't already planning to do just that. A photo op would explain his late-night visit to the cemetery, except for the missing camera.

"I'm here because . . ." Gillian pressed her fingers
to her lips. *Please, please, let this not be a mistake.* "I
could use your assistance with a problem I'm having."

"I won't be a part of your next book, if that's what
you're going to ask."

"It isn't."

His eyes narrowed.

"I promise."

He waited for her to continue, a tapping foot the
only sign of his impatience.

Discussing her father wasn't easy for Gillian, and
something she seldom did. Not because she was
ashamed, but because people tended to look at her
cooly and treat her differently once they learned
about him—which had resulted in one or two awk-
ward relationships and ended one or two more.

Oh, hell, if Nick blew her off tonight, at least she
didn't have any emotional investment.

"My father is serving a life sentence in Florence
Prison." She waited for Nick's face to register shock
at her revelation. When it didn't, she cautiously continued. "For murdering my mother."

"I know."

"You do?"

"I'm sorry. That must be very hard on you."

Nick spoke kindly, and for once, Gillian didn't feel
ostracized. Here was someone who understood her,
had seen what she'd seen. Someone she could talk
openly with and not fear any negative repercussions.
A lifetime of pent-up frustration and tenuously held
self-control broke free.

"He didn't kill her. The creature did. Radlum."
The words, so reminiscent of those she'd spoken to
the police twenty-five years ago, came out in a rush.

Nick, unlike the police, didn't smile patronizingly, pat her on the head, and roll his eyes when he thought her back was turned. He wouldn't because he'd seen Radlum, too.

She sank deeper into her chair, feeling herself unwind. Well, wasn't spilling one's guts what kept many a counseling psychologist in business?

"All the other urban legends are just an excuse," she said. "My main focus is and has always been the creatures."

"Has writing about them eased your pain or added to it?"

"I don't know." Gillian frowned. She'd asked herself the same question repeatedly and had yet to come up with a satisfactory answer. Steering their conversation back to the topic at hand, she said, "I didn't follow you to the cemetery because I wanted to discuss my writing."

"You followed me from the TV station to my apartment and then to the cemetery."

Gillian's jaw went slack. "You saw me?"

"A piece of advice for future reference. Don't wear a yellow shirt when following someone. Not unless you want to stick out like a sore thumb."

"Why did you pretend not to notice me?"

"What? And take all the fun out of it?"

Gillian sighed, disgusted by her ineptitude. "So much for being clever."

"Plus, I was curious. I wanted to see what you were after." The humor lighting his eyes dimmed. "What are you after, Gillian?"

"Proof of the creatures' existence."

"For your next book," he said flatly.

"To free my father from prison."

"You're not serious." He sat up so fast the table shook.

"His next parole hearing is in two months. I can't be certain but I believe the judge will grant his parole if I provide proof of the creatures' existence." A pressure built inside Gillian's chest, making breathing difficult. It took her a moment to identify the source of the pressure. Hope.

"You think waving a photo in front of a judge will free your father?"

"A video of the creatures would probably be better." A number of people Gillian interviewed had taken pictures of the creatures. For some mysterious reasons, all the photos were lost or damaged. "Maybe one of those heat sensor cameras. Or better yet, physical evidence. Skin. Hair. Do they have any? Whatever, as long as the samples can be DNA tested."

"You'll be laughed out of court."

"No, I won't." Gillian's assurance held fast in spite of Nick's pessimism.

"Yes, you will. Except for a small cult following, nobody believes in the creatures. You'll be lucky if the judge doesn't charge you with contempt of court."

"That's where you come in."

"Me?" Nick raised an eyebrow.

"You're an award-winning camera operator." Gillian leaned forward to compensate for the distance he'd put between them. "If you shoot the video of the creature, no one will doubt its authenticity."

"Forget it!"

Gillian didn't let his objection stop her momentum. "Coupled with your testimony, the judge is bound to be swayed."

"My testimony?"

"The video alone may not do the trick but you—"

"No." Nick stood, grabbed the two empty mugs, and headed to the kitchen where he dropped them in the sink.

She went after him. "Wait."

"I said no. End of discussion."

"Please." Tears stung Gillian's eyes, and she tried to blink them away. "My father's not well. I don't know how much longer he can tolerate prison life before his health is seriously affected."

Nick rinsed out the mugs and set them in the drainer to dry. "I feel bad for the both of you. Your father especially. He doesn't deserve to be in prison for a crime he didn't commit. But I can't get involved."

"Why not? Are you afraid of ruining your reputation? Because exposing the creatures will make your name a household word?"

"There's a whole lot more at stake here than you can possibly imagine, the least of which is my reputation."

She grabbed his arm and swung him around to face her. "Don't you think the public has a right to know about Cadamus and that you, as a member of the news profession, have a duty to tell them?"

"I'm well aware of my duty and am trying my damnedest to uphold it. Aiding your cause, touching as it is, will only result in catastrophe."

"More so than letting Cadamus run amok? He's on a killing spree. You said so yourself. At least one death a night." She stepped closer. "He can be stopped. Lives can be spared. And not just my father's."

"You don't understand."

"You're right. I don't understand." Her hand

climbed his arm to clutch his shoulder. "How can you allow this monster to murder innocent old ladies? Innocent young mothers?"

"I'm going after Cadamus." His muscles tensed beneath her fingers. "Just not the way you want me to."

"And you're doing this alone?" She remembered the cemetery and the zigzagging flashlight beam.

"Like I said before, I have a few resources."

"Not like the police. Or even the army. They have high-tech weapons they can use to locate and destroy Cadamus."

"Don't talk to the police," he said sternly. "Don't talk to anyone. Christ. What's next? The CIA?" He raked a hand through his hair, leaving the front rumpled.

It didn't, Gillian noticed, detract from his good looks.

"I was thinking of NASA. Cadamus and his kind could be aliens for all we know."

"Weren't you listening? They've been around for tens of thousands of years."

"The Smithsonian, then. The creatures are living dinosaurs."

"Somehow I don't think even the Smithsonian would know what to do with a serial-killing prehistoric beast. You'd have better luck with the police."

She responded to his stinging sarcasm with some of her own. "I burned my bridges with them years ago."

"Trust me, that's not a bad thing."

"But they'd listen to you."

"I doubt it."

"They would if you presented them with a video of Cadamus."

"I can't." There was no compromise in his voice.

"You mean you won't."

"Can't, won't, it's irrelevant."

Gillian tried guilting Nick into acquiescing. "You said you'd help me."

"You're asking for more than I can give." He turned away in order to hang the dish towel he'd been using on the oven door handle.

Then the tension got to Gillian and something inside her snapped. Giving free rein to her irritation and disappointment, she said, "Anyone ever tell you you're a pigheaded, obtuse—"

He whirled on her so abruptly she stumbled and might have fallen if not for his arm snaking around her waist and hauling her hard against him. The gasp she uttered died on her lips when he bent his head and spoke softly into her ear.

"I've been called worse and by women a whole lot meaner than you."

"Why am I not surprised?"

Common sense dictated she be afraid. Scared for her life. They were three stories up, directly over a noisy bar. Her screams would fall on deaf ears.

But the only thing scaring Gillian was her body's instantaneous reaction to Nick's proximity and whether he'd notice.

Could he hear her heart beating faster and faster? Feel her breasts, full and aching and straining against the confines of her bra? Sense her insides turning to liquid as his breath tickled the fine hairs at her temples?

The same familiarity she'd experienced when he cradled her cheek during their tryst on the cemetery service road returned. Impossible, she thought with the tiny portion of her brain still able to function.

Yet when he walked her backwards and pinned her

between the counter and his six-foot-plus frame, her arms encircled his neck as if she'd done it a thousand times before.

"You shouldn't have come here tonight," he said, his mouth dangerously close to hers.

She stood on tiptoes, reducing the distance between their lips to mere millimeters. "Why? What are you going to do?" She quite liked the scent of him, liked his arms locked around her waist even more.

"Explore those options we were keeping open."

"I'm willing if you are," she said, marveling at her newfound ability to flirt.

He exhaled and tightened his hold on her, a completely unnecessary precaution as she wasn't going anywhere anytime soon. "Don't take this the wrong way, but you shouldn't get involved with me. I'm not who you think I am. *What* you think I am. And there's a hell of a good chance I'm going to break your heart."

"Who said we're getting involved?"

"A guy can always hope."

His lips connected with hers, light as a whisper and soft as silk. Gradually, he applied more pressure. Not fast enough to satisfy Gillian, however.

The more control he exercised the more control she lost. Her tongue sought entrance to his mouth, her fingers tangled in his hair, and she aligned her hips with his so his erection nestled snugly in the junction of her legs.

Would he be this calculated, this precise, during sex? Demand she savor each step to the max before moving forward to the next? The idea of tumbling into bed with Nick, exploring every inch of his body with bold strokes and hungry kisses, filled her with delicious anticipation.

Dear Lord. She had truly gone over to the dark side.

They'd been acquainted less than twelve hours and already she was contemplating having sex with him. That was a first. She hadn't slept with a man she just met since . . . come to think of it, she'd never slept with a man she just met. Lengthy dating periods followed by discussions about contraceptives and sexually transmitted diseases was more her style.

Thankfully, lucidity returned.

It didn't last.

Nick's tongue delved deep into her mouth, his hands snuck up the back of her shirt, and his fingers made contact with her skin, sending shivers of delight coursing through her from the top of her head to the tips of her toes.

Gillian sighed. He brought out the worst in her, no question about it.

"You feel so damn good." His hands glided around her middle to encase her ribs while his mouth nibbled a path down the column of her neck. "And taste so damn good."

Hardly hearing his words over the roar in her ears, she urged him on by leaning her head back and saying his name.

All at once it felt as if the floor had dropped out from under her feet. Gillian let out a gasp. It took her several seconds to realize Nick had lifted her up.

Evidently not as much in control as he'd led her to believe, he sat her on the counter, shoved her knees apart, and, with a low groan emanating from deep in his chest, executed a little hip aligning of his own.

Gillian locked her legs around his waist and dug her fingers into his hair, pulling his mouth up for another kiss and another rocket trip to the moon.

"I can stop if you're not sure about this," he said in a ragged voice when they paused briefly for some much needed oxygen.

He would stop, too, she instinctively knew it. Just as she knew he wouldn't hurt her, not intentionally, despite his earlier warning about breaking her heart. He cared for her, and she cared for him. They shared a connection that went beyond lust, beyond the creatures. Gillian didn't understand it and didn't need to. Even dyed-in-the-wool psychologists could accept that some things just were.

"Don't stop," she breathed. *Not yet. Not for another four or five hours.*

He obliged and picked up where he left off. Nudging aside the opening of her shirt, he pressed his lips to the base of her throat. Her nipples peaked in readiness when he reached for the buttons on her shirt, fumbling in his haste to unfasten them.

"Nick, I want—"

Before she could complete her sentence, the front door flew open.

Gillian gasped and involuntarily twisted, narrowly avoiding hitting her head on a cabinet. Nick stepped back, putting himself between her and his visitor, the expression on his face one of resignation.

"Hello, Charlie," he said.

Charlie? She peeked over his shoulder into the living room to see a very old, very distinguished-looking Native American gentleman enter Nick's apartment.

"Hello, Nick." He smiled pleasantly and inclined his head in Gillian's direction as he hobbled toward them. "Dr. Sayers. It's an honor to finally meet you. I'm a big fan of your book."

Gillian covered her eyes with her hand and muttered an unladylike, "Oh, shit."

CHAPTER SIX

Nick gave Gillian credit. She handled herself with aplomb in what had to be an incredibly embarrassing situation.

"Gillian," he said after lifting her off the counter, "this is Charlie Blackwater."

Thank goodness the old geezer didn't try to shake her hand. Physical contact with a person who'd just walked in on you twenty seconds away from baring your breasts would test anyone's limits.

"Blackwater?" She smoothed the front of her hastily rebuttoned shirt. "You're related to Nick?"

"My father," Nick answered before Charlie could elaborate. Telling Gillian about the creatures was one thing. About himself, another. The Huntsmen were a surreptitious lot and with good reason. Anonymity was the key to their success.

"Really?" Gillian's eyes widened an infinitesimal amount.

Someone else mightn't have noticed. Nick did. He noticed everything about her, most of which was seared into his memory.

"Foster father," Charlie corrected, the many wrinkles lining his face shifting when he smiled. "I'm no blood relation to this rascal, for which I'm grateful."

"That makes two of us," Nick joked in return.

All three moved into the living room. Charlie made himself comfortable on the couch, his bones creaking as he lowered himself onto the cushions.

"I took him in and raised him after Radlum killed his family," he said with a grunt.

Gillian spun on Nick. "You didn't tell me Radlum killed your family."

"I didn't get around to it."

"I noticed the not getting around to it part when I came in," Charlie commented from the couch.

"I'm truly sorry, Nick. How . . . who . . . ?"

"Both my parents and my baby sister."

"Oh, God."

The sorrow in her voice evoked emotions in him he thought long buried if not dead. "Thank you. But it was years ago."

And he'd exact his revenge. Soon. Or die trying.

"It seems we have yet something else in common."

Nick nodded, feeling the commonality on a level that surprised him. He'd always suspected Gillian was special, he just hadn't figured on her becoming special to him. "I should probably take you back to your car."

Something had happened, something bad, else Charlie would be home in bed. Which meant Nick had a full night's work ahead of him and didn't need any distractions.

"Yes," Gillian agreed, retrieving her purse from the end table where she'd left it earlier. "I still have papers to grade."

"I saw the interview on the news tonight," Charlie said, stalling Gillian's departure. "Well done."

"I forgot to thank you for the excellent editing job," she told Nick. "I was expecting the interview to be awful. Celeste can be a little intimidating."

"A wolf in sheep's clothing if ever there was one," Charlie concurred.

"You're welcome," Nick said as he took Gillian's elbow and guided her toward the door, eager to escape before Charlie got his hooks in her any deeper.

They'd disagreed from the start on how much to involve her in their activities. Charlie thought she'd make an excellent addition to the team. Nick had insisted on stopping at the interview.

After tonight, he was more determined than ever to keep her clear of Cadamus *and* the Huntsmen. The risks were great and too numerous—to her, to him, to the entirety of humankind. When the creatures were dead and life had returned to normal, he'd finish what he and Gillian had started tonight.

"How'd it go at the cemetery?" Charlie asked before Nick and Gillian took two steps.

"Fine." Nick didn't break stride.

"Did Cadamus show up?"

He ground his teeth. Damn Charlie's infuriating wiliness. His arthritic joints might be shot to hell but his mind stayed razor sharp.

"Cadamus was there?" Gillian dug in her heels.

"Yes," Nick grumbled.

"And you didn't tell me?"

"I didn't see the need for it. You were already scared."

"Where was he?"

"In a tree."

"How far away?"

"From you? About a hundred feet."

"Cadamus was a hundred feet away from me and you didn't see the need to tell me?" Gillian's eyes flashed, more with fear than anger. "That's why you hustled me out of there so fast. Isn't it?"

"Very noble of you," Charlie said with obvious amusement. "Putting her safety ahead of your duty."

Nick shot Charlie a dirty look before returning his attention to her. "You weren't in danger, not immediate danger anyway." He squeezed her arm. "I wouldn't have let him harm you."

"Like you could have stopped him."

Nick didn't mention the ritual dagger stuck in the waistband of his pants. Other weapons had the ability to destroy Cadamus, but only his dagger guaranteed man's future on Earth. "He's not invulnerable. If he were, his species would number more than four."

"And he'd already fed by then," Charlie added. "He won't be hunting again tonight."

"Who was it?" Nick demanded, momentarily forgetting his mission to drag Gillian out of there. "And when?" This was the reason for Charlie's unexpected visit.

"A fifteen-year-old Hispanic boy. Right across the street from the cemetery. His death will probably be attributed to a gang slaying."

"Cadamus's sanctuary is nearby. He'll stick close to it until he becomes familiar with the city."

"That's my guess."

"What are you guys?" Gillian's brows drew together. "Some sort of special forces?"

"Concerned citizens." Nick propelled her ahead, hoping to reach the door before Charlie butted in.

"Do you work for the government?"

"Actually," Charlie pushed himself to his feet, the effort costing him, "we work for a higher authority."

"Higher than the government?"

"Charlie," Nick cautioned.

"I want to help," Gillian insisted.

"Impossible."

"I know a lot about the creatures."

"She does," Charlie added.

"More than what I've put in my books."

"Is that so?"

Gillian recognized an ally when she saw one. Removing her arm from Nick's grasp, she moved away from the door to stand near Charlie. "I don't know what you two are up to or who you work for, but if it means ridding the world of that monster, count me in."

"No!" Nick bit out.

"There are no coincidences," Charlie said, his gentle tone contrasting Nick's angry one. "She was put in your path for a reason."

"It isn't to help us."

"The final battle is yours to fight, son, but we've never operated alone. Not entirely."

"Final battle?"

Nick ignored Gillian. "She has a personal agenda."

"Don't we all?" Charlie shrugged.

"She wants to expose the creatures in order to free her father from prison."

"I see."

"She thinks she can obtain his parole with proof of the creatures' existence."

Charlie patted Gillian's arm. "I'm afraid Nick is right. We can't allow you to help us if your goal is to expose the creatures. Their existence must be kept secret at all costs."

"What if I agree to help and not expose them?"

"The answer's still no," Nick said.

"Why?"

"We're not at liberty to explain," he cut in before Charlie could answer.

"You don't trust me?"

"I can't trust anyone right now."

She hid her hurt well but not so well Nick didn't see. He remained immune. He couldn't afford not to.

"Dr. Sayers, why would you forsake your purpose in order to help us?" Charlie, the old softie, asked.

"Retribution," Gillian said with no emotion whatsoever.

"Ah." Charlie gave Nick a pointed look.

Nick felt like punching a hole in the nearest wall. Gillian had given the one answer he couldn't refute.

Gillian read the lost-dog notice taped to the No Parking signpost, the third such notice she'd come across in the past hour. With each vehicle that shot past, the corners of the flimsy paper fluttered in the breeze. It was a miracle the thing hadn't flown off to collect in the gutter along with the rest of the trash.

Beneath a description of the missing pet was a poorly reproduced photograph. Banjo, a six-month-old beagle mix, had been missing for six days.

The same number of days since Gillian and Nick had entered into their uneasy partnership.

He didn't want her working with them, whoever *them* was. For nearly a week she'd spent each evening with Nick and Charlie, and she still had no idea who employed them or if they were freelancers.

Nicholaus and Charlie Blackwater, Creature Hunters, Inc.

And she, the lowly gofer. Lowly being the key word. While she searched for lost-pet notices, Charlie, clearly the brains of the outfit, ran command center, and Nick, the apparent brawn, chased down creatures.

Gillian opened the portfolio she carried, withdrew an enlarged copy of a city map, and marked her location with a red pen. She'd gone through this same drill with each notice they'd found. Eleven lost pets in all. How many other cats and dogs had become dinner for the female creatures besides these eleven? Strays without a bereft owner sitting by the phone, praying for their return? Gillian shuddered to think.

Standing in the circle of light cast by a street lamp, she studied the map in her hands. Three pockets of activity had begun to emerge, separated by roughly six city blocks. Potential hiding places for the female creatures?

Nick had told her they were going after the females first. Half the size of Cadamus and significantly weaker, they would be easier to kill. Also, according to Nick, no female creatures equaled no procreation and no future generations. It might mean a few more deaths in the short run, but in the long run, they could conceivably wipe out the creatures for good.

Gillian didn't dwell on the extermination aspects of their operation. In spite of her tough talk about retribution, she was squeamish when it came to taking life. Any life, be it human, animal, or *monster*.

Replacing her map in the portfolio, she strolled north on Second Street. A block away, music blared, drawing hordes of fans to US Airways Arena like ants to a discarded soda can. The entertainer headlining that night's sold-out concert performance wasn't Gillian's favorite, but he could sure pack 'em in.

No one paid her the slightest heed. Nick had planned it that way, saying he couldn't have arranged a better cover. Police officers on foot and bicycles were too busy controlling traffic and people to notice a lone woman reading lost-pet notices and a lone man prowling back alleys, doing God knows what, and not checking in with her every fifteen minutes *like he was supposed to*.

Gillian unclipped her cell phone from her belt and called Charlie at Nick's apartment.

"Hi," she said when he answered. "It's me."

"What do you have?"

"Lost dog. First Street and Jefferson."

"Got it."

She waited in silence, knowing from the routine they'd established the previous three nights that Charlie was entering data into his computer and running some probability or GPS program. For a guy pushing eighty, he was amazingly talented when it came to sophisticated technology.

"Where's Nick now?" he asked after a minute or so.

"Your guess is as good as mine." Worry took the form of annoyance and sharpened her voice. She inhaled slowly to counter the effects. "He hasn't called in almost half an hour."

"I just talked to him ten minutes ago. He was right around the corner from you, behind the old Hanson Building at Jefferson and Central."

"Great," Gillian grumbled and stared down the street. She'd been walking in the opposite direction and was now three blocks from Nick. Damn him for not checking in.

Why was it he could check in with Charlie and not her? She immediately chided herself for letting Nick get to her again. It was she, after all, who'd insisted on working with him and Charlie even in the face of Nick's adamant objections. The two of them were a team and she the interloper.

"I've got to go," she told Charlie.

"Call me with anything new."

And she would. Unlike Nick.

Darting between enthusiastic concert attendees, she headed back the way she'd come. Diners enjoying the various specialty restaurants in the area spilled onto the sidewalk, adding to the confusion.

Despite her resolution to stay cool, Gillian's frustration with Nick escalated as she neared his last known location.

One of the more annoying drawbacks to having a PhD in psychology was possessing the ability to pinpoint the real reason for her irritability—which had nothing to do with Nick's lack of responsibility and everything to do with the emotional barriers he'd erected during the last six days.

He kept their conversations to a minimum, avoided her if possible, and visibly tensed when avoidance was impossible. Not that Gillian was the high-maintenance type who required constant reassurances, but his sudden withdrawal hurt. Even if she did understand it to a degree.

They'd have been "doing it" if not for Charlie's fortunate arrival, or unfortunate depending on her current mood.

No, wait.

"Doing it" was hardly an apt description.

If his toe-curling, sigh-inducing, I-didn't-know-it-could-be-like-this kisses were any indication, making love with Nick would have been the stuff of pure fantasies.

Not to mention probable disaster.

Though she hated to admit it, he'd been right to slam on the brakes, even if his approach was a little abrupt. Too much, too soon, would only complicate things. In the best interest of everyone concerned, they needed to stay focused on Cadamus, eliminating him and the females, and saving lives.

Mind-boggling sex could come later—if at all.

Another blast of hot air slammed into Gillian as a delivery van sped by in the hopes of beating a taxi to the next red light. Pushing her disarrayed hair from her face, she glanced up to see the old Hanson Building half a block away, its twenty stories set against a typically gorgeous orange and pink Phoenix sunset.

The building had once been headquarters to a savings and loan company that went belly up in the late seventies. A string of tenants came and went, and the building slowly fell to ruin. Five years ago an ingenious developer riding the revitalization wave converted the two bottom floors into a mini-indoor mall that catered to the six-figures-a-year-income crowd. The remaining eighteen stories were turned into condominiums. The top floor consisted of two penthouse apartments, one of which was owned by the reigning forward guard for the Phoenix Suns.

Gillian tried calling Nick again. No surprise, he didn't answer. Wouldn't government agents—or whatever he and Charlie were—own more sophisticated communication devises? Bluetooths at least. She hadn't completely given up on trying to convince Nick and Charlie to go to the authorities for assistance. And if she played her cards right, she still might even be able to free her father.

With renewed purpose, she jogged to make the green light and crossed at the intersection, coming to a stop directly in front of the entrance to the mini mall. Bright shop lights and elaborately decorated store windows with the latest, hottest fashions beckoned her to come inside. She resisted their siren call and instead walked the building's perimeter.

On the north side she discovered a delivery entrance discretely placed between two palm trees in cement planters. Wide enough for a single vehicle, the entrance appeared to lead to a small underground garage. Gillian debated going down into the garage and searching for Nick.

Taking her cell phone out yet again, she dialed his apartment.

"Hi, Charlie, I'm at the Hanson Building." She wished a bit of the easy camaraderie she enjoyed with Nick's foster father would rub off on her and Nick. "There's no sign of our wandering boy."

"He's having a look around inside."

"You've talked to him?"

"A couple minutes ago."

"I see."

She must have let a small note of disappointment creep into her voice for Charlie asked, "Are you okay?"

"Fine," Gillian said, conveying a cheeriness she didn't feel. If they had any hope of working together, she would have to get past her hurt. For her father's sake if not hers. "Where did you say Nick was?"

"He visited a few of the shops, pretending to be a representative of the management company, and questioned the staff. Seems they complained at length about a rat problem."

"Rats?"

"No one's seen any, but lately they've heard scratching and scurrying behind walls and in the ceilings."

"Do you think the noise is from one of the females?"

"Possibly. The Hanson Building sits dead center of the target zone. Realistically?" He released a loud exhale. "My money's on rats."

"How can I help?"

"Just stay put and wait for Nick."

"I'm capable of doing more than locating lost-pet notices, you know."

"Nick already has enough on his hands. He doesn't need any trouble."

"Trouble?" Gillian sniffed. When had she ever been trouble?

"Sorry. Poor choice of words."

"I took a self-defense class last summer at the YMCA. And I have Mace."

"Uh-huh." Charlie's distracted reply led Gillian to believe he was paying more attention to his computer than her.

Determined to prove herself a worthy team member, she blatantly defied orders and approached the delivery entrance. Passing potted palm trees, she picked her way down the ramp. In the blink of an eye she traded the dusk of early evening for semidarkness. The temperature dropped with each step she took, which, while kind of creepy, was a welcome relief from the eighty-five-degree heat.

"Wait by the main entrance outside the shops," Charlie told her. "If anyone comes snooping around, call Nick. The tenants might not buy into his act and contact the police."

"He's not presently taking my calls," she said, distracted.

"Text message him."

Gillian tried to picture a police officer patiently waiting for her to finish text messaging Nick before interrogating her. When she told the police officer why she and Nick were conducting an unauthorized, not to mention illegal, search of the premises, he'd arrest her on the spot for trespassing.

No, better to enter the bowels of the building and find Nick. Then, if one of the shop employees did call the police, he could do the explaining.

At the bottom of the ramp, she paused to get her bearings. To her left were about thirty or forty parking spaces, most of them occupied with cars or motorcycles. To her immediate right was an elevator and beside it a steel door with STAIRWAY marked in stenciled lettering. Mounted above the door was a glowing red exit sign.

Good advice that Gillian chose not to heed.

Straight ahead stretched a long, narrow corridor with security lights positioned every fifteen feet, their yellow bulbs giving off a dim, fuzzy glow. More steel doors lined both sides of the corridor, each marked accordingly. Phone room, electrical room, maintenance room, and so on. A large storage bin of some sort jutted out from the entrance to the corridor, partially blocking the entrance.

"Gillian, are you still there?"

At a loud burst of static, she pulled the phone away from her ear. "Yeah, Charlie, I'm here."

Glancing about, she gnawed the inside of her lip. In spite of the eerie gloom, the garage appeared harmless enough. So why the strange tingling sensation pricking the back of her neck?

Drawn to the security lights in the corridor and the safety they represented, she inched forward. In her ear, Charlie's crackling voice issued orders. She understood only every third word—something to do with rats. Or had he said pets?

"Charlie. You're breaking up." Interference from the ten zillion pounds of concrete above her head, but she didn't tell him that. "I'll call back in a few minutes."

She snapped her phone shut, then stopped to survey her surroundings. If she were Nick, where might she go to investigate a pest problem?

To the farthest, darkest corner of the garage, she supposed.

A terrible smell assaulted her nostrils, becoming stronger the closer she got to the corridor. What Gillian had mistaken as a storage container was, in reality, an industrial-sized trash Dumpster and the source of the terrible smell. In front of the Dumpster on the bare floor lay two or three torn plastic garbage bags, their contents strewn haphazardly.

"When's collection day?" She made a face and kicked an empty milk jug out of her path. It inadvertently slammed into the Dumpster, and the ensuing racket echoed off the concrete walls. She started and let out a gasp.

"For crying out loud." Feeling utterly ridiculous, she crossed her arms over her waist and waited for her frayed nerves to calm. "If there are any rats in the vicinity, I think I just scared them off."

She turned and when her arm inadvertently brushed the Dumpster, she sprang away and examined her exposed skin for any clinging debris. There was none, thank goodness. She wiped her arm on her pants just to be on the safe side and promptly walked into an invisible wall of stink.

"What the . . ." She drew back, her hand covering her nose and mouth, and retched.

The really disgusting odor turning her stomach inside out, she realized, wasn't coming from the Dumpster but the trash chute in the wall next to the Dumpster.

She crept forward, stuff too icky to think about crunching beneath her shoes. She grabbed the handle on the trash chute door and pulled it open. Bags of trash tumbled forward, and the smell nearly knocked her to the ground.

"Oh, shit!"

She pushed on the trash chute door but to no avail. The bags blocked the opening. Her eyes began to water, and she blinked back tears while struggling to breathe through her mouth.

"Close, damn you." Putting her full weight into it, she pushed harder . . . and jammed the door's mechanism so that it would neither close nor open. "Great. Just great."

Her thirst for adventure fully slaked, Gillian decided to return to her "post" and leave the creature-hunting to Nick and Charlie. She was clearly in over her head, helping not in the least, and probably smelled as bad as the trash chute.

She swung around just as a ding sounded and the elevator doors swished open. Nick? Her heart unconsciously leapt at the prospect.

A smartly dressed woman emerged and headed toward the parked cars, her high heels clicking on the concrete floor. Without thinking, Gillian crouched behind the Dumpster and peered around the corner. She had no wish to be spotted this late in the game.

After a cursory glance over her shoulder, the woman continued to her car, the horn beeping and headlights flashing when she activated her remote key device. Climbing in behind the wheel, she wasted no time leaving. Tires squealed as she crested the ramp at a speed exceeding safe limits. Gillian didn't blame her. She couldn't wait to get out of the garage either.

Bracing a hand on her knee, she started to rise—and caught sight of a small, brown, fuzzy rodent under the Dumpster. Before she could move, it scampered between her legs.

She let out a short scream and shot to her feet, dancing as if she were walking barefoot on hot coals.

The rat disappeared. Where to, Gillian didn't know or care. She worried there'd be more where that one came from and released a pent-up breath when none appeared.

Shaking from head to toe, she leaned against the wall, giving her wobbly legs a moment to recover.

God, she was *such* an idiot. What possessed her to think she could go it alone? Never again would she complain to Charlie about the grunt work he and

Nick threw at her. Lost-pet notices beat smelly garbage and rats any day of the week.

Feeling a bit steadier, Gillian set out.

She took no more than a single step when the lid to the Dumpster popped open. Something—a hand?—shot out and grabbed the back of her shirt.

CHAPTER SEVEN

Gillian screamed again, louder and longer this time, and twisted wildly in an effort to break free. The hand let go, only to seize her by the hair and jerk her off her feet.

Still screaming, she regained her balance and slapped at the hand. The fingers tightened their hold.

"Let go of me!" Grabbing her attacker's wrist, she dug her nails into the flesh.

Cold, hard, bumpy flesh.

Gillian's next scream died in her throat. Who, or what, had hold of her?

Adrenaline flooded her system by the bucketful. Driving her thumb into the pressure point on the underside of her assailant's wrist, she squeezed with all her might. To her relief, the fingers loosened a fraction. With her other hand, she fumbled for the can of Mace in her pocket.

Pain radiated along her neck, back, and arms. She fought it, instinct overriding fear.

The fingers abruptly released her hair. Gillian lifted her head and blinked, dizzy from the ordeal. A split second later the Dumpster lid flew all the way open, banging into the wall. She yelped, her paralyzed vocal cords once again functioning.

Before she could make a run for it, something definitely not human hurled itself at her, hissing angrily. Spittle, wet and slimy, struck her in the face as long, sticklike fingers closed about her neck.

She thrashed from side to side, gagging on the foul smell. Her last thought before she hit the ground was that she'd die not from asphyxiation but from the stench.

Her shoulders absorbed the brunt of her fall, saving her from certain head injury. Something heavy landed on her chest. A body? Through a veil of tears she saw a face straight out of a sci-fi movie, with eyes black and round and impossibly huge. The mouth hung open, revealing twin rows of razor-sharp teeth. Above the mouth were two small holes where a nose should have been.

Gillian pummeled her attacker, her fists connecting with a hard, flat surface smooth as sheet metal and just as impenetrable.

In the furthest recesses of her mind she realized she'd just found one of the female creatures . . . and it very much wanted to choke the life out of her.

Gillian was no match for the creature, which, while the size of a ten-year-old child, possessed twice her strength. Her lungs on the verge of exploding, she clawed at its hands, hoping to puncture its thick hide.

When that failed, she attempted to dislodge the creature by bucking like a madwoman.

The open mouth with its pointed teeth hovered inches from her face, the foul breath affecting Gillian less and less as survival took precedence. Lifting a leg off the ground, she tried to shove her knee into the creature's backside and knock it off balance. She encountered only empty air. In retaliation, the creature squeezed doubly hard.

Time was running out. Her vision dimming and strength ebbing, Gillian made one last effort to reach her can of Mace. The creature's legs, locked firmly around her waist, blocked her probing fingers.

"I don't want to die."

Had she spoken the words out loud? Gillian wasn't sure. Very little made sense as her oxygen-starved brain shut down cell by cell.

An image of her mother floated before her eyes, taking the place of the creature's hideous face. How tragic, thought Gillian with an odd lack of emotion, that she should die in a manner so similar to her mother.

She'd been just seven the last time she saw her mother and, sadly, her memories had faded over the years. But this smiling visage was crystal clear, perfect in every detail, and . . . speaking to her.

"Hold on, baby, just a tiny bit longer. He's coming."

Gillian wanted to ask who was coming but nothing except a weak wheeze passed her lips.

A shadow crossed in front of her mother's face, becoming darker until blackness consumed Gillian's entire field of vision. And with the blackness came freedom from pain. Her lungs no longer burned and the excruciating weight around her middle lightened.

Her tranquility was cut short by a yell that came from everywhere at once. In the next instant—or perhaps longer, Gillian's concept of time was distorted—the female creature was gone.

She gulped. Air invaded her lungs, searing them like liquid fire. Coughing uncontrollably, she rolled onto her side and hugged her middle. Her throat ached, inside and out. Her ribs, too. Rivulets of liquid spilled down the sides of her cheeks and neck. Tears, or perhaps blood?

Her coughing fit eventually subsided, and she became cognizant of her surroundings.

She wasn't alone.

The female creature was still there—Gillian could hear it hissing, smell its stench. Someone else was also there. The sounds were too confusing for her to decipher, but she thought there might be a struggle taking place.

Her breathing, though ragged, had begun to slow to a rate resembling normal. She tried to sit up and was hit with a wave of intense nausea. Putting a hand out to brace herself, she encountered the Dumpster and scooted over to lean on it.

An athletic shoe landed next to her leg. A man's athletic shoe, thank goodness. Gillian's fuzzy gaze traveled upward. Leg. Butt. Back. Head.

She knew him.

"Nick?" she croaked.

He swung around, and she saw he had the female creature by the neck, holding it at arm's length. Hissing and screeching, it flailed its long, spiderish limbs. Nick jerked backward, narrowly missing being slashed and kicked.

With his right hand, he reached for the waistband

of his jeans and withdrew an object. Gillian squinted, bringing the object into focus . . . and froze.

He had a knife. A really big one. With a shiny gold handle.

With the cry of a warrior, he raised the knife and plunged it into the female creature's chest.

A hoarse, agonizing scream filled the garage. Gillian's, not the creature's.

It convulsed for a few seconds, then went limp, hanging from Nick's grasp like a raggedy stuffed toy. He let go, and the creature landed in a heap on top of the discarded garbage.

Gillian stared in mute shock, her heart knocking against her bruised lungs. Nick bent down and removed the knife. There was, she noticed, not a drop of blood on it. He replaced the knife in the waistband of his jeans, then knelt beside her and pulled her into his arms.

"Gillian, honey, are you okay? I'm sorry I didn't get here sooner."

He stroked her hair, and she clung to him, wanting him to hold her always and never let go.

When her stomach stopped heaving and her head quit spinning, she mustered the courage to peek at the creature over his shoulder. Blood oozed from the wound on its chest, dripping onto the garage floor and forming a large puddle.

"It's red," she said in a scratchy voice.

"What's red?" Nick placed a small kiss on the top of her head.

"The blood."

"What color did you think it would be?"

"I don't know. Green maybe?"

He chuckled, the sound pleasant and comforting

and reassuring. Not like the awful sounds the creature had made. "They aren't aliens, I told you that."

"There wasn't any blood on the knife."

"You're right."

"How . . . ?"

"It's a little complicated to explain."

A picture! She should have thought of it before.

Here was her chance to obtain the proof she was looking for. Hoping Nick wouldn't stop her, Gillian reached for her cell phone, which had camera and video features. But before she could remove her phone from its case, the creature started to glow with a blinding white light.

"Look!" She sat up straighter.

Nick followed her gaze. He appeared not the least surprised when the creature dissolved into a hundred million particles that drifted up to the ceiling and disappeared.

"What just happened?" Gillian's analytical mind grappled for a reasonable explanation. One that didn't scare the hell out of her. "Where did it go? And all the blood?"

"It's been disposed of," he said and stood.

"Disposed of?" Her teeth began to chatter—from fright, or a delayed reaction to her attack. "What does that mean?" She stared up at him and might have been looking at a marble statue for all the emotion he revealed. "Tell me," she pleaded when no answer was forthcoming.

"Let's get out of here first before someone calls the cops. Do you think you can walk?"

She nodded and with his assistance, climbed to her feet. Every bone and muscle in her body cried out in agony, and she swayed unsteadily.

Nick put his arm around her and held her steady. She turned and gave one last look at the pile of garbage. Nothing remained of the female creature. If not for her injuries, she might have dreamed the entire thing.

A strange feeling came over her, not so much fear as awe.

"Who are you really?" she asked Nick.

He leaned down and brushed his lips across hers. "Are you sure you want to know? Because once I tell you, there's no going back. Not ever."

"It's a long story," Nick said. "We'd better get out of here before the police come."

Gillian, still obviously dazed, climbed into his car. He wanted to hold her, comfort her, and assure her everything was all right. But he couldn't. They didn't have time.

Besides, he was quite certain once he had Gillian in his arms, he wouldn't let her go until morning—and then only after they'd made love two or three times.

Not wise.

Taking more than one unnecessary chance, he cut in and out of traffic, making record time. Gillian revived somewhat and called Charlie to update him on everything that had happened.

Ten minutes later, they passed through the stone entrance gate leading to South Mountain Park. The road began to curve and soon they were winding their way up the side of the mountain, Nick's car hugging the steep pavement. He knew of a spot with a postcard-perfect view and a modicum of privacy.

"Okay, not a cop in sight. I'm all ears," Gillian said once they had parked.

Nick knew she deserved the truth, not a watered-down version, and he had an obligation to tell her. But that didn't make the telling any easier. Nick led her to a wooden bench facing out over the city.

He sat close to her and when she didn't scoot away, he captured her hand in both of his. The contact was for his benefit as much as hers.

Bit by bit she invaded his senses, much like she'd invaded his heart. Slowly, subtly, and completely.

"You in any pain?" he asked.

"Some. My throat hurts when I swallow. And my neck is sore."

Nick didn't doubt it. She sounded hoarse, almost like she had laryngitis.

"My arm hurts, too. A lot." She extended her arm, showing Nick a long, nasty gash that still bled profusely. She'd used the hem of her shirt to stanch the bleeding.

"Maybe I can help with that."

"How?"

"Close your eyes," he instructed and hugged her tighter. "Concentrate on your symptoms, on making them go away."

"You're kidding." She drew back and gave him a curious look.

"Humor me."

Sighing, she did as he asked. When her breathing evened out, Nick cupped the side of her face, shut his own eyes, and sent a silent prayer to the Ancients, asking them to ease her suffering and heal her wounds. She deserved their assistance. After all, she'd contributed in eliminating the female creature, almost losing her life in the process.

After a minute, Gillian opened her eyes.

"Feel better?" he asked.

She appeared surprised. "Yeah. I do."

"How's your arm?"

She looked at it, knitting her brow. "It doesn't hurt anymore and the bleeding's stopped."

"Good."

Gillian narrowed her eyes. "Who are you really?"

"I'm called the Huntsman. It's my destiny to kill Cadamus or be killed." His gaze didn't waver from hers. "And if Charlie's right, it's your destiny to help me."

CHAPTER EIGHT

"Do you, like, have special powers or something?"
Gillian asked.

"No." Nick chuckled. "I'm a regular guy. Not
faster than a speeding bullet, and I can't leap tall
buildings with a single bound."

"You did a pretty impressive job with the female
creature. I couldn't move, couldn't even breath, and
you tossed it around like a beach ball."

"Adrenaline rush. I was highly motivated."

"Seriously."

"Seriously, I've had some training."

"What kind?"

"Martial arts, mostly. Street fighting. Kick box-
ing." He didn't elaborate on the other training he'd
received or the skills passed down to him from Charlie, the only other living Huntsman.

"That's it?"

"You sound disappointed."

"Well, Cadamus can fly. Smell you from far away. Connect psychically with his prey. And he's got the strength of five men."

"I'm smarter."

"Okay, but . . ."

"No buts about it. His biggest weakness is his limited brain capacity. He can't think his way out of a paper sack."

"You're exaggerating."

"Only a little. Cadamus has three drives, and they rule his every waking moment. Survive, procreate, and kill me. In that order."

"He *won't* kill you."

Her fingers squeezed his, and when Nick turned toward her, he was met with a small, yet resolute, smile.

The city spread out before them, a glittering, shimmering landscape of multicolored lights. To their right loomed the distinctive silhouette of Camelback Mountain. Straight ahead, downtown Phoenix with its myriad skyscrapers clustered together like bean stalks reaching for the night sky.

At another time, Nick would have taken advantage of the romantic moment, leaned over, and kissed Gillian.

Squeezing her fingers in return, he let the moment pass, promising himself if they were ever in a similar situation, he'd taste her lips over and over again.

"No, he won't kill me," Nick reiterated, returning his gaze to the incredible view. "I come from a very long line of Huntsmen. We're as old as the creatures and just as enduring. After the final battle, I'll spend the next twenty-five years training my successor, whoever that may be."

"Are you saying that in all the millennia the creatures have been on Earth, the thousands of cycles, no Huntsman has ever died?"

"I'm not saying that at all. The final battle is to the death."

Nick stared at the horizon. He saw not the city but the still, lifeless body of Jonathan, his predecessor, a man he'd known only a few days. The same man who'd rescued Nick from Radlum's grasp moments before the alpha male would have killed him.

"I'll defeat Cadamus," Nick said. "I have to. He and his kind can't be allowed to multiply." Nick sat back, lifted their clasped hands to his mouth, and kissed the underside of Gillian's wrist. It was the only liberty he'd allow himself to take. "But you have to understand, I may not walk away."

"What are you saying?"

"My predecessor died from his wounds within hours of his battle with Radlum."

Gillian paled.

"Charlie trained me. He was Jonathan's teacher and mentor."

"Charlie's a Huntsman, too?"

Nick nodded. "He's dedicated his entire life to saving mankind."

"I should have guessed." Gillian didn't speak for several moments. When she did, it was to voice Nick's greatest fear. "Charlie's old. If you should di . . . don't win the battle with Cadamus, who will train the next Huntsman?"

"No one. Which is why I *can't* lose."

"Oh, Nick," Gillian said on a sob. "I've been so stupid. All this week I was in a snit because I felt you and Charlie were underutilizing me."

"Underutilizing you?"

"Yes. You and Charlie wouldn't give me any work more challenging than tracking down lost-pet notices. But here you are, fighting these alien creatures . . . okay, alien-*like* creatures," she said when he opened his mouth to object, "and trying to save lives, your own included. Could I be any more selfish?"

"It's no big deal." He stifled a laugh.

"I'm sorry." Tears filled her eyes.

Nick resisted the impulse to wipe them away. Barely. She was pretty damn cute all tore up with misery. "What happened in the garage?" he asked, changing the subject before she started blubbering. "Why'd you go down there when Charlie told you to wait in front of the building?"

She looked chagrined. "My nose was out of joint about the underutilizing thing, and I thought I could help with the investigation."

"I see." He'd be amused if he didn't feel responsible for the female creature's attack on her.

"Why do you think the female attacked me? Are they territorial?"

"Not especially. I suppose she could have considered you an intruder or . . ."

"Or what?" Gillian pressed.

"*Or* the females have adapted and become more aggressive."

Her eyes widened. "I really hope you're wrong."

"Me too. But if I'm not, we'll need to change the focus of our efforts in locating the remaining two."

"Explain something to me," she said.

"I'll try."

"What happened to the female? Granted, I was a

bit foggy, but I swear I saw it dissolve into all these particles and just disappear."

"Divine intervention."

"What?" Gillian's eyes lit as if waiting for the punch line. When none came, her expression faltered. "You're kidding."

"We call them the Ancients but they're known by other names in other cultures."

"The Ancients?" she repeated with a trace of skepticism.

"Most religions, from the very old to the very new, include good and evil counterparts. God and Satan, for example. The Ancients are the oldest form of good and evil. They're constantly at war, vying for control of man, and have been since the beginning of time. You need only examine history to see their influence. Hell, just look at what's happening today. Gangs, drugs, organized crime, terrorists."

"You can't blame the world's problems on an age-old war between divine entities."

"No?"

"I'm a psychologist, remember? *People* are good and evil. *They* choose and are responsible for the consequences."

"Whether good and evil resides inside us or outside us, the end result is the same. Terrible things are always occurring and probably always will."

"I won't disagree," she said, clearly not convinced. "But I'm not sure what this debate on man's goodness, or lack of it, has to do with the creatures."

"The war among the Ancients, their good and evil factions, is fought in different ways and on different planes. Here in Phoenix, the conflict takes place every twenty-five years between a winged creature of darkness and a mortal warrior."

"So . . . what? Cadamus is the champion for evil, and you're the champion for good?"

"In a nutshell."

"And this final battle, it's symbolic of the war between good and evil?"

"Not symbolic at all. The battle is very real and to the death." Another image of Jonathan's dead body appeared to Nick. "Many Huntsmen have died from injuries sustained during the final battle."

"The Ancients don't protect the Huntsmen?"

"There are casualties in every war."

She appeared to digest, if not accept, what he was telling her.

"Until the last few hundred years," he gestured to encompass the city, "this was an empty desert for hundreds of miles in any direction. As Phoenix has grown, become populated, the battle, its participants and strategies, have changed."

"These Ancients, they're what caused the female creature to dissolve and disappear?"

"Yes. There's never any evidence left behind for mankind to ponder over."

"What about the bodies of the victims? Aren't those considered evidence?"

"Dead humans can be explained. Dead creatures can't."

"Why hide the existence of the creatures? What purpose would it serve?"

"To level the playing field. The battle is fought by the alpha male and the Huntsman alone."

"Why alone?" She raised one eyebrow.

"There's a natural balance of power between good and evil. Any interference will disrupt that balance and result in chaos."

"Forgive me for saying so," she said with a hint of humor, "but you sound a little melodramatic. I'm half expecting ominous music to swell in the background."

"This isn't a joke," he said sharply.

"Okay, okay. But you're asking me to accept an awful lot on faith."

"Not faith. You have proof."

"The existence of the creatures," she said.

"Yes. And yourself."

"Me?"

Nick touched her throat. "When you were concentrating on your injuries earlier, I sent a prayer to the Ancients, asked for their help. Afterwards, you said you felt better."

"I'm supposed to believe the Ancients are responsible for my spontaneous recovery?"

He gave her an arch look. "How else would you explain it?"

"Mind over matter. The power of suggestion. Wishful thinking."

"Okay."

"You're mad because I'm not automatically buying into everything you've said."

"I'm not mad. You don't believe in the Ancients, and that's your prerogative." The lines around his mouth tightened. "But you *know* the creatures exist. You witnessed Radlum kill your mother, and were attacked by a female. How do you think people will react if they find out the creatures are real and not an urban legend?"

"Outraged. Scared."

"Which will lead to . . . ?"

"The creatures will be hunted down and destroyed by whatever means possible."

"That can't happen. If Cadamus is killed by someone other than me, life as we know it will end."

"You can't convince me that the destruction of the creatures is wrong."

"It's not wrong. We just have to go about it the right way."

"A battle between you and Cadamus?"

"Yes. Conventional weapons might kill him, but only the ritual dagger will send him to hell."

"That's the knife you used to slay the female?"

"It's been passed down from Huntsman to Huntsman for generations."

She thought for a moment. "Is there any way to permanently end the creatures' existence?"

"We can if we find and destroy all three females before Cadamus has a chance to mate with them."

"How hard can that be? I stumbled on the first one pretty much by accident."

"It was no accident."

"What then? Divine intervention again?"

"Charlie would say so."

"Don't go all mystical on me, Nick."

She might have been teasing him, but he noticed she hadn't let go of his hand. It was possible she believed more than she let on.

"Like in any war," he said, "each side has its advantages and disadvantages. Good may have dominated thus far, but it hasn't conquered evil. Not by a long shot. Evil simply retreats for a while, regroups, and returns to fight another day."

"What's my part in all of this?" she asked. "My destiny?"

Nick resigned himself to the inevitable. Though he'd been slow to admit it, deep down he'd known Gillian was an integral part of what was happening and had been from the beginning. A player in an age-old drama having a brand-new run.

For her sake, he hoped her participation would have a better outcome than her father's.

"Each Huntsman has a helper," he said. "Sometimes two. A person not his predecessor or successor. They're called Synsärs."

"Synsärs?" she repeated, her tongue tripping over the pronunciation.

"It's a very old word."

"Sounds Egyptian or Middle Eastern."

"Much older than that. The literal translation is 'loyal servant,' but Synsärs mean much more than that. The relationship between a Huntsman and his Synsär is a strong one, deep and abiding and lasting a lifetime. A Synsär's role differs with each Huntsman, but it's always vital and directly contributes to the eventual outcome."

"Am I your Synsär?"

"That's what Charlie thinks."

"What do *you* think?"

He stared straight at her. "Until tonight, I disagreed with him."

"What changed your mind?" Her voice had gone low and breathy and a tiny bit scared.

"The female creature's attack on you." With his free hand, he reached over and lightly brushed her neck, just above the bruises. "And these marks."

She didn't flinch. If anything, she angled her chin to give him greater access. "I don't understand."

Nick unbuttoned the collar of his shirt and tugged

the material aside. Gillian let out a small gasp. He felt heartened that she didn't cringe like some women who viewed his gnarled and disfigured flesh.

"Jesus, Nick!"

"Radlum attacked me. I was nine years old."

"You escaped?"

"I was saved. By Jonathan, my predecessor. Charlie's successor."

"The one who died," Gillian said.

Nick took a moment to rein in his emotions. Even after twenty-five years, talking about that night was hard for him. "Each cycle, a child is chosen to become the next Huntsman."

"By the Ancients?"

"Yes."

"How do they choose?"

"I'm not sure what dictates their decision. I do know the child is always an orphan whose family has been slaughtered by the alpha male."

"That's a rather gruesome selection process."

"We both carry scars from our attacks," Nick said. "Emotional and physical." Her eyes sought his and a flicker of awareness passed between them. "And now we can add an attack by the creature to the list."

"Is that why you think I'm your Synsär?"

"The creatures don't leave many survivors."

Nick kept the most compelling reason to himself. It wasn't his place to tell her about their longest-standing tie. That privilege belonged to her father.

"This must have hurt like the dickens." She turned the tables on him by reaching out and touching his exposed chest.

Nick closed his eyes and concentrated as she explored the ugly bumps, dents, and ridges left when

Radlum had ripped out chunks of his flesh. He wanted nothing, not even the sound of his own thundering heart, to distract him from the enjoyment of her caress.

She didn't hurry, her strokes alternating between curious and bold. When her fingertips dipped lower to run through his chest hair, his concentration slipped and with it his ability to restrain his desire. She need only to divert her attention to his lap to see just how much he wanted her.

"You must be tired." He sat up, ignoring the excruciating discomfort caused by the change in position. "I should get you home."

She withdrew her hand, but slowly. Nick clenched his jaw. He hadn't wanted her to stop either, but another minute of her sweet torture and he'd explode.

"What's next?" she asked, absently smoothing the front of her jeans. "Now that we've eliminated one of the females?"

"A more concentrated effort. I'm off work for two weeks starting Monday. Everyone at the station thinks I'm going on a fishing trip to a remote spot in Mexico."

Gillian brightened. "I'm finished with classes on Friday. I'll be able to spend every day with you. And Charlie, too," she added.

"Great." Nick forced a grin, unable to think of anything else he wanted more than to spend every day with Gillian.

Of course, he wanted to spend every night with her, too. And not hunting creatures.

Nick pulled up to the curb in front of Gillian's condo and came to a stop.

"Aren't you coming in?" she asked.

Her innocent question triggered a burst of anticipation in him that was anything but innocent.

Down boy.

"I don't think so," he said. "You look beat."

"I could use the company, if you're up to it."

She had no idea.

Nick hadn't been alone with Gillian since the night in his kitchen when Charlie walked in on them—and with good reason. He couldn't be trusted to keep his hands off her. Snug inside the privacy of four walls, the temptation to see where things led would be impossible to resist.

"Um . . ."

"Please."

He was no match for the pleading blue eyes she turned on him. "Just for a few minutes. I need my beauty sleep."

"Parking's around back," she instructed.

Five minutes later they were riding the elevator to her unit on the tenth floor.

Juggling three different keys, she opened one lock and two dead bolts. "Ignore the mess. My housekeeping's not up to par with yours."

On the other side of the door, she deactivated a beeping security alarm system by entering a code on a wall-mounted key pad.

"City living." She shrugged in way of apology and made a beeline for the kitchen. "Would you like anything to drink? Wine, coffee? Sorry, but I don't have a cappuccino machine."

"Water's fine. Don't trouble yourself."

"I'll just be a second. Make yourself comfortable."

Since a briefcase and stack of textbooks occupied

the overstuffed chair in the corner, Nick chose the end of the couch nearest the door. The room, while far from spotless, wasn't the mess she'd hinted at. Tastefully decorated in a classically modern style complementing its academic owner, the condo was small, yet cozy and comfortable.

"Read a lot?" he called to her, craning his neck to glimpse a title or two among the hundreds of books shoved into a pair of side-by-side, floor-to-ceiling bookcases.

"When I have time." He heard the grind of an automatic ice dispenser and a refrigerator door open and close. "Most of my books here are for research."

"Into the creatures?"

"No." The echo of her laughter carried into the living room. "Psychology. I store my research material on the creatures in the spare bedroom. There's some interesting stuff in there you might want to look at sometime."

"Sure." Nick reclined into the cushions only to sit up straight when she returned carrying a tall tumbler filled to the brim. "Thanks." He took the glass from her, noticing her hands trembled. "You okay?"

"A little shaky still." Her breath hitched. "If you don't mind, I'm going to clean up a bit and take a couple of aspirins."

"Why don't I leave—"

"You can't!" She bit her lip and then in a more controlled voice said, "I wish you'd stay. I'm not quite ready to be alone."

"All right." He understood her trepidation. After Radlum's attack, Nick had feared being alone, particularly at night. For months, he'd slept on a cot in Charlie's room. "No rush, I'll be here."

"Thank you," she whispered and disappeared down the hall.

Nick polished off half his water, not realizing how thirsty he was. Too antsy to sit, he rose, stretched, then strolled the room, pausing to study a set of framed photographs sitting on a chrome-and-glass computer desk.

The first photo was a candid black-and-white snapshot of Helena, Gillian's mother, taken shortly before her death. Nick recognized it from various newspaper accounts and the TV-7 News Center archives.

Looking at the picture, two things were clear to Nick: where Gillian had inherited her blond beauty, and why William Sayers, a one-time juvenile delinquent, petty criminal, and notorious bad boy, had turned a new leaf, becoming a devoted and law-abiding husband and father.

Next to the photo of Helena was a studio family portrait. Flanked by two doting parents, a young Gillian wore what was probably her Easter Sunday dress and a big, toothless grin. Though cute, the picture lacked the sentimental charm of the third and remaining one.

Sitting on her father's shoulders, a toddler-age Gillian waved a tiny American flag and watched a passing parade, her small round face alight with joy and wonderment. Gillian's mother stood beside them, her left hand resting on her husband's arm, her right on Gillian's chubby leg. She gazed up at them both with love and adoration.

They were the epitome of a happy family.

And like Nick's, torn apart in the blink of an eye.

He touched the corner of the last picture. He couldn't change what had happened, couldn't bring

back the dead. But he might, if they found and destroyed all three female creatures, save countless
more families from ruination.

A loud crash reverberated from another part of the
condo, startling Nick. Not stopping to think, he
bolted across the living room and hollered, "Are you
okay?"

CHAPTER NINE

"I'm fine," Gillian's sorrowful reply came from behind the closed bathroom door.

Nick hesitated, his hand hovering above the doorknob and his chest pounding. "What's wrong?"

"I dropped a jar of salve."

"Did it break?" He envisioned her bare feet stepping on glass fragments.

"No. But the contents spilled and went everywhere." She sounded on the verge of tears. "I couldn't get the damn lid off."

"Are you decent?"

"Yes, but—"

He opened the door, slowly so as not to bump her, and squeezed into the cramped space. "Here, let me help."

"Really, Nick." She had no choice but to step backward or be trampled. "I don't need your help."

The shower door rattled when she inadvertently whacked her elbow on it. "Ow!"

"You sit." Nick shut the toilet lid, clasped her by the shoulders, and gently lowered her onto the seat. "I'll clean up."

Ripping off a dozen or so sheets of toilet paper, he knelt and swabbed up the spilt ointment, which had splattered all over the floor, cabinet, and wall.

"This is truly embarrassing." She sat hunched over, her forearms propped on her knees. "I'm such a klutz."

"Relax. I won't tell."

She'd changed into a pair of gym shorts and a gray sports bra that revealed considerably more than it hid. Nick tried not to drool over the lovely expanse of bare legs mere inches from his face or the tiny butterfly tattoo floating just above her belly button.

Retrieving the fallen jar, he passed it to Gillian. "By some miracle there's a little left."

She wiped the outside clean with a towel. "I was trying to put some salve on my scrapes when I dropped the jar."

"I'll do it for you." Nick made the offer without thinking and it wasn't until the words left his mouth that he realized what such a task would involve—his fingers stroking her bare flesh. "Unless you rather I didn't."

"Actually, I'd appreciate it. If you don't mind."

Oh, shit.

He braced a hand on the counter, climbed to his feet, and said with all the nonchalance he could muster, "I don't mind."

Taking the jar from her, he moved aside. Gillian

swivelled around and presented her back to him, then lifted her hair off her neck.

Nick gulped, prayed to the Ancients for strength, and dipped a finger into the jar of salve.

He focused on her various cuts and scrapes, which were many, and not the sensation of her silky smooth skin, which was incredible. When a familiar pressure began to build in his groin, he tried staring at the ceiling. Since his mind readily supplied a very accurate picture of what his fingers were doing, that trick also failed.

Giving up, Nick stared his fill. If he were going to sport an erection, he might as well enjoy the view.

And what a view.

Her sweetly curved neck and arm draped elegantly over her head reminded him of a Greek statue, all sensuous lines and tantalizing curves. With each breath she took, her slim shoulders rose and fell. As did her breasts, the soft tops of which spilled from her sports bra.

Nick was mesmerized.

When he finished with the back of her neck, she tilted her head and sighed softly. "Can you do the sides, too?"

Now his hands were shaking. "Sure," he croaked, sounding—and feeling—like a teenaged boy who'd recently entered puberty.

Get a grip, he told himself. *You're a grown man. Not a kid.*

A grown man who very much wanted to pick up where he and Gillian had left off last week in his kitchen. He reminded himself she'd had one hell of a night and sex with him was probably the last thing she wanted or needed.

"Here, too," she murmured and lowered one bra strap to reveal a shallow cut.

Nick silently cursed. Could she truly be blind to the effect she was having on him? Not hear his pulse thrumming? Not notice the tension radiating off him in waves?

Unless she wasn't blind at all. His fingers stilled. What if she, too, wanted to pick up where they left off?

"Thanks." She let her hair drop and faced forward. "You're a dear."

You're a dear? Well, that didn't sound like any ravish-me-I-beg-of-you invitation he'd ever heard. His erection lost some of its atta boy.

"Anytime." He replaced the lid and plunked the jar on the counter.

Gillian rose, her subtle movements a tantalizing combination of innocence and provocativeness Nick found irresistible. He knew he should leave and give her some privacy, but he didn't. He couldn't. Watching her had triggered a communication shutdown between his brain and his legs.

Oddly enough she didn't seem to mind being trapped by a human wall. Lifting his right hand, she placed it on her cheek and held it there. Her skin was petal soft and warm beneath his fingers.

"I haven't thanked you for saving my life earlier."

"You're welcome."

"I'd have died if not for you." She turned her face into his hand.

He was immediately reminded of the night in his apartment when they'd been sitting at his dining table and her tongue accidently darted out to touch his palm.

And then it happened again, only this time was no

accident. She kissed his palm as she might his mouth, fully, sensuously, using tongue, lips, and teeth.

Nick tensed. Hands weren't anything he considered an erogenous zone. On the giving end, maybe, but not the receiving end. Gillian, however, was fast making a believer out of him.

"You really should stop that." His request was half-hearted, not that she listened.

Every nerve in his arm, from his fingertips to his shoulder, tingled. And the sensation didn't stop there. It moved down his spine and along the back of his thighs. He had another five seconds before his legs buckled and he slumped to the floor, completely at her mercy.

Right before he lost all respect for himself, she stopped, and Nick breathed for the first time in almost a minute.

That was, until she took the hand she'd just kissed, placed it on her hip, and slipped her arms around his neck.

Because he wasn't dead, paralyzed, or hog-tied, he wrapped his arms around her and buried his mouth in her hair. Though she felt damn near perfect and there wasn't anything else he'd rather be doing, he said, "This is a mistake."

"Sex with you couldn't possibly be a mistake."

Did she have to use the "s" word? Nick groaned, part in frustration—one of them had to keep a level head—and part in elation—his attempts to treat her like crap the past week hadn't driven her away.

"Gillian, honey, you don't know how much I want that."

"I want it, too," she whispered, toying with the fine hairs at the base of his neck.

"The timing's not right. You've had a rough night. You're scared and don't want to be alone. Those kind of emotions cloud a person's judgment."

"My judgment is crystal clear." She stood on tiptoes and brushed her lips across his. They were still moist from kissing his palm.

He licked his own lips and swore he could taste her. "That's good, because mine is shot to hell."

Her smile was shameless and a total turn-on. "Take me to bed, Nick."

"Wait."

A small crease furrowed her brow. "What?"

He deserved a medal. Here he had a beautiful woman in his arms, insisting he take her to bed, and he was bound and determined to do the noble thing.

"If you're worried about morning-after awkwardness . . ." She brushed his lips again with hers, lingering a little longer than before. "Don't be."

"I'm not." He suffered a lapse in willpower and cupped her very nice and quite shapely ass in his hands. "It's the morning after my fight with Cadamus I'm worried about."

She drew back, and Nick released her.

"You think what we're feeling isn't genuine?" she demanded. "That it's just a product of the circumstances?"

"Hell, no. I'm worried what will happen if I don't make it through the fight with Cadamus in one piece."

"You *will*."

"But if I don't . . ." He banged a fist on the doorjamb, then let his arm drop. "I can't commit to you, not right now. After this—"

"Bullshit!"

"I hate the thought of hurting you." He reached for her.

She evaded him. "Let's say Cadamus kills you. You think I'll be less hurt because we didn't make love two or three dozen times back when we had the chance? Wrong." She glared at him. "I'll be more hurt."

"Two or three dozen times?" A smile pulled at the corners of his mouth.

"Nick, if you lose the final battle, whatever happens tonight—or any night from now on—really won't matter, will it?"

"Your logic is difficult to dispute."

"I'm a psychologist." She slid into his open arms. "I've had years of training in getting people to see reason."

He lowered his head. "Thank God for college educations."

In the next second their mouths were locked together and his tongue was tangling with hers and, oh, yes, he was holding her ass again and pulling her flush against him.

Frantic to devour her, Nick backed her into the counter, and something clattered to the floor. The jar of salve?

Gillian wrenched free and panted, "Protection."

"Tell me you have some." He'd prefer not to run to the convenience store if he could help it.

"In the medicine cabinet behind me."

Nick got the cabinet door open, but he couldn't find the condoms. Probably because he was simultaneously trying to yank his shirt from his pants.

"Here, I'll get them." She twisted around and reached into the cabinet, producing two condoms.

"Is that all you have?"

"Sorry. I haven't needed any lately."

Nick took the condoms from her. "Fine. We'll improvise."

"Improvise?" She looked interested, which ignited his interest—through the roof.

Grabbing her hand, he pulled her from the bathroom. "Which way?"

"Follow me." She started down the hall with him in tow.

"Gladly."

Gillian had been right, Nick thought as they stumbled into her darkened bedroom. Making love with her tonight, and every night for the next few weeks, wasn't going to change anything.

Well, maybe one thing. If he were destined to leave this world behind forever, he'd do so a content man.

Nick did have a point, Gillian thought as she led him across the floor of her bedroom. She'd had a rough night. And it was possible the female creature's attack on her, and her subsequent fright, was responsible for this sudden and inexplicable lack of inhibition.

Though she doubted either she or Nick would regret their impulsiveness come morning, she did understand his concern. He really was a sweet guy.

And in this instance, absolutely wrong. No way was she going to regret having sex with him.

He tripped and stumbled into her, swearing under his breath.

"Careful." She caught him by the arm.

"Sorry. I stubbed my foot on the bedpost."

"I'll get the light." She switched on a small reading lamp attached to her headboard.

Immediately, the room was bathed in a soft yellow glow.

"Nice," Nick said, surveying their surroundings.

"Not too girly?"

"Uh-uh." He grinned. "Very sexy."

Unlike the rest of her condo, Gillian's bedroom had been decorated with an eye to the old-fashioned, complete with four-poster bed, decorative throw pillows edged in lace, and a five-drawer oak dresser, painted white with gold trim. Several framed prints, Monet knockoffs, added color.

"This room is my one indulgence," she explained.

"I like it." He caught a glimpse of her in the standing oval mirror by the dresser, and his grin turned sly.

"I'll get the light," she said.

"Leave it on. I have plans for that light. And that mirror."

Gillian felt a stirring inside her. Nervousness mingled with arousal. "What sort of plans?"

"I'll show you." He led her to the mirror.

She recalled his earlier remark about improvising and the stirring inside her blossomed into a blistering heat that spread fast and furious.

Professors of psychology knew a lot about sex. It came with the territory. There wasn't much Gillian hadn't heard from patients and students or read about in books and reports. But knowing didn't translate into experiencing. She wasn't one to take the initiative when it came to intimate relationships. And since the few men she'd been with hadn't either, experimenting and crossing conventional boundaries weren't part of her normal repertoire.

She was definitely due for a change.

"Come here," Nick said, his voice low and rough.

As Gillian stepped closer, he ripped off his shirt and tossed it aside. Goose bumps erupted on her arms. He had a truly spectacular physique, and the scars on his chest and shoulder only enhanced his rugged sex appeal.

When she would have gone into his arms, he placed his hands on her shoulders and faced her away from him. In that same rough voice he said, "Look at me," and nodded at the mirror. Their eyes connected in the reflection. "That's right."

A shiver of desire rocked her when his hands circled her waist, then slid up to cover her breasts, kneading her pliant flesh through the fabric of her sports bra.

She moaned, her eyelids drifting shut.

"Don't close your eyes." He rolled her taut nipples between his thumbs and forefingers. "I want you to watch."

Gillian arched her back, pressed her breast into his hands and watched both Nick's and her reaction to what he was doing in the mirror.

"You like?" he whispered and kissed her collarbone, his teeth and tongue doing truly amazing things.

"I like," she murmured as nerves she didn't know existed came alive.

When his hands moved lower to her belly, she said, "Don't stop."

Nick shot her a mischievous look in the mirror. "How 'bout we improvise a little?"

Something in his tone sent Gillian's pulse spiking and her imagination soaring. "What do you have in mind?"

"This." He removed her bra, then took her hands and placed them on her bare breasts.

Her initial reaction was to pull away but he held her hands firmly in place. "I-I don't . . ."

Manipulating her fingers so that she stroked her own breasts and fondled her own nipples, he said, "You do now."

Again, he caught her gaze in the mirror, and the pure wickedness flashing in his eyes vanquished every last bit of her resistance.

She stared at her reflection, transfixed. She wasn't averse to touching herself, but she'd never done it in front of anyone. It was a little disconcerting . . . and a lot exciting.

Nick's hand slipped beneath the waistband of her shorts. Gillian bit her lower lip in heady expectation. As his fingers found her sex, she stifled a cry of pleasure and widened her stance. He slid first one and then two fingers inside her.

"Nice," he said in her ear. "And wet." Using his teeth, he nibbled a path from the curve of her shoulder up to her ear. "I want you to watch yourself come, and I want to watch you doing it."

At the rate they were going, he'd get his wish any second.

He bent at the knees, pressed his erection into the cleft of her buttocks, and rubbed back and forth while his fingers simultaneously stroked her. Gillian gasped when he found the magical spot, the one that seemed to mystify most men. Her hands involuntarily kneaded her breasts, intensifying the sensation building within her.

"Yeah, just like that." Her muscles must have clenched around his fingers, for he said, "Oh, baby."

Though her head lolled back, she didn't close her eyes. She wasn't going to miss any of this for the world.

His thumb circled her clitoris while his fingers continued to probe inside her. She tensed, held back another moment—any longer would have been impossible—and, catching Nick's gaze in the mirror, let go.

The free fall was spectacular.

He anchored her securely against him until her orgasm subsided, all the time telling her how beautiful she was. Gillian observed the flushed, disheveled woman in the mirror and the man wearing the cocky grin who'd put her in that state and thought, *No, we are beautiful.*

"Ready for more?" he asked.

Thank goodness he was holding her, because her trembling legs were about to give out. "We might have to attempt the next one lying down."

"Works for me."

He swept her up in his arms, carried her to the bed, and deposited her on the white fluffy coverlet. She started to laugh but stopped when he shucked out of his pants and left them in a heap on the floor. His boxer briefs followed.

Gillian's heart stopped at the sight of his nakedness, then abruptly restarted, only to beat erratically. He was incredibly gorgeous. Every inch of him finely chiseled muscle and flesh.

And hers for the taking.

Crawling to the edge of the bed, and getting up on her knees, she tossed his own words back at him. "Come here."

He complied, and Gillian wrapped her arms around

his neck, fusing her mouth with his and kissing him with mindless abandon. Her hands roamed his body, from chest to stomach to ribs to hips. It was nice. *Very* nice.

But not enough. She wanted to taste him. All of him. Head to toe. And when she was done with that, she wanted him inside her, stretching her and filling her until she was ready to pass out from the sheer ecstacy of it.

She lowered her head and licked his nipple, flicking her tongue over the small nub.

Nick sucked in a sharp breath.

"You like?" she asked, again repeating what he'd said to her.

"You know damn well I like it," he said, threading his fingers in her hair.

"I thought so." She wrapped the fingers of her one hand around the thick length of his penis and stroked. With her other hand, she hefted his balls and squeezed.

He never took his eyes off her.

Inspired by his muttered encouragements, she experimented, surprising herself with her daring and inventiveness. Her plan to draw out her seduction came to a sudden end when Nick pushed her away. Gillian sat back on her calves and blinked.

"If you're not careful," he said, ripping open one of the condoms, "we won't be needing this."

"We won't?" She feigned innocence.

"No." He placed the condom over his erection.

"You did mention improvising."

"Later." Completing his task, he reached for her gym shorts. "When I come with you for the first time, Gillian, I'm going to be inside you." He hooked his fingers under the waistband. "Deep." She leaned back on her elbows and lifted her hips. "Hard." He yanked off her shorts, leaving her completely bare. "And hot."

Talking had become difficult so she kept conversation to a minimum. "Okay."

He fell onto the bed, pinning her solidly beneath him, his mouth ravishing hers. She spread her legs, and he entered her, fulfilling every promise he'd made.

"I fantasized about this."

"You did?"

"Since that day in your office."

"Only once?"

"Every goddamn night."

"Me too."

Gillian bucked and gasped and clung to him, marveling at how delicious they felt together. And yet, she craved more. Deeper, harder, hotter. More wonderful. What was it about Nick that she couldn't get enough of him? She got what she wanted when he changed the angle of his penetration.

"Oh yes," she said, willing him to keep doing what he was and not stop for anything.

"You like?" His amusement was unmistakable.

"You know damn well I like it."

"I thought so."

If she had a free hand, she'd slug him in the arm. But as it so happened she was otherwise occupied, scraping her nails up and down the muscles of his back, hoping to drive him half as crazy as she felt.

It worked, but on her, not him.

Gillian's second climax was nearly as intense as her first and every bit as pleasurable. Nick's release came on the heels of hers. She held him until he stopped shuddering, kissing his sweat-dampened face and neck.

"For the record, I'm glad you twisted my arm." His smile was lazy and sexy and so gorgeous she just had to kiss him again.

"I'm glad I twisted your arm, too." She smiled back at him, trying for sultry and failing miserably. She was too happy and too satisfied to do anything except beam.

He rolled off her, disposed of the condom, and gathered her to him. Cuddling in the aftermath, thought Gillian as she melted into his embrace, was one of the best parts of making love.

"I'm looking forward to those next two or three dozen times you mentioned." He caressed her back, her buttocks, and the tops of her thighs.

Gillian sighed contentedly, loving the sensation of his hands on her body. "We should probably pace ourselves. I'd hate to wear you out, what with the hours you've been keeping lately."

His smile lost some of its luster. "I'm going to beat Cadamus."

"Let's not spoil the mood by talking about him," she said but the damage had already been done. She smoothed the frown lines from his forehead.

He shifted and settled deeper into his pillow. "You know, I haven't given much thought to what my life will be like after the final battle." He chuckled mirthlessly. "I've always been afraid I'd jinx the outcome by making plans."

"Nick." She started to say he wasn't afraid of anything but was struck silent by the solemnity of his expression. Here was someone who carried the weight of the world on his shoulders. Platitudes were inadequate and demeaning.

"All that's changed." He pulled her closer and nuzzled her cheek. "I'm coming for you when the battle is over." His arousal pressed against her leg. "Promise me you'll be waiting."

Gillian's heart swelled. "I will. I promise."

She sealed her vow with a kiss, pouring everything she felt for him into it, which, given the relatively short time they'd known each other, was considerable.

He lay on his back and lifted her on top of him so that she straddled his hips. Her need for him instantly spiraled out of control, and she moved back and forth, gliding over his noticeably revived erection. Nick's attention remained fixed on her to the exclusion of everything else. She discovered she rather liked being the center of his universe, and played to her appreciative audience.

When he extended a hand toward her, she pushed it away. "Look but don't touch," she said in her best seductress voice.

"You really know how to torture a guy."

And torture him she did, licking her fingers and touching herself in a display that left him breathing hard and her feeling smug. Leaning forward, she brought her breasts to his open mouth.

Just as his lips closed around one damp nipple, his cell phone rang.

"Damn it to hell," he grumbled. "This had better be good." When Gillian climbed off him, he reached over the side of the bed for his pants on the floor. Digging through the pockets, he retrieved his phone and answered on the fourth ring.

"Yeah," he snapped. There was a pause during which his scowl increased. "Where?" He swung his legs onto the floor and sat up. "Oh, fuck." Another, longer pause. "I'll be right there."

"What is it?" Gillian demanded when he hung up.

Nick shook out his pants, then rounded up the rest of his clothes. "That was Charlie. The police just found the remains of another victim."

Gillian shut her eyes and grieved momentarily for the victim's family and friends. "Have they identified the body yet?"

"No."

Something in Nick's tone put her on the alert. She sat up, leaning on one elbow. "There's more, isn't there?"

"Go to sleep, Gillian."

"Are you kidding?" He put a reassuring hand on her shoulder, only she wasn't reassured. "Please," she implored. "I have to know what's going on."

Turning back to his clothes, he said in a terse voice, "The remains were found in the parking garage of the Hanson Building."

Gillian froze. "We were just there."

"And so was Cadamus. Maybe even at the same time."

"I'm coming with you." She threw off the bedsheet.

"Forget it. Not after what you've been through to-night. You stay here and rest. I'll call you in the morning."

"Don't call. Come back here instead." *I need you,* she thought, but she didn't say it.

Nick nodded, kissed the top of her head, and eased her back onto the pillow.

She pulled the sheet up to her neck. It did nothing

to ward off the icy chill creeping to her bones, which worsened at the sound of the front door slamming behind him.

Cadamus perched on the roof of the building, his feet gripping the railing, his partially extended wings acting as a ballast to steady him.

On the street below, lights flashed, tires screeched, and humans scurried about like ants whose hill had been crushed by a large foot. Noise bounced off the walls of surrounding skyscrapers, the sound deafening.

"Damn you, Huntsman," Cadamus growled, the blood in his veins boiling.

He didn't normally risk exposing his presence, but the moonless night hid him well enough, and the humans were too busy examining the remains of his last meal to notice a shadow flitting across the roof. He'd intended to share the meal with the female; however, she'd been dead and disposed of well before he arrived, thanks to the Huntsman and his stupid, clumsy mate.

Cadamus curled his right hand into a fist, pictured it clubbing the Huntsman in the side of the head. Had he arrived sooner, not stopped to feed first, the outcome would have been different, the female even now nesting in preparation to lay her eggs.

He cursed his ill timing and condemned the Huntsman to an eternity in hell. It had taken Cadamus a week to find this female. Only two remained, and he had not much time before his short life came to an end. If his race were to continue, he couldn't tolerate another blunder.

"You will know what it feels like to have my teeth

sink into your flesh, Huntsman. Just like you felt my father's teeth. Only mine will rip your heart from your chest."

Raising his nose in the air, he scented the breeze, then spread his wings and prepared to take flight. He gave one last look at the scene below. Hearing a sudden scraping noise behind him, he swung around, ready to attack the intruder. The metal door he'd been unable to breach the previous night opened slowly, and a face appeared. That of a young human boy, whose black eyes widened.

Cadamus wasn't hungry, but neither could he invite discovery. In the next instant, he swooped down on the boy. Gripping the thin chest with long fingers, Cadamus held the boy aloft, his open jaws descending on the boy's neck.

"Wait," the boy said, remarkably unafraid for one so young. "I've come to warn you."

"Warn me?" Cadamus hissed, suspicious of trickery.

"The police are on their way up here to search for the killer. You must hurry."

"Why tell me this?"

The boy wheezed from Cadamus's tight grip around his chest. "Because the Dark Ancients sent me."

"You're lying."

"No, I'm not."

Cadamus concentrated and probed the boy's mind, reading his thoughts. When he'd learned all he needed to know, he tucked the boy under his arm, dove off the side of the building, and took flight, heading for his sanctuary.

The Huntsman, it seemed, wasn't the only one to be given a human Synsär.

CHAPTER TEN

Nick dragged into the newsroom at the station right behind Celeste and was immediately assaulted by a cacophony of noise and a rush of activity. Everywhere he turned, phones rang, speakers blared, monitors flashed images, and people who weren't hunkered down over their work stations darted in a dozen different directions.

"Christ, Blackwater, you look like crap," Max said, swiveling in his chair to give Nick an exaggerated once-over. "Who fucked you over?"

"Nobody you know."

"Forget to take your happy pill this morning, did we?"

His coworker snorted and returned to his monitor, on which was displayed a man's face. Nick thought he recognized the guy, but couldn't quite place him.

God, he was tired. These constant late nights were killing him. He'd been averaging only three to four hours every night this week. Less, last night, not that he regretted a moment of the time he'd spent with Gillian.

Though he tried to talk himself out of it, he'd gone back to her condo after all, arriving there sometime around three in the morning. She'd been waiting up for him, so he knew she felt as lousy as he did today. Worse, probably, considering what she'd been through with the female creature. And being Gillian, she'd refused to take his advice and call in sick, claiming she had essays to grade before the end of the semester.

Bradley McEntee stuck his head out of his office door and hollered, "Celeste. Nick. In here. Pronto."

Celeste, who didn't look like crap, charged ahead of Nick into their boss's office. She was still riding high from their scoop on the elderly woman's murder last week. Their report on the dismembered arm had earned TV-7 the top ratings in their time slot the night of the original airing and again the next morning when the segment was replayed on the early edition—a feat no doubt helped along by the outrageous number of teasers the station ran prior to the broadcast. They came in second the following night with Gillian's interview.

Nick would be surprised if Celeste didn't already have a spot on her mantel picked out for their next local Emmy award.

Upon entering Bradley's office—a room everyone except Bradley referred to as the fishbowl—Nick shut the door behind him. The three glass walls reduced some of the racket but none of the visual distractions.

"Did Max give you the scoop on last night's murder victim?" Bradley's chair squeaked under his generous bulk.

"No, what?" Celeste brightened. With her contract coming up for renewal in another month and the threat of competition from the magnificently proportioned Linda Perez at KBCB, Celeste went after every possible opportunity to plant her face in front of the camera.

Nick leaned against a file cabinet and waited, very interested in what Bradley had to say—though he hoped his relaxed demeanor suggested the opposite.

He and Charlie had learned next to nothing about the murder victim. Admittedly, Nick had spent the night concentrating more on the victim's attacker. While Charlie had hacked into the police computer, Nick had gone straight to the crime scene after leaving Gillian's. Sneaking past the police barricade and into the building had been difficult, but not impossible. Unfortunately, he'd turned up no new information to help them locate the remaining two female creatures or Cadamus's sanctuary.

"I need you two to hotfoot it over to the Washington station right away," Bradley said. "The police have released the victim's identity and Chief Denning is getting ready to give a statement."

"Who is it?" Celeste nearly popped off her chair.

Bradley smiled like a cat who'd just swallowed a canary. "Carl Salvador."

Nick recalled the face on Max's monitor.

"*The* Carl Salvador?" Celeste practically squealed. "Ernie Orsi's right-hand man and daughter's fiancé?"

"One and the same. Fingerprint report just came back positive."

"How sweet!" Celeste positively glowed.

Nick had never understood the callousness of some

people in the news industry. But even he saw how this latest development in the case could set a news producer's and star reporter's hearts to fluttering.

Carl Salvador lived, or had lived until meeting his untimely demise the previous night, in one of the two penthouse apartments on the top floor of the Hanson Building. His future father-in-law, Ernie Orsi, a wealthy Phoenix entrepreneur, was reputed to have close connections with the Mafia. Some claimed Ernie Orsi *defined* the Arizona Mafia.

The story wasn't just big, it was gigantic.

"Do the police think Salvador's death was the result of a hit?" Celeste asked.

"They aren't saying." Bradley's smile dissolved. "Which is why you two have to head your collective asses over there and find out everything you can."

Celeste bounced to her feet before Bradley finished his sentence. "We're on it!"

Nick didn't respond quite so fast. Not because he was exhausted but because, in his opinion, covering Chief Denning's press conference was a colossal waste of time. While the chief would give a statement, he'd say essentially nothing because the police had no clue who killed Salvador. But they did know one thing: This killer was no run-of-the-mill hit man.

Hell, thought Nick, he wasn't even human.

But he couldn't very well tell that to Bradley and Celeste.

The hall outside the police chief's office was packed with reporters. Nick recognized many of them, had even worked with a few of them over the years. He liked only one or two. Reporters were generally a competitive, cutthroat lot. Not one of them gave an inch of space as he and Celeste squirmed their way into the crowded hallway.

They'd already done their obligatory footage of Celeste on the steps of the police station, and Nick had taken some random shots of officers and vehicles from different angles.

Now, lifting his camera onto his shoulder, he elbowed past a couple of newspaper reporters and took a shot of the empty podium. The police chief was scheduled to appear ten minutes ago, and tension in the hallway had reached an oppressive level.

Finally, a side door opened, and Chief Lyle Denning appeared. The sternness of his steel gray hair and bushy eyebrows was offset by the teddy-bear paunch around his middle. Escorting him were two suits and three uniforms, one of whom was a woman. The shorter of the suits whispered in his ear, and the police chief kept nodding his head even after he took his place at the podium.

The commotion came to an abrupt halt when Chief Denning raised his hand and lowered his mouth to the microphone. At least the talking stopped. Cameras and tape recorders whirred softly, BlackBerries clicked, and pens scratched across pads of paper.

"Good morning." Chief Denning surveyed the room. "I have a brief statement to make, after which I'll open the floor to questions for no more than ten minutes."

Celeste, through sheer determination and willpower, had wormed her way to within a few feet of the podium. Nick tried to zoom in for an unobstructed close-up of the police chief. Unable to get a clear shot, he resorted to holding the camera above his head and hoped for the best.

"As you know," Chief Denning began, "the body of Carl Salvador was discovered last evening at approximately nine-seventeen in the parking garage of the old Hanson Building on Jefferson Street and Central Avenue. We are still awaiting the results of the autopsy. However, it's believed at this time Salvador's death was not due to natural causes."

There was a brief flurry of activity as thirty-plus reporters documented the information either on tape, memory chip, or paper.

"Who discovered the body?" someone asked.

"A resident of the building. He's not acquainted with Salvador and not currently under suspicion."

"His name?"

"You know better than to ask that," Chief Denning admonished the reporter.

"Was it a hit?" someone yelled.

"No comment."

"Was he shot?"

"Mr. Salvador does not appear to have been the victim of a gunshot wound."

"How was he killed?" Linda Perez asked. She stood at the very front, in a better position than Celeste, something Nick was sure stuck in Celeste's craw.

"The exact cause of death is not yet known and may not be for days." Chief Denning then went on to say, "Mr. Salvador appears to have been alone and was discovered a few feet from his parked car. The car was not tampered with."

"Surely you have some idea of how he was killed," Linda Perez insisted.

"No comment."

"A blow to the head? Strangled? Stabbed?"

Police Chief Denning glowered at her. "No comment."

One of the suits beside him bent to the microphone. "We don't wish to reveal the means by which Mr. Salvador was killed as it might adversely impact our investigation."

He died from loss of blood after having the flesh stripped from his body.

"There are certain particulars about Mr. Salvador's remains that may help us narrow the list of suspects."

His heart and other organs had been ripped from his body.

"And we don't want to encourage any copycat killings."

Tonight someone else will die in an identical manner.

"Do you have any leads?" another reporter asked.

"Not presently," Chief Denning answered.

"Have you questioned Ernie Orsi?" Celeste asked.

"No comment."

"What about Salvador's fiancé, Orsi's daughter?"

"Ms. Orsi has been questioned, yes, but only for information on Salvador's recent whereabouts and activity. She's not currently a suspect," he concluded.

More questions were asked, none compelling and most receiving a "no comment" response from the chief. Nick started getting antsy.

He wanted to return to the station, throw the segment together as quickly as possible, then get back to finding the female creatures. By using the lost-pet notices Gillian tracked down, Charlie had pinpointed two possible hiding locations for the remaining females.

Nick's attention, which had begun to wander, suddenly refocused when Linda Perez asked, "Is there any connection between Salvador's murder and the recent string of deaths in downtown Phoenix?"

"We don't believe so." Chief Denning's response came a millisecond too slow.

Nick caught the hesitation.

So did Linda Perez.

"Excuse me, Chief," she said, "but there have been five reported deaths in the past seven days. All in downtown Phoenix, all within a one-mile radius, all with certain particulars about the remains. How can you stand there and say you don't believe the deaths are connected?"

Five *reported* deaths. Cadamus fed at least once a night if not twice. There were likely two or more *unreported* deaths. Missing persons whose remains—with certain particulars or not—might never be found.

"We concede to some similarities in some of the deaths," the suit said. "Rest assured, we're looking into those now and will release the facts as soon as they become available."

"Are we dealing with a serial killer?" someone asked.

"There's no evidence—"

Chief Denning's response was drowned out by a hallway full of reporters simultaneously erupting with questions. Nick caught only bits and pieces above the din.

". . . the public has a right to know . . ."

". . . safety of our citizens . . ."

". . . police accountability . . ."

". . . dismembered limb . . . old woman . . ."

Linda Perez shouted to be heard. "Excuse me, Chief Denning. Has anyone in your department talked to Dr. Gillian Sayers?"

The room went instantly quiet. Nick clutched his camera tighter and ground his teeth together. Figures Linda Perez would be the one to bring up the creatures. She might look like a centerfold model but she had the IQ of a neurosurgeon and the tenacity of a . . . well, of a reporter.

God dammit.

Why had he ever mentioned Gillian's name to Bradley in the production meeting and pushed to interview her?

Because you wanted to meet her and it provided a legit excuse.

Someone would have eventually connected the recent murders to the ones described in her book, he rationalized. The urban legends were well circulated, though not taken seriously by everybody—for which Nick was glad. The police had probably been fielding calls from scared, and in their opinion, wacky, citizens all week.

Which gave Nick an idea. Maybe Charlie could hack into the police computers again and find out if any complaints had been filed about an atrocious smell. It was worth a try, and Nick could kick himself for not thinking of it sooner.

Chief Denning tugged on the knot of his tie and looked uncomfortable. "No, we have not spoken to . . . Dr. Sayers, did you say?"

"Don't you think you should?"

"Why, Ms. Perez?" Chief Denning's tone was condescendingly patient and ripe with sarcasm. "Are you

GET UP TO 4 FREE BOOKS!

You can have the best romance delivered to your door for less than what you'd pay in a bookstore or online. Sign up for one of our book clubs today, and we'll send you **FREE* BOOKS** just for trying it out...with no obligation to buy, ever!

HISTORICAL ROMANCE BOOK CLUB

Travel from the Scottish Highlands to the American West, the decadent ballrooms of Regency England to Viking ships. Your shipments will include authors such as CONNIE MASON, CASSIE EDWARDS, LYNSAY SANDS, LEIGH GREENWOOD, and many, many more.

LOVE SPELL BOOK CLUB

Bring a little magic into your life with the romances of Love Spell—fun contemporaries, paranormals, time-travels, futuristics, and more. Your shipments will include authors such as KATIE MACALISTER, SUSAN GRANT, NINA BANGS, SANDRA HILL, and more.

As a book club member you also receive the following special benefits:

- **30% OFF all orders through our website & telecenter!**
  (Plus, you still get 1 book FREE for every 5 books you buy!)
- **Exclusive access to** special discounts!
- **Convenient** home delivery **and 10 days to return any books you don't want to keep.**

There is no minimum number of books to buy, and you may cancel membership at any time. See back to sign up!

*Please include $2.00 for shipping and handling.

YES! ☐

Sign me up for the **Historical Romance Book Club** and send my TWO FREE BOOKS! If I choose to stay in the club, I will pay only $8.50* each month, a savings of $5.48!

YES! ☐

Sign me up for the **Love Spell Book Club** and send my TWO FREE BOOKS! If I choose to stay in the club, I will pay only $8.50* each month, a savings of $5.48!

NAME: _____

ADDRESS: _____

_____

TELEPHONE: _____

E-MAIL: _____

☐ **I WANT TO PAY BY CREDIT CARD.**

☐ VISA   ☐ MasterCard.   ☐ DISCOVER

ACCOUNT #: _____

EXPIRATION DATE: _____

SIGNATURE: _____

Send this card along with $2.00 shipping & handling for each club you wish to join, to:

**Romance Book Clubs
1 Mechanic Street
Norwalk, CT 06850-3431**

Or fax (must include credit card information!) to: 610.995.9274. You can also sign up online at www.dorchesterpub.com.

*Plus $2.00 for shipping. Offer open to residents of the U.S. and Canada only. Canadian residents please call 1.800.481.9191 for pricing information.
If under 18, a parent or guardian must sign. Terms, prices and conditions subject to change. Subscription subject to acceptance. Dorchester Publishing reserves the right to reject any order or cancel any subscription.

JOIN NOW!

privilege to information that implicates this Dr. Sayers in Carl Salvador's murder?"

"She's a noted local authority on urban legends," Linda Perez said, undaunted and unintimidated. "Some of the legends bear a striking similarity to the recent murders."

"Is that so?" Chief Denning asked with blatantly false ignorance.

Nick didn't like Gillian's name being brought up. On the other hand, he was relieved to learn that the police didn't put much stock in the myths about the creatures. He couldn't afford any interference from an outside source.

Chief Denning heaved a weary sigh. "We're following up on every possible lead, none of which include winged monsters that supposedly eat people." He glanced around the room. "I'll take two more questions. Please use them wisely."

The police chief's snide treatment of Linda Perez didn't diffuse the spark of interest she'd ignited. While the last two questions were asked and answered, Nick noticed an unusual abundance of cell phone calls being placed.

His agitation returned tenfold. Shutting off his camera—something Bradley would give him hell for later—Nick pulled his own cell phone from his pocket and dialed Gillian's office at school. He had to talk to her before one of these reporters did.

He got a busy signal. Nick hit the disconnect button and swore. Advances in technology had changed the way in which Huntsmen sought out the creatures, giving them more sophisticated tools and a greater edge. He hadn't taken into account that those same sophisticated tools could also hinder his efforts. Gillian might, at this very moment, be talking to one of these reporters.

"Nick." Celeste appeared in front of him.

"What," he snapped.

"We've got to get back to the station." She glanced down. "Oh, good. You have your phone. Call Sherri and tell her to get in touch with that Dr. Sayers and set up another interview. See if she can swing an exclusive."

"Here, hold this." Nick shoved his camera at her.

"What!" She took it only because he gave her no choice.

Nick punched in Gillian's cell phone number. It rang four times, then went to her voice mail.

"Damn it to hell."

"Nick," Celeste wailed and stamped her foot. "This fricking thing weighs a ton."

"Yeah, yeah, try carrying it around all day."

With the press conference over, Chief Denning and the suits left through the same door they'd come out of. The uniforms stayed behind, guarding the door. Nick and Celeste were being bumped and jostled on all sides by a stampede of reporters racing back to their offices or newsrooms to put together their stories. Celeste barely managed to hold on to the camera.

Nick ignored her perpetual whining.

No point calling Gillian's home, he thought. She wouldn't be there until after five.

"Can you drive the van back to the station?"

"Are you insane?" Celeste shoved the camera back at him.

Nick took it from her before she dropped it, figuring the station wouldn't appreciate him damaging a piece of very expensive equipment.

"Look, Celeste. I have to go." They joined the stream of reporters heading toward the exit. "That phone call I got was . . ." He searched his brain for a reasonable excuse. "I have a family emergency."

"What family? You're an orphan."

"My foster father's sick."

"Oh, yeah, him," she said, letting Nick know she didn't include foster parents in her definition of family. "Gee, I'm sorry about that. But I can't, I won't drive the van. And besides, you have a story to edit. Work first," she chirped. "Family second."

Christ, he had to get hold of Gillian before some other reporter did.

He contemplated his options. Max could edit the piece on Chief Denning's press conference. Nick wasn't worried about that. Bradley would probably forgive him ditching Celeste and the van in order to attend a family emergency. *She* wouldn't, however, and he could kiss their working relationship good-bye. For the next few months anyway. Nick wasn't worried about that, either.

Maybe he should call Charlie.

Or maybe he should go back to the station, keep trying to get in touch with Gillian, and trust that she wouldn't say anything about Cadamus and the Ancients should some reporter finagle an interview with her.

And there was the problem in a nutshell.

Nick was crazy about her, wanted her more than he'd ever wanted any woman in his life, had been half in love with her since he was a kid. But he didn't trust her. Not where her father was concerned. She would, he feared, do anything within her power to free him from prison, including breaking her promise to Nick and triggering a chain of events that would lead to mankind's destruction.

It occurred to Nick that the person he most needed to talk to was William Sayers.

"Are the creatures real? Dr. Sayers?"

"Some people believe so."

"Do you?"

"I've interviewed dozens of individuals for my book, and they've shared some very compelling eye-witness accounts. I believe *they* believe the creatures are real."

Gillian rolled her head from side to side and rubbed the back of her neck. Beneath her desk, her leg beat a nervous tattoo. This was her fourth phone call from a reporter in the last two hours and, she promptly decided, her last. Apparently they'd only just this morning noticed the resemblance between the recent killing spree and the one occurring twenty-five years ago.

No, that wasn't possible. She'd done the televised interview with Celeste for TV-7 News Center. Maybe these reporters were simply jumping on the bandwagon. Carl Salvador's death was big news, and the series of unexplained murders in Phoenix was making national headlines.

Or could it be the media was finally taking the existence of the creatures seriously? If so, what impact would that have on her agreement with Nick to keep his alter ego a secret?

"Have any of these individuals ever offered more proof than eyewitness accounts?" the woman on the other end of the line asked.

Gillian glanced down at the name she'd written on a piece of paper when she first got the call. "No, Ms. Perez, they haven't."

She remembered what Nick told her about the Ancients never leaving any trace of the creatures behind. They'd done their job well.

Every single photograph the people she interviewed had taken of the creatures somehow mysteriously vanished. She supposed, like the female creature, the photographs dissolved into a cloud of golden particles. If she were ever going to obtain the proof to free her father, she'd have to find something that endured.

"In your book," Linda Perez said, "you recount the urban legends but don't give a reason for the creatures' brief appearances every twenty-five years. Is that because you don't know, or you don't want to say?"

None of the previous three reporters had asked that question, and Gillian was unsure how to answer it. She hadn't known the reason at the time she wrote the book. She hadn't known it until last week when Nick explained about the creatures' unusual life cycle and only last night she'd learned about the Ancients, their war between good and evil, and their respective champions.

It was a lot to swallow on faith.

She figured Linda Perez would have trouble swallowing it, too.

And Gillian had her credibility to consider, which would probably fly out the window along with her teaching position if she began spouting tales about good and evil duking it out every quarter century on a mortal plain. Analyzing the psychology behind the urban legends was one thing. Proclaiming them as real, another.

Then again, there was her father, his wrongful imprisonment, and her commitment to free him. Her book, and the research for it, had provided an acceptable cover for her true agenda: proving the creatures really existed. She need only reveal to this reporter what Nick had told her and if enough people believed her, the result might be a citywide hunt for Cadamus.

Thoughts of Nick held her back. A week ago she wouldn't have factored him into her decision. Since then, she'd worked with him, conversed with him, fought with him, and slept in the comfort of his arms.

He'd asked her to guard his secret. Interference of any kind, he'd said, would shift the balance of power from good to evil. Like the many individuals she'd interviewed for her book, he believed in things that weren't of this world. So did she, to a degree. Enough that she would honor his request.

For now.

"No, Ms. Perez. I don't know why the creatures appear only every twenty-five years. I have some theories, but nothing concrete."

"Care to share those theories?"

"I don't."

"Off the record?"

"No."

"One last question, if you don't mind."

"All right." Gillian tried not to convey her enormous relief. It had been a grueling day for many reasons, and she was exhausted.

"Weren't you yourself one of those dozens of individuals with compelling eyewitness accounts?"

"I beg your pardon?" She sat upright, accidentally toppling a stack of term papers.

"Didn't you, as a little girl, claim that a monster with wings killed your mother?"

None of the other reporters had asked this question. Linda Perez had clearly researched Gillian before calling her. "Yes. I did."

Lying was useless. Gillian's statements to the police were easy enough to substantiate, and there had been references in the many newspaper articles about her "nightmares," a term the child psychologists had chosen to describe her rants and raves.

"So, you *do* believe in the creatures?"

There was a knock on Gillian's office door. Before she could send whoever it was away, the door opened and Nick came in, momentarily distracting her. He looked awful, like he'd been worked over by someone twice his size and left by the side of the road.

"It, um, was a long time ago," she told Linda Perez. "I was emotionally distraught over finding my mother dead. The truth is I'm not sure what I saw."

The truth was she'd never forget what she saw if she lived to be a hundred.

Nick shut the door behind him and sat in the visitor chair, falling into it as if he were thankful to be off his feet at long last. His smile drooped, but his eyes sparkled and filled her with unexpected warmth.

"Do you think any of the people who claimed to see these creatures were actually covering up a murder *they* committed?" Linda Perez asked.

"Are you implying I killed my mother?" Had she not been so appalled, Gillian might have laughed at the sheer ludicrousness of the question.

"Of course not. But you might have been protecting your father."

"This interview is over," Gillian said cooly.

Nick leaned forward and braced his hands on her desk. "Who are you talking to?" he demanded in a low, fierce voice.

She turned the piece of paper with the reporters' names around so he could read them and pointed to the last one.

"Hang up on her," he said. "She's a barracuda."

Gillian didn't have to hang up. Linda Perez ended the call by saying, "Thank you for your time, Dr. Sayers," and disconnected.

"What a bitch," Gillian exclaimed after replacing her phone in the receiver.

Nick reviewed her list. "I'd say you've had a busy morning."

She sighed. "Very busy. What's with the sudden interest in me?"

"Your name was mentioned this morning at the press conference Police Chief Lyle Denning gave about Carl Salvador's death. By Linda Perez, in fact."

"My name? I have nothing to do with Carl Salvador." Other than being in the parking garage at approximately the same time he'd been killed. Her one alibi had dissolved into a thousand golden particles. And if questioned, her other alibi would probably deny he'd even been in the vicinity of parking garage. "I'm not a suspect, am I?"

"Naw. Linda asked the police chief a question about the creatures. It was bound to happen eventually. People are calling in sightings to the police right and left. Radio and TV stations, too, I imagine."

"How do you know that?"

"Charlie found a way to hack into the police computers."

"Doesn't it bother you that all these people are seeing the creatures?"

"Not as long as no one takes them seriously."

"What happens if the police start taking them seriously and go looking for Cadamus?"

Nick's good-humored smile vanished. "I'm just going to have to find him first."

Not wanting to think about Nick's battle with Cadamus, Gillian changed the subject. "No more interviews." She balled up the piece of paper with the reporters' names on it and tossed it in the trash. "I've had it. They can find somebody else to badger."

"You know how we news people are once we get hold of a story. Dogs on a bone."

He hadn't yet asked her about what she'd said in the interviews. She assumed he wanted to know.

"I didn't tell anyone about the Ancients or Cadamus, in case you're worried."

"To be honest, I was a little."

"I thought about saying something. I really did. But I decided it wouldn't serve my best interests."

"Hmm. You don't say?" One corner of his mouth curved up in a teasing grin.

She would have liked to tease him back but she was too tired and too confused and, because of Linda Perez's last question, too aggravated.

Collecting the stack of toppled term papers, she put them in order before laying them in her briefcase and said, "I think we should attempt to keep our working relationship separate from our personal relationship."

Nick chuckled. "Too late for that."

"Seriously. I'm less convinced today than I was last week that the public has a right to know about the creatures. But the jury's still out."

"And you don't want to hurt my feelings should you decide to blow my Superman-Clark Kent cover by giving Linda Perez an exclusive. Is that it?" He stood and leaned over her desk, bringing his face close to hers.

She countered the flood of sensation his nearness evoked by saying brusquely, "Whatever I decide to do will be because it facilitates my father's release from prison. I care about you, but he's my father, and I love him."

His gaze met hers and she was instantly reminded of the previous night in her bedroom when they'd stared at each other in her mirror while his talented fingers brought her to a shattering climax.

"At least you admit you care."

"I do," she breathed. More than she should. More than was wise. More than she ever thought possible.

Gillian, and not Nick, closed the last little distance between their lips. Holding the sides of his face with both her hands, she kissed him hotly and hungrily, her tongue delving deep into his mouth. She rose from her chair as if floating on air, her mouth still locked with his, intending to climb across her desk if necessary to get to him.

The depth of her need for him might have scared her if she stopped long enough to ponder it.

She wasn't expecting him to break off the kiss, but he did.

"Why don't you ask your father what he wants you to do." Nick placed his hands on her shoulders and eased her back into her chair. "His answer might surprise you."

She sat back, mildly affronted at his apparent rejection. "How would you know what my father wants?"

"Because I'm a regular visitor to Florence Prison."
He stood and started toward the door. She was too
stunned to do more than blink. "Ask him, Gillian,"
Nick said, his hand on the doorknob. "And when he's
told you, come see me, and we'll talk again."

•

Chapter Eleven

Gillian sat in the cramped booth and, through the bulletproof Plexiglas, watched her father approach. His gait was a little slower than the last time she'd seen him, his face a little more drawn, and the orange jumpsuit he wore fit a little looser around the shoulders.

Had it only been a month since her last visit? He looked like he'd aged five years.

Cancer would do that to a person.

The tumors, four in all, had been removed from his neck and back. Radiation and chemo followed. The doctors advocated a change in lifestyle. Right, like that was going to happen. They'd given him a fifty-fifty chance of the cancer not returning. But the ordeal, just two months prior, had left its mark on William Sayers. He wasn't the same man he'd once been, physically or emotionally.

Dropping into the chair opposite her, he picked up the phone and waited for her to do the same.

Gillian placed the receiver to her ear. It was cold. Like the visitor center. Like her. She wished somebody would turn down the blasted air-conditioning.

"Hello, Gillian."

"Dad."

"You okay? You look beat."

She was beat. Through and through. A ten-ounce cup of rotgut convenience store coffee purchased when she stopped for gas on the trip from Phoenix was the only thing keeping her eyelids open. That and Nick's words resounding in her ears.

Because I'm a regular visitor to Florence Prison.

Why in heaven's name would he visit her father?

Something told her she wasn't going to like the answer.

Her mind had been in a whirl since Nick had walked out of her office, and though she was dead on her feet, she couldn't sleep a wink until she learned the reason behind his acquaintance with her father.

Skipping out on her afternoon office hours, she'd jumped in her car and sped the forty miles to Florence, praying she made it there in one piece and before visiting hours were over for the day.

She succeeded on both accounts, but with only a half hour to spare. The guard who'd checked her in had frowned his disapproval at her late arrival.

"We don't have a lot of time, Dad," she said without preamble, "and I have some questions to ask you. Important questions."

He didn't appeared unnerved by her no-nonsense tone. Could it be he'd been expecting her, or was he just keeping his cards close to his chest?

"Okay. Fire away." He propped an elbow on the

counter. They could have been discussing the weather for all the interest he showed.

"Tell me about Nicholaus Blackwater."

A barely perceptible pause in the rise and fall of his chest was his only reaction.

"Nicholaus Blackwater? Don't think I know the name."

"Are you sure? He told me today he visits you regularly."

"He did, huh?"

"Please don't patronize me. I've had a really rough twenty-four hours." She toyed with the phone cord, wrapping it around her fingers.

"Answer me this first. How well do you know him?"

Well enough to have spent the night with him enjoying the most incredible sex of my life.

"We met last week," she said. "TV-7 interviewed me, and he was the camera operator."

"An interview? About your next book?"

"About the creatures."

Her father frowned. "I wish you'd forget about them once and for all and concentrate on something else."

"They're back," she said in a voice more controlled than she felt. "The next cycle has begun."

"They're not real." His voice was equally controlled, but a thin film of sweat glistened on his forehead.

"One of the female creatures attacked me last night in a parking garage and tried to kill me. The same parking garage where Carl Salvador was found dead." Gillian winced, feeling the creature's fingers around her neck, squeezing and squeezing until her windpipe closed and her lungs collapsed. She swallowed, surprised she could. "It would have succeeded if not for Nick."

Finally. Something she said got a reaction from her father.

He leaned forward. "Are you all right?"

"Yes, but—"

"Stay the hell away from Nick Blackwater."

"Why?"

"Just do it, dammit. He's crazy. He'll get you killed." Her father's face flushed a deep crimson.

Gillian refused to be put off. "Why does he visit you?"

"He's a cameraman. The news stations come down here sometimes."

She drew back and gaped at her father. "You're lying."

"Don't be ridiculous." His short burst of laughter rang false.

"What are you hiding from me?" she demanded.

"Nothing."

They stared at each other through the Plexiglas for innumerable seconds. Gillian broke the silence first.

"The creatures are real. One of them killed Mom. And I'm beginning to think you know they're real, too." She gripped the phone with such force her fingers cramped. "Tell me I'm wrong."

Her father unexpectedly hung his head and for the first time since her mother's funeral, she thought she might see him cry. Not even the cancer had done that.

Gillian wanted to cry, too, but not for the same reason. Like the rest of them, her father had pleaded with her after her mother's death to stop making up stories. Stories, she now realized, he'd known were true.

A stab of betrayal cut through her so sharp and so deep, she nearly doubled over.

"I kept hoping your fixation with the creatures would die out," he murmured. "Or at least end with your book. You always were too obsessed with them for your own good." He lifted his head and cleared his throat. "How much do you know about Nick?"

"Everything. He told me last night."

"I wish he hadn't."

"He didn't want to. Not at first. I insisted."

"You're like your mother that way." William's smile was faint and melancholy. "Once she set her mind to something, there was no stopping her."

Any other visit, Gillian would have treasured a walk down memory lane. Not today. "Nick says I'm his Synsär."

"No!" Her father lunged out of his chair. When a guard came up behind him, he sat back down and waited until they were alone again to continue. "You don't have to be a part of this. Just walk away. Nick will find someone else to be his Synsär."

Gillian noticed her father had no trouble pronouncing the word. She'd always assumed her father's role in her mother's death had been that of an innocent bystander. And while she wasn't so sure anymore, neither was she ready to consider the alternative.

"I don't know if I can walk away, even if I wanted to." In retrospect, she'd probably sealed her fate the night she decided to tail Nick to the cemetery.

Her father scrubbed his jaw, and Gillian was reminded of when she was a little girl.

Every day when he'd come home from work, he'd pick her up, swing her around in the living room of their small, rundown apartment, and rub her cheek with his five o'clock shadow while she squealed with delight. He'd worked at a gas station. She could still see the grime on his hands and smell the oil and grease that forever permeated his uniform.

"Isn't it past time you told me what really happened the night Mom died?" she asked.

"I couldn't live with myself if you wound up hating me. You're the only thing that keeps me going in here." He looked at her with such love and such desperation, Gillian's anger at his betrayal melted.

She raised her hand and pressed her fingers to the Plexiglas. "I could never hate you."

"You might. When you learn what I've done." With a resigned sigh, he asked, "Do you know who Jonathan is?"

"Yes. Nick's predecessor."

He met her gaze, and she read a mix of emotion in his expression. Love, sorrow, regret. But also something else. Resolution. She remembered as a little girl seeing the same unwavering look in his eyes. It was one of the reasons her belief in his innocence had never faltered.

Then all at once she knew, even before her father spoke. The alternative she hadn't wanted to consider.

"I was Jonathan's Synsär," he said.

"Oh, my God." The ramifications sank in one by one, boggling her mind and piercing her heart like tiny knives. "Oh, my God." She pressed her trembling fingers to her mouth only to remove them. "Why didn't you tell me?"

"You were too young to understand."

Gillian heard footsteps behind her and turned around to see a guard strolling past. He tapped his watch, signaling to her that visiting hours were almost over. She waited for him to move on before asking, "And then later?"

"I was afraid. I didn't think you'd forgive me for your mother's death if you knew the truth."

"You didn't kill her."

"Not with my own hands. But I was the reason Radlum was in our apartment that night." He lowered his voice to a gravelly whisper. "Jonathan and I had killed two females and Radlum was out for revenge. The bastard got it, too. In spades. He murdered your mother, destroyed our lives, and ensured the continuation of his kind all in one fell swoop."

Loathing radiated from her father in waves. Gillian repressed a sob when she realized her own loathing, carefully contained for years, was as fierce as his.

"Jeez, honey, don't cry. I won't talk about this anymore."

"No, go on. Please." She pulled a tissue from her pocket and dabbed her eyes. "I really want to hear the whole story. How could Mom's death ensure the continuation of his kind?"

He hesitated briefly before continuing. "We were closing in on the location of the third female. Might have gotten to it ahead of Radlum if not for what he did to your mother. Jonathan stayed with me most of the night. By the time he went out to hunt, Radlum had tracked down his mate."

"Were you and Jonathan friends before . . ."

"Yeah, we were friends. Not at first. He busted me twice when I was a juvie, and I hated his guts."

"Jonathan was a cop?"

"A good one. He tried his best to straighten me out. Came close once or twice but I kept getting sucked back in, or I guess you could say, down. When

I wasn't snorting coke, I was pushing it to support my habit. Sometimes, usually when I ran out of cash, I'd go straight for a few weeks. But I always went right back to the dope. I'd have wound up dead in some gutter or shot in the back by someone I double-crossed if not for your mother. She saved me in more ways than one."

Gillian had heard the story of how her parents met and married many times before. And though the end of visiting hours was quickly approaching, she didn't interrupt her father.

"She was from the same streets as me, but, by some miracle I'll never understand, stayed clear of the drugs and violence. I still can't figure out what she saw in a loser like me. A druggie, punk loser at that."

"Maybe she saw the same qualities Jonathan did. Someone who could make a difference. Someone who could help save the world."

"God knows I tried to do right by her. And by you when you came along. Crawling out of that hellhole in south Phoenix was the hardest thing I did next to leaving you to be raised by strangers."

"Harder than taking the blame for a crime you didn't commit?"

"That part was easy. I deserve to be in here. For what I did to your mother and you."

Something that had always eluded Gillian suddenly made sense. "You took the blame for Mom's death so that the secret of the creatures and the Ancients would remain safe. Didn't you?"

"You're wrong. I wouldn't have gone to prison if I could help it."

Right or wrong, it didn't matter. The sense of abandonment Gillian had suffered since her mother's death diminished a little.

"I think Mom forgives you. She would have understood you were trying to do the right thing and save people's lives."

"I'm not convinced my motives were that honorable."

"No? Then what were they?"

"Just once in my life, I wanted to be a hero instead of a loser. The kind of man who deserved to be married to your mother and a father to you."

Gillian touched her neck where the collar of her shirt covered her bruises. The dull stab of pain reminded her of her conversation with Nick the previous night. "Did Jonathan recruit you?"

"Yeah. One of Radlum's first meals was a kid from my old gang. Everyone assumed he'd been slain by a rival gang, including the police, and that his mutilated body was left as a warning. Members of my old gang retaliated by murdering two members from the rival gang. Threats were made and carried out. Jonathan approached me and asked me to talk to my old gang in the hopes of stopping what promised to be an all-out street war. Even though I'd been off the streets for a number of years, he thought they might listen to me. So I went to their hangout at the chop shop off Lincoln."

"And did they listen?"

"Hell, no. They were too riled up. One of them didn't like what I said, accused me of being a narc and selling out to the police. The son of a bitch jumped me. Jonathan intervened but not before the kid nearly choked me to death with an air compressor hose. I had welts on my neck for weeks."

Gillian felt the blood drain from her face. Lights

danced in front of her eyes. Were all Synsärs survivors of a brutal attack that left them marked, only to be rescued by the Huntsman they later served?

"What's wrong?" Her father's voice sounded distant, almost as if he were talking to her from the next room. "Gillian? Gillian!"

Silently, she tipped her head sideways and pulled the collar of her shirt away enough to show her father the bruises on her neck.

"Who did that?" he demanded.

"The female creature. Last night when it attacked me." She let go of her collar.

"Jesus, no!" Her father's face crumpled.

"Nick has scars on his neck from where Radlum bit him. He says it's my destiny to help him."

"You can refuse. You *have* to refuse. Don't let him feed you that bullshit about destiny."

"It's not like that. He'd really rather I not get involved."

"Then don't."

"*You* did."

It hit her in that moment the incredible sacrifices her father had made for the good of a world that had given him nothing in return.

"That was different. I had no clue what I was getting into or the danger I would put your mother and you in. Nick can handle himself. There's a reason he was chosen."

Then wasn't there a reason she'd been chosen, too?

The buzzer rang, and a guard announced the end of visiting hours.

Gillian had only a minute left and a hundred things she wanted to say to her father to help him understand what she herself was just beginning to.

"Please, honey," he said. "I'm begging you. Don't make the same mistake I did."

She thought of how the creatures had killed countless people and destroyed countless lives. She wanted nothing more than to see the monsters wiped off the face of the earth forever.

"I have to." The sense that she was part of something greater than herself filled her. "I love you, Daddy, and I promise I'll be careful."

"Why?" he croaked.

She stood and pushed her chair in under the counter. "Maybe I want to be a hero, too. The kind of woman who deserves to be your daughter."

Unable to say more because of the lump in her throat, she hung up the phone and turned to leave.

With Nick staring over his shoulder, Charlie laid a map of the Phoenix downtown area on the desk in front of him. Using a red pen, he drew a circle around a spot halfway between the cemetery where the old woman's remains were found and the Hanson Building. "Here." He marked another spot seven blocks north of the first one, this one in the neighborhood of Gillian's condo. "And here."

"You sure?" Nick studied the map.

"I've allowed a one-percent margin for error."

"What's that translate into? Thirty feet in any given direction?"

"If that much."

Charlie had wasted no time putting Nick's idea to use. In the past three days, there had been a total of seventeen complaints made to the Phoenix Police Department about obnoxious smells, the source of which remained a mystery. Taking it one step further,

Charlie cross-referenced the locations with those of general disturbance complaints and came up with eleven matches.

Cross-referencing those with the lost-pet notices Gillian had tracked down, Charlie narrowed their search for the remaining female creatures to two city blocks about a mile apart.

"This is even more interesting." Charlie drew two additional circles on the map. "These represent the cemetery and the Hanson Building." Next, he drew straight lines between all the circles. The results were a distorted star. "Now compare it to this."

He laid a clear plastic transparency, one with considerably more circles and lines, over the map.

"These circles represent the locations of Radlum's sanctuary twenty-five years ago and the hiding places of the two female creatures Jonathan eliminated, as well as your apartment and Gillian's condo."

"Nice work," Nick said, seeing how closely the two sections of downtown Phoenix corresponded.

"I'm not done." Charlie placed a blown-up copy of the map from Gillian's book next to their map. The boundaries of both were in nearly perfect alignment.

Nick experienced a jolt, his gut instinct telling him they were on target. "I think we've just found our females."

"Only if they haven't moved."

He tapped one of the prospective hiding places with his finger. "Isn't this where Iglisia de San Pedro is?"

"Yeah. And behind the church is a row of old houses. Both were originally built in the thirties."

"I remember." Nick hadn't set foot inside Iglisia de San Pedro in the last twenty-five years but he could still see the richly adorned altar with its life-size crucifix clearly in his mind. "That neighborhood is one of the few left that hasn't been renovated." Pushing old memories aside, he tapped the other circle. "This is the Phoenix Exhibition Center."

"I understand the management is very upset. They're hosting a big art show this weekend, and they're afraid the horrendous smell coming from the back of the building will drive customers away."

Nick pictured the Exhibition Center in his head. "The place is huge. And not easy to get into. We're going to have our work cut out for us there."

"On the plus side," Charlie commented, "so will Cadamus."

"True."

It was still a mystery how the females wound up so far apart, considering the eggs were laid together in a subterranean nest. Their best guess was that during the first year the creatures spent in a larvae state, they traveled, crawling along the ground or burrowing beneath it. About the size and shape of a rolled-up blanket, they could, even in a well-populated metropolis, remain undetected.

Separating also made sense from a survival standpoint. Should one of the female creatures be detected or damaged during their lengthy metamorphoses, there would still be two left.

On the downside, they weren't easy for the alpha male to find.

"What was the date of the last complaint?" Nick asked Charlie.

"Yesterday. I'll check again for any new complaints." He got up out of his chair and stretched. "Tomorrow. I'm beat and you look ready to drop at any second." He gathered his wallet and few personal possessions from the desk.

Nick's spare bedroom had been converted into a makeshift communication center, complete with two computers, three monitors, a printer/scanner/fax machine, satellite TV, police scanner, and a few other pieces of high-tech equipment Nick didn't understand and thought Charlie might have obtained through questionable means.

They could have passed for a covert government operation if not for the lack of weapons. Nick didn't bother with any save the ritual dagger, which he carried with him at all times concealed beneath his clothing.

He glanced at his watch. It was almost seven-thirty, and he still hadn't heard from Gillian.

She'd been gone all afternoon and evening, since he'd left her office. He knew because he'd sat on the steps of the building across from hers and waited until she left, fifteen minutes behind him. Then he drove by her condo building and when he didn't see her car parked in her assigned space, assumed she'd gone to Florence Prison.

Nick had been out of line dropping the bombshell about Gillian's father the way he had, but if she were going to play Lois Lane to his Superman, she needed to know exactly what was at stake and what she was in for. Who better to tell her than her father, Jonathan's Synsär?

"You want to crash here?" Nick hitched his chin at the futon couch in the corner buried under a mountain of research books, maps, newspapers, and magazines. "We can dig out a hole for you."

"No thanks. I prefer to sleep on something more comfortable than a sack of potatoes."

"Wimp. And you call yourself a Huntsman."

"Former Huntsman. I passed the torch a long time ago. And into very capable hands, I might add."

Nick clapped him on the shoulder. "I learned from the best."

"And you'll do an equally good job training your replacement."

He hoped so. The next Huntsman had not yet been revealed to him and with each passing day, he wondered if that was because he wouldn't defeat Cadamus.

Picking up Charlie's map, he examined it again. "I'm going to head out later tonight. Check on the Iglisia de San Pedro and get the lay of the land."

He could check on Gillian, too. Her condo wasn't far from the church.

"Why don't you get some sleep instead? Running yourself ragged won't do anyone any good except Cadamus."

"I'll think about it. Tomorrow is my last day of work, and I do have a full schedule." After that, he'd be fishing in Mexico, or so everyone at the station would think.

He walked Charlie to the door of his apartment. "Be careful driving home."

"Aren't I always?" Charlie grabbed his helmet hanging from the coat rack beside the door.

Two minutes later, Nick heard the roar of Charlie's motorcycle.

He decided to take a shower, then see if he was still in the mood to go adventuring afterward. The urge to confirm Gillian's safe arrival home hadn't abated, but he was feeling less and less like doing his Huntsman thing.

Looking at his watch again, he swore. She could have driven to Florence and back twice in the time since visiting hours were over.

He grabbed his cell phone and punched the speed dial number for her home. After one ring, he hung up. More than likely she was mad at him and wouldn't answer anyway. In which case, a face-to-face meeting would be better than a phone call.

His shower lasted seven minutes, just long enough for the tiny hot-water heater his landlord refused to replace to run dry. Nick had no sooner turned off the spigots when he heard the whine of a motorcycle on the street outside. The driver—Charlie?—came to a stop beneath his window and revved the engine repeatedly. Sliding one pane open, Nick peered out the window, a rush of adrenaline chasing away his exhaustion.

Unable to see anything, he slammed the window shut and reached for a towel. He was nearly done drying off when a knock sounded at his door. Wrapping the towel around his waist, he beat a path to the door, hollering, "Hang tight. I'm coming." Whatever had brought Charlie back must be important. Hand on the knob, he swung the door wide.

And had the face-to-face meeting with Gillian he'd been hoping for.

Good thing, too, because she looked ready to spit nails.

CHAPTER TWELVE

"Where's Charlie?" Nick leaned sideways and looked past Gillian.

"I don't know," she snapped.

"Hmm," he mused. "I thought I heard a motorcycle."

"You live above a sports bar. You must hear motorcycles all night."

"True."

Evidently fed up with small talk, she shouldered past him and into his apartment.

"Come in," he said to her back, and shut the door, a grin stretching from ear to ear. Spitting nails or not, he was glad to see her. And if the price was a verbal lashing, he'd gladly pay it.

For a while anyway.

She spun around and gave him a cool once-over. "Get dressed."

"Are we going someplace?" He moved away from the door.

"I refuse to argue with you while you're wearing nothing more than a bath towel."

"Mind telling me what we're arguing about so I know what to wear? A raincoat in case you're going to sling mud. Kevlar vest in case I have to dodge bullets."

"You knew all along my father was Jonathan's Synsär."

"Ah." Nick nodded. "Suit of armor."

"Stop making jokes. This isn't funny."

"No, it isn't," he said, sobering for her sake. "But if you don't mind, I'll stick with the towel. I get the feeling I'm going to need every available advantage in this argument."

"I'm a psychologist, Nick. You have nothing on me when it comes to playing games."

He could think of a few things he had on her, but those were more along the lines of bedroom games, not head games.

Unfortunately, the scowl she aimed at him discouraged all notions of sex. Okay, not all, but most. Nick couldn't be in the same room as Gillian without imagining her naked, her legs spread wide, and him plunging—

"Why didn't you tell me my father was Jonathan's Synsär?"

Adjusting the towel more securely around his waist, he headed toward the kitchen. "Some cappuccino?"

"No, thanks." She dogged his heels. "Do you have something stronger?"

"Beer? Wine? A stiff drink?"

"Yes."

He hadn't expected that. "Rocks or straight up?"

"Rocks." She leaned her back against the counter and observed his every move without the slightest hint of sexual interest.

So much for strutting around half naked.

Opening a cupboard above the stove, he removed a bottle of Chivas Regal that Celeste had given him in the holiday gift exchange last year. Three years working together, and she had no clue he was a Bud man.

He twisted the top off the unopened bottle and filled two tumblers, then added several cubes to each drink until the dark golden liquid reached the brim.

Passing one of the drinks to Gillian, he said, "Cheers," and, raising his glass, took a swallow. The scotch whiskey went down nice and smooth, except for the slight burn at the end. "Not bad."

Gillian knocked back half her drink in one gulp.

"Wow. I'm impressed." Nick's eyebrows shot up. "Where'd you learn to handle hard liquor?"

"Faculty cocktail parties." She set her glass down on the counter and fixed him with an unwavering stare. "I wasn't going to come here tonight."

"I'm glad you did. I was worried about you."

"I went to Florence." The alcohol hadn't mellowed her by any means. Her tone was as edgy as her movements.

"So I gather. Did you find the answers you were looking for?"

"Some. And came away with a whole set of new questions."

Drink in hand, she strode into the living room and made herself comfortable on his couch. Maybe the alcohol had affected her after all, for she toed off her shoes and nudged them under the coffee table.

Too bad she was still pissed at him because she made a delectable picture, sitting there with her skirt hiked up above her knees, her feet bare, and her long legs tucked up beside her on the couch.

"Comfy?" He sat down next to her, adjusting his towel. She appeared less bothered by his lack of clothing. Too bad. It had been fun while it lasted.

"Don't get any ideas," she snapped. "It's been a long day, and I'm tired."

So was he. But not so tired his body didn't react to her proximity.

"Why didn't you tell me about my father?" she repeated her earlier question.

"It wasn't my place. And truth be told, I probably wouldn't have said anything if the female creature hadn't attacked you last night."

"Is this some kind of family curse? Am I the latest in a long line of Synsärs?"

"Not that I'm aware of."

"So why me?"

"I think the Ancients pick someone who can be the most help to the Huntsman. Someone with strength or skill or knowledge. Whatever's needed. That individual is led to the Huntsman years before the alpha male appears."

"You and I just met last week."

"You met *me* last week. I've known you for twenty-five years."

She appeared to consider that, so he gave her something else to mull over. "You probably think your research into the creatures stemmed from your mother's death and wanting to free your father from prison. What if, in fact, you were guided into researching them in order to help me?"

She made a face. "You really buy into all of this mystical, magical, each-of-us-has-a-destiny-to-fulfill stuff."

"Hell, yes, I do. Haven't you seen enough to believe it, too?"

Rather than answer him, she polished off her drink and placed the empty tumbler on the coffee table. "What would you have done if my father hadn't told me about his relationship with Jonathan today?"

"Honestly, I'm not sure."

"Would you have told me?"

"Would you have wanted me to?"

"Yes."

"Let me get this straight." Nick set his drink down on the coffee table next to Gillian's. "You wanted to learn about your father being Jonathan's Synsär, would have wanted me to tell you about him even if he hadn't, and yet you're mad at me. Me, the one who suggested you see your father in the first place. Am I the only one who doesn't see the logic in this?"

"You lied to me."

"I did no such thing."

"You lied by omission."

"I respected your father's right to tell you his story himself. In retrospect, maybe I shouldn't have pushed the issue, especially since it hasn't earned me any brownie points."

"I'm glad you did," she said, still sounding a whole lot more mad than glad.

"Then why the hell are you ragging on me? Come on, Doc," he needled when she didn't respond. "You're the expert on what makes people tick. Analyze yourself."

"I think I've had enough." Gillian rose, remarkably

steady for one who had just imbibed a full glass of eighty-proof alcohol, and straightened the front of her skirt.

Nick stayed seated. "What say I take at stab at it? You're not mad. Not really. Anger is a defense mechanism. What you are is hurt. By your father and by me. If we cared about you, we would have told you the truth from the beginning. How'd I do, Doc?"

She turned and started for the door. "You suck as a psychologist."

He grasped her hand and held fast, stopping her in her tracks. "You're also confused. And scared. Scared of the danger involved in helping me, since one of the female creatures did almost kill you, and you're scared that you're not up to handling the responsibility that's been laid on you. I've had twenty-five years to accept my duty, to train for it. You've only had a week."

"A day," she said, her voice scratchy.

"An afternoon."

"My father says I can walk away. That you'll find someone else."

"I don't want another Synsär." He tugged on her arm, unbalancing her, and she fell onto his lap. "I want you. I have since that first time I saw you coming out of the police station in the care of a woman officer. It was the day after your mother died. Jonathan took me to the station to see you. He told me you were William's daughter and about what happened to your mother."

She squirmed to get away, but he was a whole lot stronger and pinned her arms to her sides.

"There isn't one thing you're feeling right now that I haven't. Times fifty. Times a hundred. You ask yourself, why me? What did I ever do to deserve this?"

"It's easier for you." She was breathing fast and hard, but some of the fight had gone out of her. "You believe."

"So do you." He lowered his head and brushed his lips across hers, feeling the zing from that brief contact clear to his toes. "If you didn't, you wouldn't have come here tonight. That beautiful, intelligent, analytical mind of yours isn't ready to accept what your heart and soul know is true." He nuzzled her neck, then trailed light kisses along the ridge of her collarbone.

"That's the biggest bunch of crap I've ever heard."

She curled her arms around his neck, pulled him to her, and deepened the kiss. No longer resisting—him, at least; her fate was another matter—she arched against him, her low, throaty moans driving him wild.

Sliding over onto the next cushion, he lifted her off his lap and deposited her on the couch so that she was half lying, half sitting with her back to the corner. Her eyes went wide with anticipation when he reached under her skirt and between her legs.

"You're mine," he said, his hand fumbling to breech the barrier of her skimpy panties. "The Ancients chose you to be my Synsär." He gave up, ripped the thin fabric aside, and drove his fingers inside her. "But I chose you to be my lover. And you chose me. Don't ever forget that."

"Yes. Oh, yes."

She was hot and wet and so ready for him he thought he'd come right then and there.

"You now know everything there is to know. There's no going back. If you stay with me tonight, you stay for good. Until the end."

"I'm not going anywhere."

Their gazes locked, and Nick felt his connection with her grow, solid and sure and unbreakable.

"Good."

Shoving her skirt up to her waist, he tugged her panties off, sliding them down the length of her legs and over those sexy bare feet of hers. His mouth went dry at the sight of her nakedness.

God, she was so beautiful. And his.

"You were sent to me, Gillian," he said, his hand caressing her belly, her neatly trimmed pubic hair, and the insides of her thighs. "Not because you're an authority on the creatures, or because of your father, or because you have a talent for stumbling on female creatures without trying." She gasped when his fingers probed her feminine folds and stroked her clitoris. "They sent you to me so that I'd have someone to fight for. Someone to live for. Someone to show me what life can be like when this is all over."

"Oh, Nick."

Dropping onto the floor, he knelt in front of her, parted her legs, and buried his face between them.

She said his name again and again as his tongue delved inside her and he tasted her heat, something he'd been aching to do since that first day in her office.

Cupping her ass in his hands, he lifted her hips off the cushions, giving his mouth greater opportunity to tease and tantalize, nibble, suck, and lick.

She was so sweet and so responsive. Every soft cry of pleasure, every buck of her hips and tremor of excitement set him off.

Her climax came quickly, thrilling him almost as much as it did her. He continued to kiss her until her spasms ended, savoring the last of her juices. Then, he stood.

His towel had long since fallen off.

Gillian stared at his erection with huge, hungry eyes. Sitting up, she reached out and took it into her hands, closing her fingers around the rigid length.

Nick groaned. "Wait. I've got some condoms in the bedroom."

"We don't need them." Gillian settled herself directly in front of him. "Not yet."

Whatever she had in mind, he was completely ready for it.

Bending her head, she took his cock in her mouth, swirling her tongue around the tip, raking her teeth up and down the sides. Nick willed himself to hold out for more than a minute. It wasn't easy. Gillian gave great head.

"Maybe you should stop," he croaked.

"I don't want to." Her fingers squeezed his balls, applying the perfect amount of pressure.

"Baby, I'm not going to last much longer."

"That's the whole point." She licked her palm, then used it to stroke his cock, faster and faster.

"Oh, shit." Nick felt the first hot surge low in his groin and drove his fingers into her hair. When he was fully spent, he tilted her face to his, caressed her cheek with his thumb, and said in a voice shaking with emotion, "That was incredible."

"I've never . . . um. . . . done . . ."

She could have fooled him. He dropped onto the couch beside her, unable to stand, unable to breath, unable to recall a time when sex had been so damn good.

"Well, thank you then for letting me be the first." He drew her into his arms, tenderly kissing her forehead, her eyelids, and lastly, her mouth. "You still mad at me?"

"Yes. But not about my father."

He sighed. "What have I done now?"

She ran a hand over his chest, skimming the scars there. "I'm mad because I spent eight years getting my degree, four years teaching at a top university— and you, who've had no training, figured me out."

"Actually, I've had plenty of training. Being behind the camera and observing people, particularly in crisis situations, has taught me a lot about human nature."

"I suppose it would." After a few minutes, she stirred and asked, "So what now?"

"First, we get a good night's sleep, something we both really need. In the morning, I'll make us some cappuccino and omelets. Then, I go to the station and you go to school. Tomorrow night we meet back here, don our red capes and blue tights and try to save the world. Charlie ran a new analysis tonight. He thinks he's narrowed down the hiding places for the two remaining females."

"That's great." She gave him a shy half smile. "But I was asking about us."

He rose, taking her with him, and headed them both toward the bedroom. "We spend every available minute we can together."

And while he didn't say it out loud, they both understood if he didn't beat Cadamus in the final battle, it might be all they ever had.

Miguel scurried past the high iron fence of the cemetery. Though it was late at night and very dark outside, he wasn't scared. For the first time in his eight years, he knew what it was like to be cared for and protected.

He would never be alone again, never be hungry,

never be mistreated. No longer would he be forced to watch his father beat his mother black and blue and then drink himself into a mindless stupor. Or watch his older sister turn tricks on the fire escape for drug money.

The Dark Ancients had saved him.

While he lay on the bare kitchen floor, dying from the bashing his drunken father had given him to teach him a lesson, the Dark Ancients had appeared to him. In a multitude of voices that sounded like the most beautiful music Miguel had ever heard, they offered him the opportunity to trade one miserable life for a new one full of hope and promise.

In exchange for this glorious gift, he need only serve Cadamus, the winged creature of darkness, for as long as he was needed. It had seemed a fair exchange to Miguel, and at the same moment he drew his last breath, he was lifted by strong, invisible hands and carried away, out of the kitchen and up to the sky.

He'd awakened later in a strange alley, miraculously healed and unsure of how much time had passed. Hours, days, he couldn't remember. But he knew what he had to do and where to find Cadamus. The Dark Ancients had given him his instructions while he slept in their gentle hands, and everything else he needed to know for his new life.

Now, just one day later, he was a different boy. Strong when he had been weak. Brave when he had been afraid. Smart when he had been dumb. Needed when he had been of no good use to anyone.

Crossing the mostly deserted street, Miguel ran around the side of an old building that had been condemned years earlier. The neighborhood gangs sometimes used the vacant offices for parties or stashing stolen goods or conducting drug deals. Lately, they'd stayed away as if sensing something more ominous than them had taken over the building.

They were right.

Miguel trotted down a set of rickety metal stairs. At the bottom of the stairs was a battered door, which he pushed open and slipped through. It was pitch black inside the building, but Miguel traveled with confidence. He'd practiced his route repeatedly before leaving, determined to make Cadamus proud of him.

Zigzagging through the maze of rooms, only a handful of which had four walls still standing, he found the door to the basement. His footsteps echoed eerily as he descended yet another flight of stairs into the furthest, dampest, coldest part of the building.

A half-dozen steps from the bottom, Cadamus swooped down on Miguel from out of the darkness, talonlike fingers grabbing Miguel by the arms and lifting him so high the top of his head bumped the ceiling. He tried not to breathe in the stench of Cadamus's foul breath or flinch at the still-damp blood covering his body.

"You're late."

"I'm sorry. It was far away." The errand Cadamus had sent Miguel on took over an hour, even with him running both to and fro.

Pain erupted violently in his head, and he yelped as Cadamus's mind reached into his, extracting the information Miguel had learned. He didn't understand most of what he'd seen or heard, but Cadamus apparently did, for he grunted with satisfaction.

"Good."

He put Miguel down, turned swiftly around, and

glided down the remaining steps to the basement floor, his feet not touching the stairs.

Miguel followed him, happy to have done well and basking in the praise.

Cadamus met Miguel at the bottom of the stairs and shoved something at him. "Here."

Miguel's heart raced as he felt the object with his hands. It was a plastic sack, like those from grocery or convenience stores. He tried not to be repulsed by the sticky fluid on the sack or think about whom Cadamus had killed to get this most precious gift.

Reaching inside the sack, Miguel removed the first object. It was a large bag of chips. He dropped to the cold, hard floor with a cry of delight and rummaged through the remaining items. Besides the chips, there was a package of beef jerky, a two-liter bottle of warm soda, two packs of cigarettes, and a magazine.

He tossed the cigarettes and magazine aside, then dove into the food. Ripping open the bag of chips, he shoveled handfuls of the salty delicacy into his mouth, barely stopping to breathe. The beef jerky, tougher and harder to chew, took longer to eat. He swallowed everything down with the warm soda.

It was the best meal he'd ever had.

Cadamus, Miguel realized with a burst of joy, had brought him food, proof he cared. No one except Miguel's mother had ever brought him food.

"I'm going now." His protector stood over him, tall and strong and everything Miguel wanted to be one day. "You rest. I have need for you again in the morning. Early."

The Dark Ancients had explained to Miguel how he was to be Cadamus's eyes and ears during the day.

It was his job to go where Cadamus couldn't, and bring back information.

"Okay."

Miguel obediently lay down, right there in the remains of his dinner. He didn't care that the floor was filthy or that rats by the dozens were waiting in the shadows to devour the crumbs that had fallen from his mouth.

"Do not leave," Cadamus ordered and, leaping over Miguel's head, flew up the stairs.

His dictate had been unnecessary, for Miguel had no intentions of going anywhere. Ever.

Chapter Thirteen

Gillian waited on the landing outside of Nick's apartment, holding a travel mug of cappuccino he'd insisted she take with her. In the distance, the sun peeked over the tops of buildings, its yellow rays brightening the otherwise drab gray of the city.

Traffic on the nearby street had yet to reach a congested level and wouldn't for another hour. This time of the morning, the streets were safe for joggers, and, like children let loose at recess, they were out in droves.

Gillian wasn't much of a morning person, preferring to sleep in until the last possible minute. Probably because she had a tendency to stay up late, grading papers or researching. Mornings like this one, however, could make a convert of her.

She'd awakened in Nick's bed just as dawn broke, his arm draped possessively across her middle, his breath fanning her cheek. For several long, languid minutes she'd lain there, watching him sleep in the pale light filtering through the blinds and contemplating the strange and miraculous events that had brought them together. Not merely as lovers, which in itself was wonderful, but as partners in a cause.

She was his Synsär, just as her father had been Jonathan's Synsär. It was a role she'd come to embrace with all her being. Her anger at Nick last night wasn't because he'd lied to her. That was a convenient excuse. She'd been mad because he'd known all along about this special relationship of theirs and hadn't said anything.

Then again, he was probably right to have kept quiet. She'd needed to discover her destiny for herself and come to grips with it on her own. Only then could she fully commit to him and be a worthy helper.

She glanced back at the apartment door, wondering what small task was delaying him. As promised, he'd fixed omelets for breakfast shortly after they got up. They'd gotten up only after they made love.

Their joining hadn't quite equaled the emotional intensity of the previous night but it was still immensely enjoyable and a very nice way to start the day. Yet another reason for her to become a morning person.

Her thoughts drifted to work. This was her last day until summer school started in a few weeks. Usually, she experienced a brief bout of melancholy at the end of each school year. Not today. She couldn't wait to finish up in her office, sit through her last meeting, turn in her students' grades, then hurry back here to meet up with Nick and Charlie.

She made a mental note to bring a spare toothbrush and some clean underwear with her.

The door to Nick's apartment opened and he stepped outside, closing and locking the door behind him. He smiled at her, and she resisted the urge to run into his arms for another lingering kiss like the ones they'd already shared numerous times this morning, in the shower, while dressing, and over breakfast.

"You ready?" he asked, coming toward her.

"Yep."

He'd dressed for work, wearing his camera-jockey clothes—baggy jeans and a ratty T-shirt. She liked him better in his black shirt and pants. Gillian had put on her outfit from yesterday and was planning on stopping home first to change before heading to campus.

She preceded him down the three flights of stairs and together they walked to her parked car.

"Want me to drop you off at the station?" She leaned against her car hood, admittedly stalling and eager for one more minute in his company, if not five.

"I'll walk."

"You sure?"

"It keeps me in shape."

She recalled him naked in the shower, her hands soaping his chest and shoulders. "I can vouch for that."

One last kiss, she told herself, then she'd go home. Setting her travel mug on the car's hood, she melted against him. But one kiss turned into two and three.

"What time will you be back here?" He tugged on an earlobe with his teeth.

She tipped her head back to give him better access. "Around five, five-thirty." Suddenly remembering what Nick had said last night before they went to bed, she extracted herself from his embrace. "What's the new analysis that Charlie ran? You forgot to tell me."

"He thinks he's figured out the hiding places for the remaining female creatures."

"You're kidding! That's great. Where?"

"Iglisia de San Pedro and the Phoenix Exhibition Center."

"Wow. The Exhibition Center. That place is gigantic."

"Yeah. We're going to need your superspecial female-creature-flushing skills for that one."

"Very funny." She punched him lightly in the arm.

"Ouch!" He feigned a pained expression and cradled his arm.

"Oh, please." She rolled her eyes as if exasperated. Secretly, she was enjoying their frivolous banter. She'd always been the serious type, and it had defined her past relationships with men. Nick brought out an unfamiliar and playful side to her. One she liked.

"Seriously," she said, returning them to the topic of Charlie's latest analysis. "Isn't Iglisia de San Pedro that old church near Washington and Second Avenue?"

"Yeah. The female creature could be hiding there or in one of the houses behind the church. We're not sure yet."

"Which place are we checking out first? Church or Exhibition Center?"

"Church. Less ground to cover."

Gillian sighed resignedly. "I've got to go."

"Me, too. I don't have to be at the station for another forty-five minutes, but I thought I'd walk by the cemetery on my way. Cadamus's sanctuary is near there. It has to be. I'm going to look around for any more signs of it."

"Call me later? I'll be in my office most of the day except for a departmental meeting from eleven to twelve."

"I should have a break around noon."

She stood on tiptoes to claim yet another last kiss

and might have stayed indefinitely if not for a loud clattering that came from beneath the stairs.

Thinking something—or someone—fell, Gillian and Nick both looked over. A small figure darted out from under the stairs and ran away, reminding Gillian of a startled cat racing for cover.

"Who was that?"

"I don't know." Nick craned his head over the row of parked cars. "Looks like a kid."

"What was he was doing under there?"

"Watching us, I think."

"Oh." Gillian felt a stab of guilt. "We should probably exercise a bit more decorum in public."

Nick opened her car door for her, and she slid in behind the wheel. "Okay. But in private, I don't want to hear the word decorum, much less exercise it."

Reversing out of the parking space, Gillian waved good-bye to Nick and pulled onto the street, merging with traffic. She'd forgotten all about the little boy until she saw him again—at least, she thought it was him—running down the sidewalk about a block from Nick's apartment.

"Strange," she murmured and slowed her speed as she drove past him.

If he recognized her, he didn't give any indication. He just continued running, his gaze fixed straight ahead, his thin arms pumping like tiny pistons.

Creeping along the alleyway behind the Iglisia de San Pedro, Gillian kept one eye glued to the ground in front of her and the other on the sky above her.

Cadamus had been in the area recently. And while her mind assured her he wasn't there at that exact moment—the sun had just set, and Cadamus came out only at night—her nerves were nonetheless drawn tight as bowstrings.

She and Nick had visited the church grounds the previous night and seen signs of Cadamus, among them disturbed and broken branches in the sprawling trees growing alongside the church, scattered feces beneath the trees, and fresh scratch marks on the windows and door in back of the church.

To the best of their knowledge, Cadamus hadn't located his mate. Nor, unfortunately, had they. A wedding with hundreds of guests had kept them at a distance.

Since the stench originated within the church, something they'd learned from snatches of conversation overheard while skulking around the parking lot, it stood to reason the female creature was hiding somewhere inside. So far, no one working for or attending the church had discovered the source of the smell.

Thank goodness.

Iglisia de San Pedro boasted a large membership and was very active in the community. The church's doors were open twenty-four/seven, and everyone was welcome. According to the bulletin board posted in front of the church, a variety of classes were held most weeknights from September through the middle of June. Not thirty minutes ago, Gillian had watched children dashing up the sidewalk in small, boisterous groups, on their way to a youth group meeting.

She would hate for one of them to encounter the female creature, who, sensing Cadamus's presence, might become restless and venture out of its hiding place. No child would stand a chance against its superior strength and vicious nature.

Hearing a rustle in the tree branches above her

head, she skidded to a stop and looked up just in time to see a pair of large black wings unfold.

Her cry of alarm was smothered by her heart, which had lodged in her throat. Seconds later, she watched the black crow fly off, his screeching caw answered by one of his buddies on a nearby telephone wire, and she felt utterly foolish. She also felt greatly relieved.

"You okay, senorita?"

Gillian nearly jumped out of her skin at the unexpected voice. She spun around to see the lined and weathered face of a very old Hispanic woman staring at her from over the top of a wooden fence, her snow-white hair knotted in a tight bun atop her head. "Um . . . yes. I'm fine."

Where was Nick? He'd gone to check out the recycling bins behind the church while she made another pass through the alley before it got too dark to see anything. They were supposed to have met up five minutes ago but he, as usual, was late. Neither had he checked in by cell phone.

"Sorry to bother you." Gillian started to walk away from the old woman. Nick had cautioned her to invite as little attention as possible.

"I saw you here before. Yesterday. Are you looking for *el monstruo?*"

"I beg your pardon?"

"*El monstruo.*" The monster.

"Have you seen it?" Gillian blurted, then could have bitten her tongue for her burst of impulsiveness. Way to maintain a low profile!

"*Si.*" The woman nodded emphatically. "*Anoche.*" Last night.

"What time?"

"Ooh." She crinkled her face. "Maybe one or two. Very late."

"What happened?" The hell with Nick's warning, Gillian thought and stepped closer. She smiled kindly, hoping to encourage the woman. Her plan worked.

"I heard a noise, like someone had dropped something very big. I do not sleep good these days. My bones hurt all the time. How do you say . . . ?"

"Arthritis?"

"*Si.*"

"About the crea . . . the monster. You heard a noise?"

The woman nodded again. "I came out onto the porch and saw the monster. It flew from that tree over there"—she raised her hand and pointed to one of the trees by the church—"to the roof."

"What did it do on the roof?"

She knitted her brow. "It walked around, trying to get inside the church. After a while it flew away."

"Back to the tree?"

"I do not know."

"Did anyone else see it besides you?"

"No." The woman appeared crestfallen that she couldn't be of more help to Gillian.

"Are you sure it was the monster you saw?" Gillian wanted to believe the woman, but she was old and it had been dark that time of night.

"Oh, *si.* I am very sure. It looked just like the other one."

"What other one?" Had the woman spotted the female creature? "Was it smaller?" Gillian gestured with her hands.

"Big. And with . . . How do you say *en inglés?*" The woman flapped her arms to mimic flight.

"Wings?"

"*Si*, wings."

Could there be two alpha males? "When did you see that one? And where?"

"*Hace veinticinco años*." Twenty-five years ago.

She'd seen Radlum! "Here? At this church?"

"Across the street and down the block. At the market."

"Really?"

Gillian couldn't wait to tell Nick. Radlum's nocturnal wanderings probably had no bearing on Cadamus's or the fact a female creature chose the church as a hiding place. Still, the occurrences couldn't be dismissed as pure coincidence.

"That was where the family was killed," the old woman said. "At the market."

"Family?"

"There were four. A husband and wife and two children. Only three died," she said in a dramatic whisper. "The boy, he lived."

Nick, Gillian thought with an ache in her chest. This was the neighborhood where his family had been murdered. Why hadn't he told her?

"The police said it was an accident." The old woman continued with her story. "But I knew better. It was *el monstruo*."

If only she weren't running late, Gillian would have liked to interview the old woman some more. "Thank you for your time. You've been a big help."

"I hope you catch him."

"I hope so, too." Catching Cadamus would be preferable to him engaging in battle with Nick and possibly killing him. She didn't think Nick would see it that way, however. "You'd better go back inside. And don't come out again tonight."

"Adios, senorita." The woman gave a small wave of her hand and disappeared behind the fence.

Gillian's cell phone rang just as she reached the edge of the church parking lot. She flipped it open and put it to her ear after verifying the caller ID.

"Where are you?"

"Miss me?"

"Quit being cute."

"Look to your right."

She spied him at the northeast corner of the church near the entrance to the tree-lined walkway that lead around to the front of the church.

Without saying good-bye, she hung up and trotted across the parking lot toward him. Night had fallen while she'd been talking to the old woman. If their luck held, Cadamus would return in a few hours, closer to midnight, when it was darker outside.

"Are you doing okay?" Nick asked, meeting her halfway.

"I'm fine."

"You sure? You look a little flustered." He took her by the arm and lead her back the way he'd come.

"Why didn't you tell me this was where your family was killed?"

"Because it's not."

"Okay. The market down the street, then."

"Charlie needs to keep his mouth shut."

"He didn't tell me."

"Who did?"

They stopped beneath one of the trees. On the nearby street, traffic zoomed by, yet on their side of the fence, tranquility prevailed. Iglisia de San Pedro was a charming oasis in the midst of a noisy, dirty city.

"I just had the most interesting conversation with an old woman who lives in one of the houses behind the church." Gillian hitched her thumb in the general direction. "She claims to have seen *el monstruo* last night, flying from a tree to the roof of the church."

"That's good."

"Good? I thought the fewer people who know about the creatures the better."

"Cadamus is feeling the pressure. Taking more chances. Time is running out, and he hasn't found a mate yet. He'll make a mistake soon, and if all goes well, we'll be there to take advantage of it."

"Well, get this. Cadamus isn't the first alpha male the old woman has seen. She told me about spotting Radlum twenty-five years ago." Gillian took Nick's hand and observed his expression for any evidence of distress. "If being here bothers you, we don't have to stay."

"It doesn't bother me, and we do have to stay."

"Nick . . ." She gazed at him with concern.

"Gillian, no PhD-in-psychology bullcrap tonight. Please. I don't need to vent. I don't need to cry. I don't need to let it all hang out or get in touch with my inner grief."

"It's all right if you do. We're near the place where your family was killed."

"I *live* near where my family was killed. I pass by the market twice a week at least. Trust me. I have no old baggage for you to analyze."

"I'm just saying if you feel like talking, I'm here for you."

"For Christ's sake." He groaned. "Knock it off already. If any of us has unresolved issues, it's you."

"Me?"

"You live in the same building where your mother was killed."

"I bought a condo there because the location puts me close to my research." Realizing she'd raised her voice, she made an attempt to lower it.

"You bought a condo there because connecting every day with your mother's death enables you to stay focused and committed to your goal."

"Which is my research."

"Which is getting your father out of prison."

"Is this more of *your* armchair psychology? Or should I say behind-the-camera psychology?" She was vaguely aware she didn't sound anything like the professional she considered herself to be. But so what?

"Can we continue this conversation later?" Nick said through gritted teeth.

A group of men and women were strolling across the parking lot toward them. More came from across the street. Gillian guessed they were arriving to pick up their children from the classes and escort them home.

"Sure," she grumbled.

He took her by the shoulders and though it was dark outside, she could discern his features clearly. Maybe because she'd committed every detail of his face to memory.

"We're here to do a job. An important job. Even if I was upset, which I'm not, I'd put my feelings aside."

He was right, of course.

"And if that weren't enough," he bent and grazed her cheek with his lips, "I have you. You're all the psychology I need to get me through any rough time."

She smiled, moved despite herself. "You're playing me."

He smiled back. "A little."

"It's working."

"I see that." He let go of her shoulders, took her arm, and together they started up the lushly land-scaped walkway to the front of the church. "Let's go."

"Where?"

"I think the time has come to expand our search."

"Oh." While they'd inspected the exterior of Iglisia de San Pedro, its premises, and the nearby houses, they'd yet to go inside because of the wedding the previous night. She was curious about what he had in mind and might have asked if they weren't suddenly surrounded by people.

Climbing the uneven stone steps, Gillian and Nick passed through two sets of ornately carved wooden doors into the foyer. The church was reputed to be friendly and welcoming, but most of the glances cast their way were leery if not downright suspicious. Un-derstandable. They stuck out like sore thumbs in the predominately Hispanic community.

"So much for not drawing attention," Gillian mut-tered under her breath.

The parents veered off to the left, heading toward another part of the church. Classrooms, Gillian sur-mised, or perhaps a rec room. She could hear the dis-tant din of children's voices and feel the floor beneath her feet vibrating from stampeding feet.

"This way," Nick said.

"This way" turned out to be the sanctuary. It was like walking into another world.

The church was old, the traditional decor beauti-fully ornate, the artwork priceless, and the elaborate stained-glass windows a study in religious history. The church also smelled. Not bad, but noticeable.

Gillian recognized the odor, and the hair on the back of her neck stood on end.

She must have involuntarily hesitated, for Nick had to practically drag her along with him. They walked down the center aisle between rows of polished pine pews. The stench decreased the closer they got to the altar.

A man dressed in black religious garb stood near the altar, his back to them.

"Are you sure about this?" she asked in a hushed whisper.

"Absolutely." Nick let go of her hand. "Whatever I do or say, just go along. Got it?"

"Okay."

She recalled that he'd pretended to be a representative of the management company when they were investigating the supposed rat problem at the Hanson Building. He probably had a similar ruse in mind.

"Father Juan?" Nick said when they approached the man.

The priest turned and examined Nick for several seconds. Somewhere in his early fifties, his eyes were lively and intelligent and alight with kindness. "Do I know you, my son?" His English was practically flawless.

"It's been a long time, Father. Twenty-five years." Nick extended his hand. "I'm Nick Lawler."

Father Juan's confusion lasted only a few seconds longer, after which he broke into a huge grin. "Nicholaus. How good it is to see you." He clasped Nick's hand and used it to pull him into an exuberant embrace. "What brings you here after all these years?"

CHAPTER FOURTEEN

"I'm here on business," Nick said after extracting himself from Father Juan's bear hug.

"Religious business?"

"Not exactly." Nick gestured to Gillian. "This is my associate, Jill Sands."

She tried not to start at the fake name Nick used to introduce her. "Hello, Father. It's a pleasure to meet you."

He shook her hand with boundless enthusiasm. "Whatever stories Nick has told you about me are completely untrue. I swear."

"Actually," Gillian smiled thinly at Nick, "he hasn't said much about you at all."

"No?" Father Juan asked, his disappointment evident.

Gillian rushed to make amends. "But what little he did tell me was a gross exaggeration. Now that we've met I can see you're really very nice."

Father Juan's belly laugh filled the sanctuary. He gripped Nick's arm and studied him with renewed interest. "I would never have recognized you."

"Twenty-five years is a long time. I wasn't sure you'd still be here."

"The members haven't run me off yet," Father Juan said with humor. He appraised Nick and nodded approvingly. "I'd say the passing years have been good ones. You've grown into a fine-looking man, Nick. I see purpose and strength in your eyes, feel it in your handshake. Your parents would be proud." He turned to Gillian. "Did Nick tell you he and his family used to attend church here?"

"No. He didn't." It seemed there was a lot he'd forgotten to mention.

"We lost touch after the tragedy that took his parents and sister." Father Juan crossed himself, then smiled. "But now you've come back." His bushy eyebrows shot up. "And on business."

"Yes."

Though Nick professed to carrying no leftover emotional baggage, Gillian could have sworn there was a slight catch in his voice.

"What kind of business?"

"We're here about the odor and the complaint you filed." Nick reached into his pants pocket, pulled out his wallet, and extracted a business card that he handed to Father Juan. "Jill and I are field investigators for the City of Phoenix Department of Health Hazards."

"Health Hazards?"

"You have a lot of members in your church. A lot of children. Whatever is causing this smell could, and I stress the word *could*, be a health risk to them. It's our job to find out what we can, hopefully without having to shut down the church or quarantine its members."

Gillian watched in amazement as Nick delivered his bogus story without even blinking an eye. He was so convincing, Gillian almost believed him. Father Juan did, judging by his expression.

"I had no idea the problem was so serious. We thought maybe a dog or cat got stuck in the air-conditioning vents and died."

Little did he know how close he was to the truth. Only it was lots of dogs and cats. Meals for the female creature.

"We're hoping that's all it is." Nick smiled reassuringly.

"You don't think it's a . . . a . . ." Father Juan looked stricken. "A person?"

"No. Absolutely not." Nick let just the right amount of doubt creep into his voice.

"How can we assist you?" Father Juan was hooked. So hooked it didn't occur to him to ask what the heck field investigators from the City of Phoenix were doing there at eight-fifteen at night and not eight-fifteen in the morning.

"Jill and I will need complete access to the church, inside and out. And while I know you want to help, we have to work alone. Because of the health risk. Until we learn what's causing the smell, we can't allow anyone near. You understand?" Nick finished on a grave note.

"Yes. Of course." Father Juan glanced at Gillian, and she gave him a sympathetic, we're-sorry-to-cause-so-much-trouble smile.

"Where's the odor the strongest?" Nick asked.

"It's hard to tell exactly. The kitchen area, I'd say. That's where we first noticed it. I'll show you the way." He gestured for them to follow him down the aisle, filling them in on various details as they walked, including the church's recent drop in attendance.

At the entrance to the sanctuary, they were met by a young woman, her pretty face etched with worry. "Padre Juan. *Por favor. Puedo yo dirigirse a usted?*"

"*Si*, Amaia. *Que pasa?*"

She spoke in rapid Spanish. Gillian's two years of high school foreign language classes couldn't begin to keep up. But she did understand body language, and Amaia was clearly beside herself with worry.

Father Juan spoke to her, his tone reassuring, then turned to Nick and Gillian.

"I'm sorry. I have to go."

"Is there a problem?" Nick stepped forward.

"Amaia's daughter didn't meet her after class, and she's concerned." Father Juan shrugged. "Stevie is usually a very responsible girl. I told Amaia I would help her look."

"You go on," Nick offered. "I remember the way to the kitchen."

Father Juan smiled affectionately. "I hope that's not all you remember about Iglisia de San Pedro."

"It's not."

"Come back again, Nick, when you're not working."

"I will."

Father Juan went with Amaia, who appeared enormously relieved at having him accompany her. Gillian could see why. The priest had a positive effect on people. He'd certainly had an effect on Nick. Though curious about Nick's childhood, she let the subject pass. Another time, when they weren't so pressed, she'd query him.

"What next?" she asked. "I'm sort of new at this health hazzard field investigation stuff."

"Follow me. I'm about to give you a crash course."

They went left, down the same corridor the parents had taken earlier to fetch their children. The hall was considerably quieter now, vacant except for a few stragglers using the restrooms.

"Exactly how many fake business cards do you carry in your wallet?"

"A lot."

"Charlie's handiwork?"

"He's a wiz with desktop publishing programs."

"Is Lawler your real name?"

Nick nodded. "I didn't take Charlie's last name until about a year after my parents died."

The kitchen was large, the fixtures and appliances in it, antiques. Long counters with yellowed Formica tops, probably installed sometime in the sixties, were riddled with cracks and gouges. Exposed pipes ran floor to ceiling on the wall behind a double sink the size of a bathtub, the paint covering them peeled away in most places. Cupboard doors hung at odd angles, the church members' prayers the only thing preventing them from falling off.

The kitchen also smelled. Terrible. Wherever the female creature was hiding had to be nearby.

"Search all the cabinets and cupboards," Nick told her. "I'm going to check out the pantry and storage rooms."

Gillian opened and closed cabinet and cupboard doors, of which there were many, finding nothing more dangerous than a large assortment of mismatched cookware, glassware, and silverware. Still, she tensed with each cupboard or drawer she opened. In all likelihood, the female creature wasn't lurking behind the twenty-gallon soup kettle or inside the oven, but Gillian couldn't stop her hands from shaking.

"Find anything?" Gillian asked Nick when he came out of the pantry. He'd spent a good twenty minutes going through the rooms from top to bottom.

"Nothing."

"Me either." Together they surveyed the kitchen. "What do you think?"

"I think we keep looking. The smell is definitely stronger in this part of the church." He glanced up at the ceiling, studying it astutely. Irregular brown patches identified water leaks. One of them surrounded a large metal grille sorely in need of cleaning. "Well, lookie there."

"I noticed a stepladder in the corner by the refrigerator."

"Did you happen to notice any screwdrivers while you were rummaging through drawers?"

"As a matter of fact, I did." She went to fetch them.

When Nick returned with the stepladder, Gillian presented him with three different screwdrivers. "Take your pick."

"This'll work." He selected a flat head and stuck it in his back pocket. Setting up the ladder, he climbed nearly to the top and promptly make a face. "God, it reeks up here."

He undid the screws one by one, dropping them in Gillian's waiting hands.

She, in turn, placed them on the counter. "You're not going to break anything, are you?"

"If I do, I'll leave enough money in the collection plate by the door to pay for it."

"What's this about a collection plate?"

Gillian and Nick both swung around to see Father Juan enter the kitchen.

"Did the kid show up?" Nick asked, his demeanor nonchalant.

Gillian marveled at his ability to switch gears so rapidly. Less than a minute ago he'd been a bundle of energy, intensely focused on his task.

"No. Amaia's gone home to see if Stevie went there. Since she hasn't returned, I'm guessing all is well." Father Juan observed Nick, openly curious. "Do you think the source of the smell is in there?"

"Possibly. We'll know soon."

Nick had ceased removing screws to chat with Father Juan. Gillian suspected he didn't want Father Juan around when he pulled the grille off just in case the female creature was behind it.

"Those ducts haven't been used in years. Not since the central air-conditioning system was installed . . ." Father Juan scratched his chin. "Thirty or more years ago, I'd say. Before that, fans were used to blow cool air from the basement through the ducts."

"Is this the only room with ducts like this one?"

Father Juan frowned contemplatively. "I think so. But I'm not sure. I only know about the fans because some of the older members told me."

Seconds passed with no one speaking. Father Juan finally got the hint and said, "Guess I'll leave you two to your work. Stop by the office and say good-bye when you're done. I trust you remember where that is, too." He winked at Gillian. "Nick spent more than his share of Saturday mornings in there rather than catechism class."

"Did he perhaps have a behavior problem?" Gillian pretended to be appalled.

"A tiny one." He pinched his thumb and index finger together to indicate a small amount.

"Why am I not surprised?"

Only when the door to the kitchen had closed behind Father Juan did Nick remove the last of the screws. Inserting his fingers between the slats, he tugged on the grille. At first, it resisted his efforts, then finally gave, sending a shower of debris raining down upon them.

Gillian coughed and fanned the air in front of her face. "Can you breathe up there?"

"Barely." Nick had climbed another step on the ladder and had his head inside the opening.

"Does it smell?" Gillian tipped her head back, trying to see past Nick.

"I can't tell. The inside of my nose is numb." Bracing his hands on the edge of the opening, he scaled the last step on the ladder and hoisted himself into the duct. He just fit, his shoulders clearing the sides by no more than an inch.

Gillian waited, chewing her bottom lip.

A minute later, he called, "Coming?"

She grimaced, realizing too late she should have clarified the Synsär employment terms before accepting the position.

Between the stench, the dust, and the heat, breathing was almost impossible. Nick shimmied along the duct floor on his stomach, battling cobwebs and feeling his way in the suffocating darkness. The duct was wide enough to accommodate him, but only about eighteen inches high, which meant he and Gillian couldn't crawl on all fours. As a result, their progress was slow and arduous.

"You doing okay back there?" he said over his shoulder.

"Yeah."

"That's a pretty weak yeah."

"To be honest, I'm feeling pretty weak right now."

"You want to go back?"

Nick reminded himself that Gillian had only recently traded her safe and comfy academic job for one that put her in constant danger and tested her physical limits.

"I'm okay." She collided with his feet again, the third time since they'd started. "Sorry."

"No problem. We're a little tight in here."

And they couldn't see two inches in front of their faces. She must be scared, and he suspected she didn't want him getting too far ahead of her. If the stench weren't growing stronger, he'd consider going back.

Then again, the duct was too narrow for them to turn around and he was sure Gillian would be even less thrilled at blindly backing out. The best alternative was to continue forward until they hit an exit.

"How much farther do you think?" Gillian asked, her voice strained, her breath coming in short, ragged bursts.

"We have to be close." Talking had become difficult for Nick. The stench was everywhere, and he felt as if he were drowning in his own sweat. "Using fans to blow cool air to the kitchen wouldn't have worked unless the basement were located nearby."

"I hope you're right."

His hand encountered something hard and sharp, and he drew to a stop. "Wait."

Gillian collided with his feet again. "What is it?"

Nick felt cautiously ahead of him and detected more sharp objects, some with pieces of fur stuck to them, some completely unidentifiable, which was probably just as well.

"I think I found the female creature's dinner remains." The pile of dead animal carcasses appeared to be huge.

"Oh."

He thought he heard Gillian gulp.

"The female's not here, not that I can tell, anyway." He waved his hand through the air in front of him and listened intently. The creaks and groans of a hundred-year-old building were all he heard. "If it were here, it probably took off when it heard us coming." Or relocated to a new hiding place, which meant they'd have to start searching again from scratch. "Let's keep moving."

Nick wriggled forward, dragging himself over the female creature's meal remains. Bones gouged his skin, poking and pricking. Sticky substances clung to his hands and clothing. He didn't want to know what the hard, pebbly stuff was.

Eyes watering, chest heaving, and muscles aching, he moved on. "Hang in there."

"Like I have a choice."

"Try closing your eyes."

"Very funny."

He could hear the scraping and crunching as Gillian crawled through the mess. He could also hear revulsion in her voice and a determination that made him proud. Gillian possessed more strength than she realized. The trick for her would be learning to tap into it.

"We're almost through."

The debris had started to thin. In another minute, Nick was completely free of it. Air, marginally less stale and tepid, reached his nostrils. Thankful, he breathed deeply.

"Slow down. I found an opening in the duct floor."

Groping carefully with his hands, he calculated the size of the opening. He could fit, but barely. The more important question was where did the opening lead? Down, yes, but to the first floor or all the way to the basement? If the latter, it would be one hell of a drop.

Feeling the air in front of him, he determined there was no wall or other barrier blocking their path. The duct they were in continued on, but for how long and to where?

Nick made a decision. "I'm going down the opening."

"You sure?"

Gillian sounded done in. He doubted she could take much more of crawling through the ducts.

"Yeah. Stay where you are. I can't go through the opening head first so I'm going to have to crawl over it and then slide down backward, feet first."

"What if you fall?"

"It's narrow. I should be able to grip the sides with my feet."

He tried to make it sound easier than it would be. If the drop were only to the ground floor, no more than ten or twelve feet, he'd be fine. If not . . . well, he'd cross that bridge when he came to it. That, and the even bigger bridge of how to get Gillian down.

The opening was the same size as the duct they were in. Slithering over it was a little precarious, particularly when Nick's belly was suspended above all that empty air. Rather than drag his feet across the opening, he lowered them into it, then slowly, slowly, eased the lower half of his body into the duct.

His back muscles trembled, as did his arms, and his spine bent at a severe angle that threatened to snap it in half. Sliding the last few inches, he hung to the sides of the opening. His feet scraped the duct walls, unable to find purchase. Little by little, his fingers started to give.

Just when he thought he'd have to let go and hope for the best, the soles of his shoes make contact with the duct walls. Resting for a moment, he took several deep breaths and then straightened his cramped fingers.

His feet slid, but not fast. Bracing his palms on the wooden walls of the duct, he tried to slow his descent still more. Stream after stream of blistering pain shot up his legs. His ankles, bearing the burden of his body weight, were on fire. Splinters pierced his palms, his forearms. Nick bit down so hard he thought his teeth might break.

As his strength drained, he picked up speed. No way would he make it all the way to the basement in one piece.

Suddenly, Nick's feet crashed into something solid. A wave of pain ripped through him from toe to head. Sinking to his knees, he crumbled into a ball and gasped for breath, his legs and arms shaking uncontrollably.

"Nick?" Gillian called from above.

"Yeah." He sucked in large chunks air. "I'm fine. Just give me a minute."

Feeling around with his hands, he discovered he'd

landed in a crawl space about five feet long by four feet tall. Not exactly a room at the Ritz, but a welcome relief from the duct. About three feet to his left was another opening in the floor. The air wafting up from it was cleaner and cooler.

"I found the duct to the basement," he called to Gillian. "As soon as I turn myself around, we'll get you down." When she didn't answer, he called again. "Gillian."

"I'm here."

"What's wrong?"

"Just thinking about climbing down the duct. Or, I guess I should say, trying *not* to think about it."

"You'll be fine. It's not far, and I'll be right here to catch you." Raising his arms over his head he rose slowly so that he was standing in the duct. "Ready when you are."

"Okay." She sighed expansively. "I'm crawling across the opening."

"Take it slow." He coaxed her along. "Worse-case scenario, you fall four or five feet right into my arms."

She groaned and swore and cried out once. But she kept going.

Nick cursed the darkness, wishing he could see. In the next second, when she slipped and gave a loud, "Oomph," he was glad he couldn't. Watching her struggle and not being able to help would drive him crazy.

"I'm across the opening." Exhaustion, or maybe tears, had clogged her voice.

"Good job, sweetheart. Now, lower your feet into the opening." She did as he instructed. "That's it."

He could sense her legs flailing above his head, hear them bang into the sides of the duct.

"Nick."

"Don't worry. I'll catch you. Another foot or two. Then you're home free."

She started kicking. Furiously. "Nick!"

"Try to relax."

"Oh, Jesus, Nick!" she screamed.

He heard the hissing then, and every nerve in his body exploded. "Let go, Gillian," he hollered. "I'll catch you."

An ear-splitting screech rang through the duct, bounced off the narrow walls, and reverberated inside Nick's head.

The female creature. Christ, where had it come from?

"Damn it, Gillian. Let go!"

"I can't," she yelped, her legs thrashing above his head, just out of his reach. "It's got me."

The creature's hissing and screeching increased, smothering the sounds of Gillian's struggle.

Nick extended his arm as high as it would go and jumped. The back of his fingers brushed one of Gillian's feet.

"Stop kicking."

She didn't.

Crouching as low as he could in the cramped space, he jumped again, both hands extended.

His fingers grabbed empty air.

He tried jumping again and this time succeeded in latching on to the heel of a shoe. When he fell back down into the crawl space, Gillian, thank God, came with him, landing on top of him in a convulsing, howling heap. They tumbled backward into the crawl space. Nick slammed into the floor with a thud.

Recovering quickly, he tried to untangle himself from Gillian and shouted, "It's okay." She inadvertently kneed him in the groin. "Take it easy." He groaned. "You're safe."

She twisted around and, sobbing, threw her arms around his neck. "Oh, God, Nick. It had me by the hair and wouldn't let go."

He detached himself from her frantic embrace. "We have to get you out of here."

"What about you?"

"I'm going after the female."

"You can't!"

The subject wasn't open for debate. He pushed Gillian toward the opening. "There's another duct here. It should lead to the basement." He hoped.

She gasped. "I can't go down it by myself."

"You have to."

"No. I'll stay here." She shook her head vehemently. "Waiting for you."

Above them, the female creature hissed and spat, warning them to leave and never come back. Nick had to somehow climb back up the duct before it took off and relocated to a new hiding place.

"Listen to me." He gripped Gillian firmly by the shoulders and brought his face close to her. "The drop isn't far. I'll hold on to you the whole time."

"I'm afraid."

"You won't fall more than a few feet." He didn't mention the opening could lead to yet another duct or that she might land on something besides an empty cement floor and crush her legs. "Once you're in the basement, find a door or window. Some way out."

A strange, rhythmic thumping echoed through the duct above them, and the walls rattled. The creature's hissing grew angrier, its screeching louder. When the hell had the females become so aggressive? Nick really had to talk to Charlie if—no, when—they got out of this predicament.

"If after fifteen minutes I haven't come down, call Charlie." He thrust Gillian aside. "He'll know what to do."

"I don't want to leave without you."

When she would have clung to him, he pushed her ruthlessly toward the opening. "Feet first."

"Nick, please."

His hands tightened around her upper arms. "I know you're scared. But you have to get out of here." Giving her the briefest of kisses, he helped her position herself so that she was sitting on the edge of the opening with her legs hanging over the side. "Ready?"

"Not really."

"You'll be fine."

"Promise you won't let go?"

"I promise."

He nudged her butt off the edge of the opening with his knee.

"Wait!" She stiffened, resisting him. "Not so fast."

"We don't have a lot of time, sweetheart."

Hooking his hands beneath her arms, he lowered Gillian inch by inch until only her head remained above the opening. She whimpered once or twice when his grip momentarily slipped.

"Relax," he told her. "There's no—"

A loud whump cut Nick off, followed by a frenzied pounding. The walls of the duct began to shake as if the ground were trembling. But it wasn't. Only the duct.

Too late Nick realized what was happening.

In the next instant, the female creature landed on his back.

Spitting and hissing, it clawed at him, going for his

head and neck, ripping at his hair. He twisted violently in a useless attempt to dislodge it, knocking Gillian around in the process. She kicked and floundered, making it harder for him to maintain his hold on her.

"Damn it, Gillian. Stop moving."

"Don't drop me!" she yelled, desperately grappling for a handhold.

The female creature clamped her fingers around Nick's neck and began to squeeze. Though small, it was strong and agile and able to see better in the dark. It would also choke the life out of him in a matter of minutes unless he did something.

If he could just get to the ritual dagger in his pants, he'd have a fighting chance. But in order to accomplish that, he needed both his hands, which, at the moment, were holding on to Gillian.

Tiny spots of bright light danced in front of his face, an indication he was starting to fade.

Sending a prayer to the Ancients, Nick made the only choice he could. He let go of Gillian, rolled sideways, and reached for the ritual dagger.

As he pulled it out, Gillian's scream of terror reached inside him and tore his heart clean in two.

CHAPTER FIFTEEN

•

Gillian's scream turned into a grunt when her butt impacted a hard, flat surface with such force it felt like her brain shook loose from the inside of her skull.

Breathing took effort. So did sitting up. She lay down to wait until the world stopped spinning . . . and promptly rolled off whatever it was she'd landed on. The sensation of flying, for the second time in as many minutes, lasted only an instant before she slammed into a concrete floor.

Afraid to move for fear she'd take another dive, she remained motionless, contemplating the recent small miracle bestowed upon her.

She hadn't died. She'd quite possibly broken every bone in her body but was alive to tell about it. Walking might be an altogether different story.

So much for Nick and his promise not to let go of her. Oh, God, Nick!

Pushing herself to a kneeling position, she glanced

around, attempting to get her bearings. Wherever she'd landed—the basement, she hoped—was as pitch black as the ducts had been. From high above her came evidence of a struggle. Banging, thumping, the creature hissing and screeching.

Gillian instinctively looked up, though she could see nothing.

What the hell was happening? Was Nick all right?

Suddenly, an inhuman shriek rent the darkness. It escalated in pitch and volume, then abruptly ceased, leaving only silence.

Dead silence.

Suddenly in a hurry, Gillian climbed awkwardly to her feet. It wasn't easy. She hurt everywhere.

Attempting a few faltering steps, she cried, "Nick? Are you there?"

No answer.

She turned blindly around, only to run into a large, solid object. Skimming her hands over the top, she determined it was a wooden table or possibly a desk. She'd landed on the top of it, then rolled off onto the floor.

Which meant the opening she'd fallen through must be right above her head.

"Nick," she called again. "Please answer me."

Oh, God. What if something terrible . . . no, she wasn't going to think that way. Nick was the Huntsman and the chosen champion of the Ancients for a reason.

But still only human. And the creatures weren't.

Gillian tried to hoist herself onto the table. Her muscles and aching joints refused to cooperate, but her heart insisted she couldn't sit around and do nothing. After several more attempts, she still hadn't managed to swing her leg high enough to clear the top of the table.

She remembered that Nick had told her to find a way out of the basement and, if he didn't appear within fifteen minutes, to call Charlie.

Like hell.

She wasn't going *anywhere*, calling *anyone*, until she knew for certain what happened to Nick.

But what if the female creature suddenly came through the opening into the basement and attacked her? It had done exactly that in the crawl space. On top of the table, Gillian would be a sitting duck. In her bruised and battered state, she doubted she'd fend off the creature for long.

"Nick! Answer me."

"Hold on. I'm coming."

Gillian's legs, weak to begin with, went out from under her, and she slid to the floor. Only when she tasted her own tears did she realize she was crying.

"Are you okay?" she hollered in a choppy voice.

"Yeah."

Thank you, thank you, thank you.

She heard scraping and bumping and then a heavy thud. He must be coming through the opening.

Sniffing back her tears, she wiped her nose with the back of her hand and called, "There's a table or desk directly beneath the opening." Gripping the edge of it, she pulled herself upright and waited for her wobbly legs to steady. "The duct ends and—

Nick landed with a bang not two feet from her.

Gillian yelped and stumbled backward, losing her balance and nearly taking another dive onto the cement floor.

"Where are you?" he called, scrambling off the table.

"Here."

He found her, wrapped her in his arms, and held her tight. Wonderfully tight. Everything-is-going-to-be-okay tight. His embrace felt so good, her joy at learning he was alive so great, she didn't care that he'd broken his promise and let her fall.

"What about the female creature?" she asked when he'd relaxed his hold enough for her to talk.

"It's gone. Only one left now to worry about."

Gillian didn't insist on details. She'd rather not know how the female creature had perished. All she cared about was Nick and that he was safe. They were both safe.

"Are you hurt?" she asked.

"A few cuts and scrapes. No big deal."

She suspected he was minimizing the extent of his injuries. But then, he did have the help of the Ancients. Maybe they'd already intervened and healed him like they had her that night on South Mountain after the first female creature's attack.

"Did you find a way out of here?" he asked.

"I didn't have a chance to look before you . . . arrived."

"Let's split up." Placing a hand on her shoulder, he nudged her away from him. "You take that wall, and I'll take this one. Feel along with your hands. Yell if you find anything."

She disliked his plan for obvious reasons. "Can't we stay together?"

"We'll cover more territory this way."

Gillian didn't budge.

He came to stand beside her. "It's been one hell of a night. For both of us. But we'll be out of here soon and back home." He stroked her hair, tucking one of the many wayward strands behind an ear. "We just have this one last problem to tackle."

He said "this one last problem" as if it were no more challenging than locating a missing set of car keys.

"What if there's no way out?"

"There is. All this junk didn't simply appear one day. Somebody carried it through a door. And we'll find that door faster if we split up."

She had to agree with his reasoning even if she didn't like it. "Fine. We'll split up." How bad could it be? So she'd step on a few mouse droppings and walk into a few cobwebs?

He cupped her cheek in his hand and brought his mouth to hers. His tongue traced the seam of her closed lips seeking entrance. She sighed, opened her mouth, and leaned into his kiss. Her contentment was short-lived.

In the next instant, Nick had left her side, and Gillian resigned herself to the problem of getting the hell out of the basement.

It proved more difficult than she'd first imagined. Objects were constantly in her path. Boxes, crates, cartons, storage racks, and furniture. She wormed over and under, squeezed around and between each and every obstacle on the off chance someone had stacked something in front of a door or window.

To keep her hopes high, she pictured herself having a long, scalding-hot shower, followed by a mug of Nick's cappuccino. No, wait. A shot of his Chevis Regal. That would hit the spot.

Every minute or so Nick said something to her, and she answered. His comments were more conversational than anything else, leading Gillian to believe he was talking to her in an attempt to keep her fears at bay.

It worked.

"I found something," Nick called excitedly after about fifteen minutes of searching. "A window."

"Great!" Gillian started walking toward the sound of Nick's voice. She traveled slowly, running into an obstruction every other step and having to cut around it.

All at once there was a loud crash and the tinkle of glass shards falling onto the floor.

"What happened?" Gillian threw caution to the wind and rushed forward, only to slam into a . . . she had no idea what it was. A lawn mower maybe? Her big toe throbbed.

"The window's small, but I think we can fit through it," Nick said. "You can, for sure. Watch your step," he warned as she neared. "There's broken glass everywhere."

Fresh air poured into the basement. Gillian didn't think she'd ever smelled anything sweeter.

The window turned out to be large enough to accommodate both of them but very high off the floor. They had to construct makeshift steps using an old coffee table, a trunk, and two boxes placed on top of each other in order to reach the window.

Nick went first after clearing the last bit of broken glass away from the window with the rag he'd used to protect his hand when breaking it. Once outside, he pulled Gillian through the window. The sharp edge of the window frame scraped her stomach as he dragged her out, but she could not have cared less. The discomfort was minor compared to the delight of finally escaping the air ducts and the basement.

Gillian stood next to Nick and brushed herself off. After a moment, she gave up. She'd need a power washer to rid herself of all the filth and grime covering her.

"Where are we?" She glanced around.

Nick was picking bits of glass out of his shirtfront and sleeves. "East side of the church." He inclined his head. "The parking lot's over there."

"Are we going back inside to talk to Father Juan?"

"Yeah, we probably should. He said he'd wait for us in his office." He grinned. "And I ought to put some money in the collection plate to pay for the broken window."

"What are you going to tell him?"

"The truth, more or less. We found the remains of some dead animals, and that's what was causing the stench. I'll suggest they use fans to blow out the air ducts like in the old days. With the female creature eliminated, the stench should dissipate in a few days."

Hand in hand, they began strolling toward the walkway that lead to the church entrance. Security lights on the back of the building lit their way and all of the parking lot, which was empty except for Nick's car. Father Juan, Gillian assumed, must live within walking distance.

She was about to suggest they offer to drive him home when a small figure darted out from behind one of the trees and ran in the direction of the parking lot.

Gillian recognized the boy immediately. "It's him." She shook Nick's arm. "The kid who was watching us the other morning at your apartment. What's he doing here?"

"I don't know," Nick said, "but I'm going to find out." He sped off after the boy, who cut diagonally across the parking lot and headed in the direction of the alley where Gillian had met the old woman.

Gillian chased after them. Her tired muscles, already pushed to their limits, were no match for Nick and the boy. They rounded the corner leading into the alley before she was halfway across the parking lot.

She kept going, her run slowing to a jog and then to a fast walk, and reached the alley a good three minutes after Nick and the boy.

Lights from the church, though distant, provided sufficient illumination for Gillian to see. She might have screamed at the terrifying sight unfolding in front of her if her aching lungs could draw in enough air.

Cadamus—it could be no other—stood over the bloodied body of a woman. Gillian recognized her and became instantly sick to her stomach. It was Amaia, the mother with the missing daughter who'd come into the sanctuary looking for Father Juan.

In his arms, Cadamus held a young girl, unconscious or dead, Gillian wasn't sure which. His wings were fully extended, his teeth bared, and his eyes burned with an animalistic glow. He stood only five feet tall, but his wings and heavily muscled body gave the impression of someone—some*thing*—much larger.

For a moment, Gillian was transported back in time to the night of her mother's death. She'd awakened for an unknown reason and crept down the hall to her parents' room, planning to sneak into bed beside her sleeping parents. Instead, she'd found Radlum, crouched over her dead and dismembered mother—and her father missing.

Radlum's eyes had burned with the same animalistic glow as Cadamus's did now.

Dear God, it couldn't be happening again.

"Put her down," Nick said, his voice low and lethal.

Gillian turned. Her attention focused exclusively on Cadamus, she hadn't noticed Nick until he spoke.

"Nick, what are you doing?" Her hand flew to her mouth and she staggered backward when she saw that Nick held the boy by the hair, his grasp ruthless.

"Whatever happens," he said from the side of his mouth, "don't interfere." Twisting the boy's head at a severe angle, he pressed the tip of the ritual dagger into the boy's neck, right where his jugular vein pulsed. "I repeat," he told Cadamus, "let her go."

The boy's eyes were huge, and he trembled uncontrollably, but he didn't cry out.

"Don't hurt him," Gillian whimpered. "He's just a boy."

"Shut up, Gillian."

Her mind struggled to make sense of a situation that defied reason. Nick wasn't a killer. He was a good and kind man . . . and sticking the tip of the dagger into the boy's neck so hard that blood trickled from a tiny wound. Suddenly light-headed, she reached for a nearby fence post.

"Listen to your mate," Cadamus growled.

His voice, coarse and guttural, sent a wave of shivers crashing through Gillian. A memory of Radlum surfaced, one she'd apparently repressed all these years. He'd spoken to her father before he escaped through the bedroom window. What was it he'd said?

A mate for a mate.

At first, the words didn't make sense to Gillian. Then they did. Chilling sense. Radlum had killed her mother because of her father's part in exterminating the female creatures.

"Let her go." Nick's eyes never left Cadamus. Nor did his grip on the ritual dagger waver. "Or the boy dies."

Cadamus hissed and lifted the girl higher. "You think I care what happens to the human child?"

He flapped his wings, their movements slow and oddly graceful for something born in the deepest corner of hell. Dirt and small pebbles flew through the air, powered by the gusts of wind his massive wings generated, and striking Gillian in the face and on the arms.

"Then you won't mind if I slit his throat wide open," Nick said.

"Do with him what you must, Huntsman." Cadamus rose up in the air, stopping to hover when he reached a height of ten feet. He held the unresponsive girl by the wrist and dangled her over Nick's head as if she were a treat and he a dog. "And I will do with this one what I must."

Gillian watched, wishing there was something, anything, she could do.

Cadamus flew higher. Fifteen, eighteen, twenty feet off the ground. Suspended above them, he looked even larger and scarier than he had on the ground, while the girl looked smaller and more vulnerable. Light from the church reflected off his dark, scaly skin, turning it an incandescent silver. Wind from his great wings pummeled Gillian, and she was forced to shield her face against the assault.

But she didn't dare turn away. She couldn't.

As loathe as she was for Cadamus to abscond with the girl, she was equally loathe for Nick to hurt the boy. Yet one, if not both, of those dismaying possibilities was inevitable.

Cadamus floated above Nick, taunting him with the limp girl hanging from his grasp. Nick didn't respond. He continued to press the ritual dagger to the boy's throat, his stony expression void of emotion save for a commitment to carry through with his threat.

This can't be happening.

Yet it was, and Gillian could do nothing to prevent it. She was a trained psychologist. Her method of helping people was to talk with them. Clearly, neither Nick nor Cadamus was in the mood for a discussion.

Cadamus dipped suddenly and swung the girl in front of Nick's face.

"I grow weary of your games, Cadamus." Nick raised the dagger as if to strike the boy.

"No!" Gillian shouted and lunged at Nick, prepared to put herself between the ritual dagger and the boy if necessary.

She didn't have to.

Without warning, Cadamus released the girl. She tumbled downward on a collision course with the ground.

In the next split second, Nick shoved the boy aside and dove for the girl, his arms fully extended. The boy ran—not away from Cadamus but straight toward him. At the same instant Nick caught the girl, Cadamus swooped down and snatched the boy.

The last thing Gillian saw as they disappeared into the night sky was the boy clinging to Cadamus's neck and Cadamus's arm locked protectively around him.

"Gillian!" Nick called.

The weight of the falling girl had knocked him to the ground. He lay in the dirt with the girl on top of him.

"Take her," he said, his voice wheezing, his breath short. The entire left side of his face was scraped and bleeding.

"Is she alive?" Gillian asked.

"Yes."

She couldn't lift the girl, who was surprisingly heavy for one so thin. Instead, she pulled the girl off Nick and settled her as comfortably as possible beside him. When she was done, she glanced over her shoulder at Amaia. It was probably fortunate the young girl wasn't conscious to see her dead mother. Gillian knew firsthand a child never really got over the experience.

"I'll call nine-one-one." Gillian reached for her cell phone.

"No."

"Nick. She needs medical help."

"She's fine." He rolled onto his side, then sat up.

"How can you say that? She's unconscious. Dying for all we know."

Taking several deep breaths, Nick stood and reached for the girl. "Let's get out of here."

"Get out of here?" Gillian stepped back and glared at Nick as if he were a stranger and not the man she'd spent the last few nights with.

"Hurry."

"What about the girl's mother?" She flung her hand in the direction of Amaia. "We can't just leave her."

"It's too late. There's nothing we can do." Nick gently lifted the girl in his arms and cradled her against his chest. Still breathing hard, he set out for the parking lot at a brisk walk.

"Where are you going?" Gillian trotted after him.

"Home."

"Home? My God, Nick. What the hell is wrong with you?"

He didn't answer.

"You held a knife to that boy's throat."

"I was never going to hurt him. It was a bluff."

"A bluff," she shouted. "Are you insane?"

"It worked, didn't it?"

"Cadamus took the boy."

"He won't harm him."

"And you know this how?"

"He wanted the boy. Why else would he have given me the girl?"

They'd reached his car. Nick shifted the girl to one side and dug in his pocket for his keys.

"You can't take her, Nick. You have no right."

"I have every right."

Gillian grabbed his arm and swung him around to face her. An amazing feat considering how much stronger he was than her.

"I won't allow you to leave with her. I'll call the police and report you for kidnapping if I have to."

Even as she said it, Gillian wondered if she really could make such a call. What reason would she give the police for them being there? Surely not that they were inspectors from the city. And what if the police blamed them for Amaia's death? Stranger things had happened. To her father, for one.

And yet, they couldn't just take the girl, could they?

"She needs medical attention," Gillian pleaded. "She needs to be taken to a hospital, her family located and notified."

"This girl is the next Huntsman." Nick opened the car door while balancing her with one arm. "And she's going home with me."

* * *

Another female was dead.

Cadamus didn't have to read the boy's mind to learn of it. A sudden decrease of pheromones in the atmosphere was the first indicator. His inability to make a psychic connection the next.

For the second time in almost a week, the Huntsman had destroyed Cadamus's mate mere hours, mere minutes, before he reached her. He would not allow a third time.

He'd envisioned himself impregnating all three females and securing a place in history as the supreme forefather of his kind. Now, because of the Huntsman, Cadamus could conceivably end up as the last of his kind.

For that, the Huntsman must pay with his life—and that of his mate's.

"Are we going home?" Miguel asked, his small face buried in Cadamus's neck.

"Yes."

The boy had served him well, proving to be a reliable and obedient helper. Cadamus didn't mind exchanging the worthless female child for him. He should probably reward the boy with some food— find another meal for himself, too, since he'd left the last one back in the alley.

Cadamus ducked behind a large, square post. He wasn't flying as much as leaping from building top to building top and only when safe. The moon was too bright tonight and there were too many humans milling about on the streets. He was well aware of the danger their mechanized weapons presented. There was a limit to what his armor-plated hide could protect him from.

Not that he minded dying. No, indeed, his premature death by the hands of someone other than the Huntsman would guarantee that the balance of power shifted into the control of those Dark Ancients Cadamus served.

But he'd not yet mated, not yet ensured a future generation. Until then, he must exercise caution.

Afterwards, he'd seek out the Huntsman, or let the Huntsman find him, and embrace his destiny.

CHAPTER SIXTEEN

Gillian chewed on a thumbnail and watched Nick gingerly load the girl into the backseat of his car, buckling the seat belt around her waist. She'd yet to rouse, and Gillian was starting to worry.

"How can you be sure she's the next Huntsman?"

"Inside information."

"The Ancients spoke to you?"

His answer was to straighten, shut the rear driver-side door, and meet her gaze head on.

Gillian stared into the same expression of resolution she'd seen on her father's face the other day at Florence Prison. She knew any arguments she offered would fall on deaf ears.

To have such faith. To be so confident.

She grappled with a thousand doubts while Nick's eyes conveyed a conviction that laid waste to every uncertainty. He was taking the girl home with him because he believed that it was his duty as dictated by the Ancients, and the surest, perhaps only, means of protecting mankind's future.

Was it?

What would happen if she called nine-one-one as she'd told Nick she would, and he were picked up for kidnapping?

Disaster.

Whether Gillian believed in the Ancients had no bearing on the creatures. They existed. If Nick weren't there to eliminate the last female creature, Cadamus would find it, reproduce, and a new generation would be born.

Nick placed his hand on the door handle. "Are you coming with us?"

Gillian could hear in her head all the other questions he wasn't voicing out loud.

Are you still my Synsär?

Can I count on you?

Do you trust me?

Do you care about me?

She rubbed her throbbing temples. Too much had happened tonight for her to think straight. She was physically depleted, mentally exhausted, and emotionally drained.

Perhaps the best course of action would be for her to go along, see that no harm came to the girl, and try to talk some sense into him. That was what she'd been trained to do, after all. Talk sense to people.

She went around to the other side of the car and slipped into the passenger seat next to Nick. "Are you going to stop by Father Juan's office?"

"No. I'll phone him tomorrow." Nick started the car and drove out of the parking lot.

Gillian heard sirens in the distance and wondered if

emergency vehicles were en route to the alley. Someone—perhaps the old Hispanic woman—must have heard the commotion and called the police.

Come to think of it, lots of someones should have heard the commotion and come running. Had they been afraid of Cadamus or just plain afraid of getting involved?

"People are bound to be looking for her, you know." Gillian inclined her head at the unconscious girl.

"Probably."

"You don't think that's a problem?"

"Not really."

"She could have family."

"My guess is, now that her mother's dead, she's an orphan."

If what Nick said were true and the girl was indeed the next Huntsman, she was alone in the world. From what Gillian had learned, orphan status was a prerequisite for being a Huntsman. In a way Gillian didn't like to admit, that worked to everyone's benefit. Less distractions. Nothing to lose. No ties, no commitments.

Unless you got romantically involved with your Synsär.

Nick had been an orphan. So had Charlie. He'd told her about his childhood one night while they were waiting for Nick to return from buying supplies. And about Jonathan. How he and Nick were alike in many ways and also how they differed. Charlie told her Nick was more easygoing. Evidently Charlie had never tried to win an argument with him.

Gillian approached Nick from another angle. "What if the police talk to Father Juan?"

"He won't tell them anything. He has no reason to

connect us with Amaia's death or the girl's disappearance."

"He might give them our names. Mention that we were there investigating the smell and never returned."

"If he does, he'll give them your fake name and my birth name. Nicholaus Lawler doesn't exist anymore and hasn't for twenty-five years. I think we're pretty safe."

"But we left without talking to him. That's bound to make him suspicious."

"It may. But I'm sure I can relieve his suspicions with a phone call tomorrow. And besides, the girl went missing while we were in the church talking with him. We have an airtight alibi."

"And if the old woman in the house behind the church talks to the police?"

"She's just another wacko citizen caught up in the recent monster craze."

"You have an answer for everything."

"I try."

Since Gillian was getting nowhere fast with Nick, she dropped the subject and instead studied the girl in the backseat.

"Stevie," she said, suddenly remembering. "Her name is Stevie. That's what Father Juan said."

"You're right."

Traffic was lighter than usual for nine-thirty at night. They'd reach Nick's apartment within a few minutes.

"Why is she still unconscious, do you suppose?"

"She's not unconscious. Not exactly."

"What would you call it exactly?"

"More of an altered state of consciousness as opposed to unconsciousness."

"Hypnotized?"

Cadamus was capable of reading minds. Maybe, thought Gillian, he'd done something to the girl. Put her in a trance.

"No. She's here physically, but her consciousness is elsewhere."

"Elsewhere? Like in another city?"

"On another plane of existence. She's with the Ancients."

"Doing what?"

"Receiving her instructions."

"Okay." Gillian sighed long and loud. She really was too tired to keep up this conversation with Nick. Slouching in her seat, she leaned her head back and closed her eyes. "I've reached my limit of *Twilight Zone* stuff for one night. How about we go back to the discussion of me calling the police and reporting you for kidnapping. That conversation made sense, from my perspective anyway."

"What the hell are you doing here, Gillian?"

His unexpected anger took her aback. She opened her eyes and stared at him. "I beg your pardon."

"Is it to obtain proof of the creatures so that you can free your father?"

"How can you say that after this past week?" *And after all the times we made love.* She swallowed back her hurt.

"Then why don't you trust me?"

"I do." She remembered him letting go of her hands after he'd promised not to, and her crashing fall to the basement. "Most of the time."

"You can't pick and chose, you know. Say 'I believe in the creatures but not the Ancients,' or 'I accept my role as Nick's Synsär but not that Stevie is the next Huntress.' It's all or nothing."

"She's a kid, for crying out loud. A kid who just lost her mother. How can you expect her to make a decision that will affect the rest of her life? Force her to abandon everything and everyone she knows for a purpose she may not fully understand?"

"I did."

Gillian's rebuttal died on her tongue.

"Jonathan did, and so did Charlie. Huntsmen who accept their calling do so willingly and because they're ready."

Nick turned the car into the single-lane driveway leading behind the strip center and the stairs to his apartment.

"Are you saying she has a choice?"

"She does. If she wakes up and remembers nothing about tonight, it means she refused. The Ancients will have erased her memory of them and Cadamus. If she remembers, she's chosen to answer her calling."

Nick pulled into his parking space and shut off the engine. Charlie's motorcycle was in its usual spot. Every light in the apartment was burning at full wattage.

"Stay with Stevie," Nick said, his voice low and soothing in the darkness of the car's interior. "Be the first to talk to her when she wakes up. Decide for yourself. I'll abide with whatever decision you make. If, afterward, you want me to turn her over to the authorities, I will. You have my word."

"You seem awfully sure."

"I am. Of a lot of things." He found her hand and folded it inside his. "If you agree with me she's the next Huntsman, I swear to you I'll take good care of her. I'll raise her as if she were my flesh-and-blood daughter. Like Charlie raised me. Like Jonathan would have if he'd lived. Coach her softball team. Ground her for wearing too much makeup." He squeezed Gillian's fingers. "Being a Huntsman is more than saving mankind. I get to be a dad, too."

Nick would make a great father. Something Gillian had missed out on. Of course, her father loved her, but he hadn't been there for her. Not like other fathers. She didn't want Stevie to suffer the same dismal childhood she had.

Tears unexpectedly filled Gillian's eyes, and she blinked them back.

"You could be part of it, too."

"What?" she asked, her voice thick.

"Raising Stevie."

"Oh, Nick."

"I know it's too soon to talk about where our relationship is heading, but when this is all over . . ."

He didn't finish whatever it was he'd intended to say because Charlie was coming down the last flight of stairs, a flashlight in his hand. Nick opened his door just as Charlie reached the car.

"Don't you answer your goddamn cell phone?" he barked.

"I had it on vibrate."

"How did it go?"

"We got the female."

Charlie's irritation instantly vanished. "Good."

"And something else."

"What?" Charlie quirked one eyebrow. "Or should I ask, who?"

"How's she doing?"

"The same."

Gillian looked up to see Charlie come through the

door to Nick's spare bedroom/communication center. After bringing Stevie inside, they'd quickly cleared off the futon couch and made it into a bed for her. She'd not so much as flickered a single eyelash since Nick put her in the backseat of his car more than two hours before.

Gillian had stayed constantly by her side except for one quick potty break. The kitchen chair she'd been sitting in was starting to feel like a torture device.

Charlie wheeled over the old threadbare secretary chair from the desk, and sat down next to Gillian.

"What's Nick up to?" she asked in a hushed whisper, though she'd begun to believe Stevie wouldn't wake up even if a piano fell through the ceiling onto the bed.

"He was camped out on the couch, going over a floor plan of the Phoenix Exhibition Center I got on-line for him, but then a little while ago, he dozed off."

"I'm sure he's tired. He hasn't gotten much sleep lately."

"Neither have you. You're both working too hard."

Gillian was grateful that the room was lit only by a small night-light and Charlie couldn't see her flushed cheeks. If she and Nick spent more time sleeping and less time making love, they wouldn't be so tired.

"I suppose some of the pressure's off now," she said after a moment, "what with two of the females being eliminated. The worst that can happen is Cadamus mates with the remaining one, and the cycle starts all over again."

Far better, she supposed, than him mating with all three females and the next Huntsman having to face and defeat a small army of the creatures.

"There's still the final battle," Charlie said. "Nick won't truly relax until that's over with."

Gillian hadn't forgotten about the battle, she just chose not to dwell on it.

"Why haven't any Huntsmen ever eliminated all three females before? We've found two and while it wasn't easy, it wasn't impossible either."

"Don't overestimate your abilities or underestimate the creatures'. Now that he's lost two of the females, Cadamus will grow more daring *and* more dangerous."

"Like tonight."

"Exactly. He took a big risk showing himself in the alley and engaging in a confrontation with Nick, especially with houses right there."

"To be honest, I was surprised."

"His desperation is something that could work in our favor or against us."

Gillian thought of her mother. Radlum's attack on her had created a distraction that allowed him to reach the last female ahead of Jonathan. Would Cadamus try something similar and just as devastating?

"You should be careful, Charlie."

"As should you. Those of us closest to Nick are the most vulnerable."

For once, Gillian was glad she had no family in Arizona. She reached out and tucked the bed sheet around Stevie's neck, not that it needed tucking. "How long do you think she'll . . . be like this?"

"It depends. Usually a few hours."

"Did Cadamus know she might be the next Huntsman? Is that why he taunted Nick with her?"

"I doubt it. None of us knows who the Ancients will choose until that person is revealed to us."

"Did the Ancients speak to Nick? Is that how he knew?"

"Yes."

"He says she can refuse the calling."

"That's right."

"Has any child?"

"A few, but not many. The Ancients tend to choose successors wisely."

"She's a pretty girl," Gillian said thoughtfully.

"Very."

She'd studied Stevie's features at length during her vigil. Stevie's mother, Amaia, had been Hispanic. Clearly, Stevie was of mixed ethnic backgrounds. African-American and possibly Anglo, too. The diverse combination had come together beautifully.

Her coffee-colored complexion was flawless, and her long black hair a tumble of loose corkscrew curls. A nose just a tad too straight to be called button sat in the center of a face just a tad too round to be called oval. Gillian suspected beneath those unflickering eyelashes were large, dark eyes not unlike her mother's.

What color were the boy's eyes? Gillian hadn't noticed. And where was he right now? In Cadamus's sanctuary? Hungry and alone? Whether Stevie accepted her calling or not, she would be cared for, either by Nick, family, or foster parents. Did Cadamus care for the boy? Did he feed him, shelter him, protect him?

"I was thinking," Gillian said after a momentary silence. "The old woman I spoke to in the alley, the one who'd seen Radlum . . ."

"Yes."

"If he were sighted at Iglisia de San Pedro and one of his offspring showed up there twenty-five years later . . . well, is it possible that the church is where the female made her nest and laid her eggs? We know the females separate and travel while in their larvae state. But what if only two of the females travel and the third one remains in the general area of the nest?"

"Hmm." Charlie furrowed his brow in concentration. "It's possible, I suppose."

"And since the last female is at the Exhibition Center, as far as we know anyway, that might be where it will lay its eggs if by chance Cadamus locates it before we do."

"That's a very interesting theory. One we could perhaps explore if Cadamus does succeed in reproducing, which, unfortunately, all alpha males have."

"And if we could find the nest and destroy the eggs before they hatch, then we'd wipe out the creatures."

"Except for the alpha male."

"What do you mean?"

"The female makes two nests, one for the female eggs and a different one for the alpha male."

"Oh. I didn't know that."

"Females or not, the alpha male would still go on a killing spree after he hatches. But I like the way you think." Charlie nodded. "Destroying the female eggs would, one way or another, bring about the end of the creatures. You should tell Nick about your theory."

"I guess."

Gillian realized he'd taken for granted that she and Nick would be together when, in fact, they'd yet to fully decide on their future together.

"Is everything okay with the two of you?" Charlie asked after several moments of silence.

"Of course."

"You sure? He seemed a bit tense and you're a bit preoccupied."

Gillian was yet again grateful for the dim lighting.

Charlie's questions, asked with genuine concern, were touching on a subject she wasn't comfortable discussing.

"I've had a tough night." She fingered the hem of her shirt. "I fell through an opening into the basement and landed pretty hard. I don't know if Nick told you."

"He did. Are you all right?"

"I'm fine, other than a few . . . make that a lot of bruises."

"So, what's bothering you? You don't have to tell me if you don't want to," Charlie amended. "It's really none of my business. Except that I care about you. And Nick."

Gillian chewed her bottom lip. The irony of the situation didn't escape her. Usually, she was doing the listening while other people spilled their guts. She would have declined Charlie's invitation if not for the gnarled hand he placed on her knee. Before she knew it, the words were tumbling from her mouth.

"I witnessed a side to Nick tonight I've never seen before." In her mind, she pictured him in the alley, pressing the ritual dagger to the boy's throat. "He told me he was bluffing, but I swear to you I believed he was going to kill that boy."

"He had to be convincing in order to fool Cadamus."

"You didn't see him." Though the room was warm, she rubbed her arms as if chilled. "It was like looking at a stranger." Certainly not the man she'd made passionate love with all week. "What if Cadamus hadn't dropped Stevie? What would Nick have done?"

"Turned the boy over to the authorities." Charlie

leaned forward and rested his forearms on his knees. "Nick's no murderer."

"I never said he was."

"But you had your doubts."

"For a moment, back in that alley, I did think Nick might do something drastic." She shivered slightly. "Something he would have regretted for the rest of his life."

"No. Not possible."

"Why? Because a Huntsman doesn't have any regrets?"

"Oh, we have regrets. Lots of them. Rest assured." Charlie turned his head toward her and exhaled deeply. "Do you think Nick wanted to let go of you in that crawl space? Of course he didn't. But he needed his hands to fight the female creature. If he'd kept holding on to you, both of you could have died."

"I understand that."

And she did. The logical half of her, leastwise. The purely emotional half still remembered those few seconds of absolute terror before she smashed into the table in the church basement, and the sense of betrayal she'd felt that Nick had broken his promise.

"It was the same with the boy in the alley," Charlie said. "Nick gambled on the boy being important to Cadamus and that if he threatened the boy, Cadamus would relinquish Stevie. He followed his instincts, and it paid off. Twice."

"Things could have gone very differently."

"But they didn't. You survived your fall relatively unscathed, and Stevie's safe."

"You say that with such confidence."

"Hardly. Being a Huntsman isn't easy. We have to make difficult decisions. Choose the lesser of two evils.

It's part of the job and why the Ancients only select those individuals who are up to the task, able to carry the burdens of responsibility and guilt, of which there's much. And someone who believes unconditionally."

"That's the hard part. The believing unconditionally. I'm not a person of strong faith. My life hasn't exactly encouraged it."

"Are you sure? Something enabled that little girl who lost both her parents and spent years knocking around the foster care system to grow up into an intelligent, respected, successful college professor and author. Why not faith?"

"Hatred is more accurate."

"You're not a hateful person, Gillian. But you are committed to seeking justice for your family. So is Nick. And perhaps Stevie."

"She's so young. If she is communing with the Ancients—and I'm not a hundred percent sure I buy that—how can she possibly answer a calling that will change the entire course of her life?"

"You met Father Juan tonight." Charlie sat up straight and rubbed his elbow as if the joint ached.

"Yes."

"What did you think of him?"

"I liked him."

"Would you consider him a man of faith?"

"Very much so."

"If you were to ask him how old he was when God called him to serve, he would tell you he was thirteen. It was Easter Sunday, and he was walking down the center aisle of church toward the altar to receive communion. That was forty years ago, and he's not once wavered in his conviction. Nick was nine years old when the Ancients called him. I was ten. You were seven when you decided what you wanted to do with the rest of your life."

"You're wrong. I didn't choose to make psychology a career until my junior year at college."

"I'm talking about freeing your father from prison."

"Yes, but—"

"Is that any less of a calling than Father Juan's or Nick's?"

"I wouldn't label seeking justice a calling."

"Would you label revenge?"

"Hardly."

"And yet, those two drives motivate every Huntsman to accept the calling."

Gillian opened her mouth to respond only to shut it. "You have quite a way with explanations. Maybe I should let you teach my classes one day next semester."

He grinned, and the wrinkles in his face deepened. "I'd be delighted."

Impulsively, she leaned over and kissed his cheek.

His eyes brightened. "What was that for?"

"Trying to make me feel better."

"Did I?"

"You gave me some things to think about."

Stevie stirred, diverting Gillian's attention from Charlie.

"She's waking up," he said.

Leaning forward, Gillian put a reassuring hand on the girl's arm. Visiting the Ancients or just unconscious, she was bound to be disoriented when she came to. And frightened.

Her head rolled from side to side and her lips moved, but only unintelligible murmurings came out.

"You're all right, Stevie, honey. Everything's fine."

Gillian bent closer, then jerked back suddenly when Stevie's eyelids snapped open.

She took one look at Gillian, one at Charlie, then said, "Where's Nick?" in a voice calm and strong and not a bit like that of a child.

Gillian knew then with a faith she hadn't possessed minutes ago that she was staring into the face of the next Huntsman.

CHAPTER SEVENTEEN

Nick sat bolt upright, instantly awake. The site plans of the Exhibition Center he'd been studying before nodding off went flying onto the floor.

Gillian stood before him, solemn. "Stevie's awake. She's asking for you."

"Okay." He blinked the sleep from his eyes and pushed a hand through his rumpled hair. "How are you doing?"

"I'm fine."

"Sore?"

"Some."

"Gillian." He stood, thought about reaching for her, then hesitated. "I know you'd rather I turned Stevie over to the authorities—"

"No, it's okay. I've changed my mind."

"You did?"

"Yes."

"Did something happen while I was asleep?" He narrowed his gaze at her.

"I met your successor."

"I see."

"She's rather persuasive."

He smiled. "She must be, if she was able to change your mind."

"She wasn't the only one. Charlie can also make a solid case when he wants."

This time, he didn't hesitate reaching for her. To his enormous relief, she came willingly into his arms. He kissed her hair, her temple, her forehead. "I'm sorry I dropped you when we were in the air ducts, and I hate like hell that you're mad at me."

"I'm not mad."

"You were," he said.

"A little." She exhaled softly and rested her cheek on his chest. "But no more."

"Those must have been some interesting conversations you had with Charlie and Stevie."

"Come meet her. You'll like her." Gillian extracted herself from Nick's embrace and took his hand, her face alight with anticipation. "She reminds me of you. Or what you were probably like when you were her age."

"Agreeable and well behaved?"

"Headstrong, single-minded, and prone to mischief."

"Sounds like Charlie's been telling tales on me again."

They went through the door into the spare bedroom. Nick let Gillian lead him, preferring to lag behind. He'd accepted his role as future father for many years, but now that the moment was upon him, he was admittedly nervous. Being a Huntsman, saving mankind from obliteration, paled in comparison to the challenges of being a new parent.

How had Jonathan felt the first time he'd seen Nick? Or Charlie, who'd raised two children, the second one unplanned?

Nick remembered his initial meeting with Jonathan and, a week later, with Charlie. He'd felt a whole lot more scared than Stevie looked.

She peered around Charlie, who vacated his post by the bed to let Nick by. "Hi," she said, a tentative, hopeful smile on her face.

"Hi." Nick approached slowly. "I'm Nick."

"My name is Estabana Maria Carmella Rodriguez. Most people call me Stevie. I'm eight years old." Her bottom lip quivered ever so slightly. "You were probably hoping for a boy, but I promise I'll try harder than any stupid boy ever has and make you proud of me."

Nick's heart melted, and his legs lost their strength. He sat in the chair Gillian pushed over to him.

"You're wrong. I was hoping for a girl."

"Really?"

"There have only been a few Huntresses, but they were all great warriors."

"Will you tell me about them someday?"

"Most definitely."

Her expression grew sorrowful. "The Ancients said my mother died."

"I'm sorry, sweetie."

Stevie nodded. "Your mom died, too?"

"My mom and dad both. And my little sister."

"That sucks."

"It does."

"I don't have any brothers or sisters. My dad left before I was born. I never met him."

"That sucks, too."

"So, you're gonna be kinda like my dad?"

"Kind of. Except I won't ever leave." He tugged on one of her flyaway curls. "And I'll cry like a baby when you grow up and leave me."

She gazed at him with huge, tearful eyes. "What's gonna happen to my mom now that she's dead?"

"Do you have any family in Phoenix?"

"No." She sniffed.

"Then I'm not sure. But I'll find out for you."

"She was born in El Paso, Texas. She took me there once to visit a couple years ago and meet my grandmother and cousins." Stevie's voice wavered. "I think she'd like to go back there if she could."

"Charlie and I will make the arrangements." Nick didn't know how they'd manage, but they would.

"Thank you." Stevie swallowed.

Gillian was right. He liked his new daughter. They were going to get along just fine.

"Are you tired?" he asked.

"I'm kinda hungry. I didn't think I would be after . . . everything, but I am."

"What's your favorite food?"

"Pepperoni pizza."

Nick grinned. "I think we can arrange that."

"Cool."

"Yeah, cool." Only Nick wasn't thinking about pizza when he said it.

"You want a glass of wine or something before bed?" Nick asked.

"No, thanks."

He and Gillian were cleaning up the kitchen after putting away the leftover pizza. He rather liked that after five straight nights of staying with him, she knew her way around every inch of his place. It implied she was comfortable there, maybe comfortable enough to move in with him.

"It's really late. I have to go." She hung the dish towel she'd been using on the oven door.

"Go! Where? What are you talking about?"

"Back to my place."

"Why? You brought a change of clothes over. And a toothbrush."

"Because I don't think I should stay tonight. Not with Stevie here. We want to set a good example for her."

"She's asleep."

"She'll wake up eventually."

"So much for being comfortable," he grumbled.

"What?"

"Never mind."

"And you two should have some alone time to get to know each other."

Nick wanted some alone time all right. With Gillian. For a couple of hours, anyway. He grabbed his keys off the counter. "Come on. I'll drive you."

"I can take a cab."

"Forget it."

"What about Stevie?"

"Charlie's here. He can watch her for a while."

"He's asleep on the couch."

"He'll be here in case she wakes up."

"I don't know . . ."

"Your place isn't far. If I need to, I can be back here in ten minutes."

"Okay. I guess."

"And you have the nerve to call *me* headstrong."

Once they were in his car and on the road, Gillian asked, "What do you think that boy's relationship to Cadamus is?"

"I've been wondering the same thing myself."

"Do the alpha males typically have human Synsärs?"

"I'm not aware of it happening before. But this generation of creatures seems to have evolved more significantly than previous ones. Especially the females."

"What would their evolution have to do with a human Synsär? A child at that?"

"The only explanation I can come up with is that the Ancients are evening the odds."

"Evening the odds?" She knitted her brow.

"The city's experienced some phenomenal growth in recent years, and the creatures have lost their natural territory. Advances in technology have also made it easier for us to hunt them. I'm guessing they're due for an edge. A human can act as Cadamus's eyes and ears during the daylight hours when he's confined to his sanctuary. Which could explain why the kid was spying on us."

"But he's just a boy."

"Kids are easily manipulated. Used to being told what to do. Not like adults, who are cynical and skeptical. Can you see a grown man willingly obeying Cadamus?"

"Kids usually scare more easily than adults," she said. "But that boy wasn't afraid of Cadamus. And Cadamus, well, for lack of a better description, is fond of the boy. I watched them fly away. He held the boy in a protective, almost paternal embrace."

"Spooky to think the creatures are capable of tender emotions and not just hate, anger, and revenge."

"Very spooky."

They drove the rest of the way to Gillian's condo in silence. When they arrived, Nick pulled around to the back of the building and the visitor parking spaces.

"I thought we agreed you were dropping me off and going home."

"No, we agreed I'd drive you home and that Charlie would watch Stevie while I was gone." Nick parked in an empty space and shut off the engine.

"Your place is home with your new daughter."

"My place is also with you." He reached over, cupped her cheek, and stroked her silky skin. "Just because Stevie's come into my life doesn't mean there's suddenly no room for you."

"That's a really sweet thing to say but—"

"Let me come up for while."

"Another night would be better."

"Stevie will still be at my place, and I might not have a babysitter."

Gillian closed her eyes and groaned. "You're incorrigible."

He leaned across the console and kissed her. "Admit it. You find my incorrigibility impossibly sexy."

"True." Placing two fingers on his lips, she drew back. "But I'm strong enough to withstand temptation."

"Prove it. Invite me up."

"Nice try." She grabbed the passenger door handle and yanked. "But there's nothing you can do or say that will convince me to change my mind."

"How about 'I love you'?"

She stopped with the door half open and one foot on the ground. "Okay. Maybe there is one thing you can say." Stepping out of the car, she ducked her head back inside and said, "Fine. You win. Come on up. But only to talk."

"Don't count on it," he muttered under his breath.

She did everything within her power to transmit don't-touch-me signals, from walking impossibly straight as if her vertebrae were welded together, to refusing to meet his gaze head on, to maintaining a safe distance between them at all times.

Nick found her icy treatment of him a total turn-on.

She lost some of her composure at her front door. While she fumbled with her numerous keys and locks, he pressed close to her back and tickled her hair and ear with his fingertips.

"I won't crumble just because you're putting the moves on me. I can resist you and your juvenile attempts at seduction." She disengaged the last dead bolt and flung the door wide open.

"Do I detect a challenge?"

"Not at all," she said crisply and deactivated the alarm system. "I'm simply stating a fact.

Nick shut the door behind him. "Then resist this."

Grabbing her arm, he swung her around and trapped her against the door. Chest to breasts, hips to hips, thighs to thighs. She remained stiff as a board, but something flickered briefly in her green eyes. Nick pressed his advantage by lowering his head and capturing her lips in a mind-numbing, tongue-tangling, toe-curling kiss.

"We're supposed to be talking," she said, forcing the words out between ragged breaths.

"I like a woman who talks during sex. It gets me hard." He shoved his fingers under the hem of her shirt and around to her back where he deftly unhooked her bra. When her breasts were free, he cupped them in his hands. "Your turn. How do you feel about me?"

"I care about you."

He brushed her nipples with the pads of his thumbs. They instantly tightened to firm little buds beneath his touch. "I see that."

"I think we have a solid beginning for a relationship, one on which we can build."

"You have amazing breasts." He bent and took one of her nipples in his mouth, sucking hard until she let out a soft moan.

"We weren't discussing my breasts."

"That's right." He straightened and reached for the waistband of her jeans and the single snap that separated him from paradise. "Let's see. Oh, yeah. Relationships. Ours. Solid foundation."

The snap finally gave, and Nick ripped her zipper open with a thankful grunt. He dipped his hand inside her panties and between her legs. She was gloriously, satisfyingly wet. He went right to work and smiled to himself when she jerked and gasped with delight.

"Don't equate normal human physiology, i.e., lust, with genuine emotion," she warned in a voice that sounded more like a kitten's purr than a tiger's snarl. "Just because I desire you doesn't mean I return your love or that I ever will."

"Liar."

He pushed her jeans and panties down over her hips, stopping to remove them and her sneakers.

While he was down there, he decided to give her something else to think about regarding their relationship. He spent several minutes teasing her swollen clit with his tongue. For someone who refused to admit the full extent of her feeling for him, she certainly called out his name plenty of times.

They'd spent enough nights together, and long, languid mornings, for Nick to be intimately acquainted with each and every nuance of Gillian's body. He knew all her most sensitive spots, how much pressure to apply, and what to do with his hands while his mouth made love to her. When he sensed her approaching orgasm, he abruptly stopped.

She groaned in frustration. "So close."

He parted her feminine folds with his thumbs and blew on her. "Talk dirty to me and maybe I'll finish the job."

She shivered. "Fuck you."

"That's a start." His cock swelled in response to her very un-Gillian use of foul language. "But I was thinking more like *I'd* fuck *you*."

"Do it. Now."

He blew on her again and followed it up with a single lick of his tongue. "I might. But first, tell me how you really feel about me."

"I . . . I . . ." She whimpered when he inserted the very tip of one finger inside her and then removed it. "I like you a lot, and I think we have a possibility of a future together," she rambled in one long sentence.

"Good, but not quite good enough." He tongued her between the legs one last time and stood. "You'll have to do better."

"Damn you, Nick."

He silenced her with a kiss while unbuckling his

own jeans. Reaching into his back pocket for his wallet, he pulled out a condom, then tossed the wallet onto the floor. He stepped back, shucked out of his clothes, and put on the condom.

Gillian slumped against the door, her legs parted, her lips moist, and her rose-tipped breasts peeking out from beneath her disheveled shirt.

Damn, but he was one lucky man.

"Tell me you love me," he said and circled her waist with his hands.

"I'm not quite there yet." Her eyes stared into his and gleamed with a feral hunger that set his already boiling blood on fire.

"How 'bout I get you there and then you tell me."

"Get me there first."

Nick lifted her off the floor, lowered her onto his throbbing cock, and preceded to get them both there as fast as he could. She sped the process along by wrapping her legs around his middle and tangling her fingers in his hair.

Gillian came first, mere seconds ahead of him. As he spilled into her, she brought her mouth to his and said, "I love you, I love you, I love you," against his lips.

Gillian knocked on Nick's apartment door. A moment later, it opened.

"Morning." Charlie's greeting lacked his customary perkiness.

"You look terrible. Are you all right?" She hadn't intended to be so blunt, but his haggard appearance took her aback.

He stepped aside to let her in. "Sleeping all night on a lumpy couch isn't good for a man of my advanced age."

"I'm sorry. It's my fault." Gillian had no idea what time Nick left her condo. She'd fallen asleep with him in her bed and woke up alone six hours later. "I shouldn't have let Nick drive me home last night."

She really shouldn't have, for Charlie's sake, but she was secretly glad she did.

He looked her up and down before shutting the door. "You appear in good spirits this morning, as does Nick. I guess one night of lousy sleep is worth it if you two made up."

"We weren't fighting."

"Have you had breakfast? Nick's cooking pancakes. Stevie's in the kitchen with him."

"How's she doing this morning?"

"Pretty good, considering everything she's been through."

"It's going to take some time. She has a lot of adjustments to make. Losing her mother, her home, her friends. Living in a new place and having a new parent. Plus, she has the rest of her life mapped out, or at least the next twenty-five years, and the responsibility of being the next Huntsman. That's a huge load for anyone to handle, much less a girl of eight."

Charlie gazed at her, tired. "You done spouting psychology again? Because I could use some breakfast."

"What is it with everyone lately?" Gillian huffed and followed Charlie into the kitchen. "I do not constantly spout psychology."

The aroma of pancakes and bacon shut her up.

"Morning!" Nick took a break from cooking to give her a quick kiss on the lips. "How do you like your bacon, soft or crisp?"

"Medium." She went over to the dining table

where Stevie sat with Charlie. "Hi, Stevie. I'm Gillian. Do you remember me from last night?"

She nodded, albeit hesitantly. "Are you Nick's girlfriend?"

"I am. I'm also his Synsär. Do you know what that is?"

"Someone who helps the Huntsman. The Ancients told me. They said I'd have one when the time was right."

"You will."

Stevie's gaze traveled from Gillian to Nick. "Is my Synsär going to be my boyfriend and am I going to have to kiss him?"

Gillian laughed. "No. My father was Jonathan's Synsär. Jonathan was Nick's predecessor. He and my father were good friends."

"Your dad was a Synsär, too?"

"Uh-huh."

"So if you and Nick have a kid, will he be my Synsär?"

"Um . . ." Gillian's cheeks grew warm under Stevie's, Charlie's, and Nick's simultaneous scrutiny. "I don't think it's really up to us." She glanced around for a handy distraction. "Anything interesting on the news this morning?"

Nick had placed a small portable TV on the end of the counter. He had it tuned to the TV-7 morning news show but muted the volume, she guessed in deference to Stevie's sensitive emotional state should the station run a story on her mother's death.

"Usual stuff," he said in a tone that led Gillian to believe the station did indeed run a story on Amaia and possibly the mysterious disappearance of her daughter.

Gillian poured orange juice for everyone and set

out the dishes. There wasn't enough room at the two-person dining table, so she and Nick stood at the counter and ate.

"What's on the agenda for today?" she asked.

"Charlie's going to find out what he can on Stevie's mother's body," Nick answered in a low voice.

"How?"

"I'm not sure. He's got some ideas. If we have to, we can contact Stevie's grandmother in El Paso, pretend to be with the coroner's office, suggest they call someone and arrange to have the body shipped back, then give them the number."

"You might want to take her shopping." Gillian studied Stevie. "She's going to need some things. Clothes, shoes, a hairbrush, toys."

"Fake papers," Nick added.

"Seriously?"

"I can't go through legal channels for obvious reasons. If I'm going to pass her off as my daughter or foster child, I'll need documents. A birth certificate or some kind of guardianship papers. Whatever Charlie can finagle."

"You make it sound like all you have to do is pick up the phone and place an order. One phony birth certificate, please," she mimicked.

"It's not much harder than that if you know the right people to call."

"I was joking."

"I'm not. We live in Arizona. A border state. Fake documents are big business."

Gillian was aware there were people crossing the border without green cards. But she'd never thought about it in terms of business.

"We'll have to move soon, too," Nick said around

his last bite of pancake. "Get a bigger place. She can't stay in the spare bedroom, not with all the junk I have piled up. And we're too close to her old neighborhood. Someone is bound to recognize her sooner or later."

"I suppose you're right." Gillian's last bite of pancake went down like a piece of jagged rock.

Where would Nick and Stevie move? And how far away from her?

"I was thinking of someplace midway between ASU and the TV station," he said. "So neither of us has too far to drive to work."

"Neither of us?"

"You're coming with us." It wasn't a question.

Gillian didn't respond. Not because she wasn't sure how to but because something on the TV had caught her attention. She pointed with her fork. "Look."

On the TV's small screen flashed a shot of Celeste standing on the street outside the Phoenix Exhibition Center. Nick turned up the volume.

"—art show starting tomorrow," Celeste said into the microphone. "A team of specialists has been retained to locate and hopefully eliminate the source of the mysterious and offensive odor permeating the building."

Behind Celeste, several unmarked white vans were lined up at the service entrance in the rear of the Exhibition Center. Technicians in blue jumpsuits, hoods, and masks carried, dragged, or pushed equipment from the vans through the service entrance.

"Celeste," one of the coanchors back at the station said, "what impact is this mysterious odor and cleanup campaign going to have on the art show?"

After a beat, Celeste answered, "Well, Shawn, a

spokeswoman for the management staff assures us the art show will open tomorrow as scheduled. This popular annual event is attended by thousands of individuals throughout Arizona as well as southern California, New Mexico, and even Colorado, with a portion of the proceeds going toward a scholarship program supporting aspiring artists."

"So ticket holders out there have nothing to worry about, is that right?" the coanchor asked.

Behind Celeste, more vehicles pulled in and parked behind the vans. Small groups of people wearing business suits huddled together, engaging in animated, if not downright agitated, conversations.

"That's what we're told, Shawn. The show will open tomorrow morning at eight o'clock and continue through six o'clock Sunday evening. Tickets are still available for both days."

The scene switched back to the station where Shawn and his attractive coanchor launched into another, unrelated story.

Nick muted the volume again and said in a low voice, "I think our shopping plans just went to hell in a handbasket."

"What are we going to do?" Gillian asked.

"Head to the Exhibition Center."

"Can I come, too?" Stevie said from the table.

" 'Fraid not, sweetie." Nick went over and gave her syrup-covered cheek a wipe with his napkin.

"But I need to learn how to be a Huntress."

"You have plenty of time for that. Don't worry. But right now, Gillian and I have a lot of work to do."

"Be careful."

"We will."

Gillian watched the interaction between Nick and

Stevie and marveled at how quickly they'd developed a rapport. She'd been right about Nick: He was going to make a great dad. And wrong about thinking they should turn Stevie over to the authorities. The girl was far better off with Nick, someone who truly cared about her and her welfare, than in state-provided foster homes. Gillian only wished she'd been half as fortunate after she'd lost her parents.

"I'll stay here and watch Stevie today," Charlie offered.

"Thanks." Nick started to grab his keys off the counter, then stopped and turned to Gillian. "Can we take your car? That way I can leave mine for Charlie and Stevie."

"Sure." She nodded.

Now that they'd switched to creature-hunter mode, her nerves were humming, and her pulse was racing. A few minutes later they headed out the door and down the stairs.

"What will happen if that team of specialists finds the female before we do?" she asked when they reached her car.

"They won't."

"You can't be sure."

"I have to be sure." Nick yanked his door open and climbed into the passenger seat. "Now drive. Fast." When they were on the road, he asked, "What size jumpsuit do you wear?"

"He took the girl home with him." Miguel sat on the bottom step of the basement stairs, stuffing the food Cadamus had brought for him into his mouth. He'd returned only minutes earlier from his latest errand. "She's there, now."

"Good."

The news that the Huntsman found his successor pleased Cadamus enormously. The Ancients must know there would be need for a future hunter. And that meant Cadamus was sure to locate the last female before the Huntsman, and impregnate her.

Good news, indeed.

Cadamus strutted around the basement of his sanctuary. Midday was approaching. He should rest for the coming night, but he was unable to relax. The female called to him, the scent of her pheromones strong in the air, and his body responded with a will of its own.

Tonight, he would mate. Tomorrow, or the next day, he would face the Huntsman and seal both their fates.

"What will happen to me when you're gone?" Miguel asked, finishing the last bit of his food.

"I do not know," Cadamus grumbled.

"Will the Dark Ancients take care of me?"

Such an absurd question. Cadamus turned his back on the boy, dismissing him.

"Please."

He felt the boy's hand, small and gentle, on his wing. "You will have to take care of yourself," he said over his shoulder.

"May I serve your children?"

Cadamus swung around to face Miguel, who stared up at him beseechingly. The only human to ever be unafraid of him. "Why would you do that?"

"To repay you."

Cadamus had never touched a human out of kindness. He did so now, extending his hand and awkwardly patting Miguel on the head. It felt strange but not altogether distasteful.

"Yes. You may serve my children, if that is your choice."

"You should sleep now," Miguel said.

The boy was right. Without another word, Cadamus retreated to his customary resting place on the floor by the wall. Sitting cross-legged, he encased himself in his wings, forming a cocoon. Sleep, however, continued to elude him.

Some minutes later he felt the boy's presence beside him. Only when Cadamus laid his hand on the boy's thin back was he at last able to drift off.

CHAPTER EIGHTEEN

"Duck!" Nick said and pushed Gillian onto the hard asphalt. Throwing himself down beside her, he flung an arm over her waist and dragged her with him behind a low block wall. "Don't move and don't make a sound," he whispered in her ear. "No matter what happens."

She did as she was told.

As the cluster of golden particles, all that were left of the third and remaining female creature, floated up toward the night sky, four security guards charged from around the corner of the building, scanning the area with their high-powered flashlights.

Gillian tensed when one of the beams swept the air mere inches above their heads, and lingered momentarily before it finally moved on.

"Did you see which way they went?" one of the guards hollered.

"No, but they can't be far. Let's split up. Ron, you

and Hector take the south side, Larry and I will take the north."

How long did they have, Nick wondered, until Ron and Hector found them? He and Gillian couldn't stay where they were. Neither could they run to her car parked three blocks away. Their plan to eliminate the female creature had gone off without a hitch . . . up until the end.

They'd not put enough thought into their escape plan once the job was done.

Between the crews and vendors setting up the art exhibits and the so-called specialists hired to find and remedy the source of the smell, the Phoenix Exhibition Center had been overrun with people all day. Rather than sneak inside, Nick and Gillian decided to wait and see if all the commotion frightened the female creature and drove it out of its hiding place in search of a new one.

Their long shot paid off.

Not thirty minutes ago, right as the Exhibition Center was closing for the night, the female creature crawled out of a drainpipe on the back side of the building. Nick and Gillian were waiting, having staked out the most likely places from where the female creature would emerge.

Killing it had been easy. Unfortunately, its dying screams had alerted the security guards, who came running, leaving Nick and Gillian in serious danger of being caught.

The low wall behind which they hid rose up to join with a wrought-iron fence too high and too precarious for them to scale. Their best bet was to make a mad dash across the large circular driveway leading away from the service entrance and to the street near where Celeste had filmed her report that morning. Once on the street, Nick and Gillian could sneak behind buildings and maybe get away.

Raising his head slowly, Nick peered over the top of the wall. One of the guards was heading in their direction, his flashlight beam aimed in front of him. Nick and Gillian had at most one minute before they were discovered.

Only one guard, Nick reminded himself. The odds probably wouldn't get any better. He lifted himself to his knees and prepared to spring.

Gillian cranked her head around, her eyes silently asking him what the hell he was doing.

He inclined his head in the direction of the guard and whispered, "I'll distract him, you run to the car."

Her eyes told him she thought he'd lost his mind, but her tiny nod assured him she'd follow instructions.

The guard came closer, his footsteps thudding on the asphalt. Suddenly, Nick heard a different sound, the rustling of wings. Gillian heard it, too. They both looked up to see a black shadow streak across the sky, land on the roof, and disappear behind a small communications tower.

"Shit," Nick exclaimed.

"Who's there?" called the guard.

In the next instant, all hell broke loose.

Nick leapt out from behind the wall, startling the distracted security guard and landing a right hook to the man's chin. The guard staggered backward, dropping his flashlight and reaching for his gun. Nick was faster. His shoe connected solidly with the man's groin.

With a grunt, the security guard doubled over, clutching his injured privates with both hands. Nick grabbed the fallen flashlight and with only the teeniest stab of guilt, brought it down on the man's head. He toppled like a fallen tree and lay on the asphalt.

Nick turned to discover Gillian still standing there. "You were supposed to run for the car," he snapped.

"I didn't want—"

"Let's go! Now." He grabbed her arm.

Not waiting to see if more security guards were coming, the two of them tore across the driveway, only to come to a grinding halt when they hit the locked service entrance.

"Hurry!" Nick hollered and pushed Gillian toward a chain-link fence.

"I can't climb this."

"You're going to have to."

He grabbed her by the waistband of her jeans and tossed her at the fence. She automatically dug her fingers into the spaces between the links and held on. Before she could protest, he planted his hands on her ass and boosted her higher.

Sirens wailed in the distance. High-beam security lamps mounted to the building's rooftop flashed on, bathing them in bright fluorescent light.

The fence rattled and shook as Gillian awkwardly scaled the top and swung a leg over to the other side. Nick didn't wait for her and started climbing the fence. He reached the top just as she swung her other leg over and began carefully climbing down the other side. She was taking too damn long.

"Sorry," he said and gave her an unceremonious shove.

She dropped like a stone the last five feet, landing on her feet.

Nick jumped to the ground beside her, grabbed her

hand, and started running. She had trouble keeping up with him, probably because her legs hurt.

"My car's that way," she said, gasping for breath.

"Forget the car. Your plates can be traced."

"Where are we going?"

"Iglisia de San Pedro."

With any luck, the basement window would still be broken. If the police were looking for them, they might not think to search inside a church.

"That's a half mile from here," Gillian objected, slowing down.

"We can make it." Nick dragged her after him. He considered calling Charlie, only to dismiss the idea. He didn't want Charlie leaving Stevie alone or waking her up in order to bring her along. It was too dangerous for a young girl, even one destined to be a Huntress.

They left the sidewalk and cut behind an office building, through a line of neatly trimmed hedges, and emerged in the building's parking lot.

Stopping to rest beneath one of the steel parking shades, Nick spared a moment to look around and assess their situation. If they stayed off the streets and stuck to a back route, they could afford to travel at a slower pace. But it would take them longer to reach the church and safety.

The sirens ceased wailing, first one and then the other. Nick watched through the building's breezeway as a pair of police cars pulled into the driveway leading to the Exhibition Center.

"Break's over," he said. They sprinted from one parking shade to the other until there were no more. "Come on," Nick called, giving her no time to rest.

Twenty yards into the open, they were spotted—not by the police, but Cadamus.

He dived at them, clubbing Nick on the shoulder as he swooped past. Ignoring the sharp stab of pain, Nick kept running. So did Gillian.

"What are we going to do?" she yelled.

"Head for the street." Nick had wanted to avoid being seen. He wanted to be killed and eaten by Cadamus even less. "He won't follow us there. Too many people."

They veered to the right, their destination a narrow passage between a fast-food restaurant and a medical complex.

Cadamus made another dive at them, the gust of air from his wings nearly knocking them off their feet. He grabbed Gillian by the arm, ripping her from Nick's grasp and lifting her high in the air.

She let out a bloodcurdling scream.

"A mate for a mate." Cadamus snarled at Nick, his lips stretched back in a hideous grimace—or was it a smile?—revealing his many sharp teeth.

Gillian twisted and thrashed, pummeling Cadamus with her free hand. He fended off her assault as if she were no more bothersome than a pesky housefly. Nick watched them ascend and felt a part of his soul being wrenched away.

"No!" he cried. "Release her. It's me you want."

Now is not the time for battle.

The Ancients' voices reverberated in his head.

"Coward," Nick called to Cadamus.

Wait, the Ancients said.

"The hell I will." Nick reached in his pants for the ritual dagger. Drawing it out, he raised it over his head, took aim, and hurled it at Cadamus.

It missed the creature's chest but pierced his right wing, leaving behind a gaping hole before dropping with a clank onto the ground.

Cadamus yowled, his hideous face a mask of agony. Like a broken kite, he tipped and faltered, lost altitude, and let go of Gillian before her added weight dragged them both down.

She fell only a short distance, landing on her hands and knees. Nick ran over and dropped down beside her. Confirming for himself that she was alive and relatively sound, he rose and turned to face Cadamus . . . who wasn't there.

Damn it to hell. Where could he have gone so fast, injured as he was?

Nick scanned the nearby rooftops. No inky shadow. No rustle of wings. No shriek or hiss.

"You okay?" He returned to Gillian and helped her to stand.

"Why the fuck am I always falling?" she snapped.

Nick pulled her into his arms, held her until she stopped shaking, then gently reminded her that they needed to get away. No one had come running to investigate the disturbance, but that was no guarantee their brief encounter with Cadamus wasn't observed and even now being phoned in to the police.

"Hold on a second, sweetheart." He went over to where the ritual dagger had fallen, inspecting it before returning it to the sheath inside his pants. As he'd expected, there wasn't a single drop of blood on the gleaming gold blade.

"I'm not sure I can walk all the way to Iglisia de San Pedro," Gillian said when they started out again.

She was lucky she could walk at all.

"I have another plan." Checking first for any police cars, they emerged on the opposite side of the passage.

"Won't Cadamus come after us?"

"Not while he's hurt and we're surrounded by people."

Nick led her through the side door of the fast-food restaurant, which, according to the advertisement in the window, was open until two A.M. They seemed to be the only customers over the age of twenty and not affiliated with a particular street gang.

He nudged Gillian toward the restrooms. "Go in and clean up a bit."

She didn't have to be told twice. Nick did likewise.

He washed his hands and face, using the stiff paper towels to dry off. Next, he straightened his clothing, which had taken a beating.

The door to the men's room banged open, and Nick was joined by a tough-looking kid who glowered at him with undisguised dislike and distrust.

Having recently stared into Cadamus's face, Nick was unimpressed by the kid's attempt to intimidate him.

"Evening." He smiled, splashed some water on his hands and ran his wet fingers through his hair.

The kid flipped him the bird before entering the single stall.

When Nick was done he went in search of Gillian. A quick glance around the dining area assured him she hadn't yet emerged from the restroom. Leaning against the wall, he waited. She came out a few minutes later, tidier than when she went in but still visibly distraught.

He stared at her, unable to tear his gaze away from her disheveled clothing and scraped hands. It struck him in that instant that if things had gone differently, if he hadn't drawn the ritual dagger and thrown it at Cadamus, he might have lost Gillian forever.

For the first time since the day they met in her office, Nick doubted his conviction that she was his Synsär. Maybe he'd been wrong. Maybe he should have let her walk away when she'd suggested it instead of insisting she stay. Then, she wouldn't constantly be hurt and constantly be in danger of losing her life.

But if he hadn't insisted she stay, they wouldn't now be together and in love.

Hell of a choice.

Nick closed his eyes and sagged against the wall. A minute. That was all he needed for the sledgehammer inside his head to stop pounding and the steel band around his chest to loosen.

"Are you all right?" Gillian came over and took his hand, comforting him when he should have been comforting her. "You're shaking."

"Am I?"

Funny. He hadn't lost control once since the night his family had been slaughtered behind the market and Jonathan rescued him from Radlum's clutches.

"I'm not hungry," Gillian said when Nick asked her what she wanted to eat.

"Me either. But if we don't order something, the manager will kick us out."

"I'm not sure that's a bad thing." She turned her head, discretely checking out their dining companions.

"Your father once belonged to a gang."

"Why do you think I'm scared?" she murmured. "You should hear some of the stories he's told me."

"If the police don't storm the place in the next ten minutes, we'll leave." He propelled her ahead of him to the counter. "Come on. The rest will do us both good."

Gillian couldn't agree more. She'd taken another licking, the second one in as many days, and Nick didn't look so hot himself.

He'd dismissed his shaking hands as a delayed reaction to all the excitement, but she had her suspicions. She'd witnessed him eliminating three of the female creatures, and holding the ritual dagger to a young boy's throat. Not once did his pinky so much as twitch.

She studied him from the corner of one eye. Something else had gotten to him tonight.

Cadamus.

What else could it be? And if that were the case, was Nick up to facing him in the final battle? A battle to the death. One where the entire fate of mankind rested on him winning.

"May I help you?" a disinterested clerk inquired.

"Coffee, please."

Nick ordered a large soft drink and large fries, offering to share half with her. They found a booth both far enough away from the gang members and close enough to the door should the need arise to make a hasty escape.

After guzzling his soda, which appeared to refresh him, Nick said softly, "My guess is either the police have stopped looking for us or never started in the first place."

From the window beside their table they had a clear view of the street in front of the Phoenix Exhibition

Center. Nothing appeared out of the ordinary. But neither had the two police cars driven away, which meant they, and the patrolmen, were still at the Exhibition Center.

"We can't be sure."

"No. But other than knocking out a guard and possibly trespassing, we didn't do anything illegal."

"Assault and trespassing are enough to get us arrested." Gillian blew on her coffee before taking a sip.

"No one saw us."

"Except for the guard."

"For a total of two seconds. In the dark. He won't remember anything." Nick reached across the table and patted her hand. "Relax. The police have a whole lot more serious crimes to worry about than one thwarted burglary attempt, which is how they'll probably write it up."

"I suppose so." Gillian picked up a french fry, not to eat but to twirl between her fingers. The action, small as it was, helped to calm her. "Everything happened so fast. Cadamus attacked us, and the next thing I knew, I was in the air."

"It's my fault. I should have done a better job protecting you." Nick's face hardened.

"Are you kidding?" Gillian lowered her voice when a couple of the gang members swivelled around in their seats to glare at them. "You saved my life. If not for you, I'd be dead." She shuddered to imagine her fate had Cadamus carried her off.

"If not for me, you wouldn't have needed saving."

"Hey, is that what's bothering you?"

"By asking you to be my Synsär, I've put you in danger."

She dropped the french fry, reached across the table, and pressed her palm to his cheek. "I want to be your Synsär. *My* choice. The hell with destiny."

Nick covered her hand with his and took several deep breaths before speaking. "I couldn't have done it without you."

"We're a team."

"We are."

And they would be in everything else to come, except for the final battle. That was a trial Nick would have to face alone.

A cheering thought suddenly occurred to Gillian. "Do you realize what we did tonight? What *you* did?"

He raised an eyebrow.

"We eliminated the last female creature. No Huntsman has ever done that before."

"That's true." Nick's frown turned contemplative.

They'd been too busy running from the police and then Cadamus for reality to sink in. Now that it had, Gillian's spirits lifted.

"The creatures have been wiped out. Cadamus has no mate and can't reproduce. There'll be no future generations of little Cadamuses running around, terrorizing people. Once you beat him in battle, the war between good and evil will be over forever."

Nick pushed the remainder of his food aside.

"You don't agree?"

"The war is hardly over. It's constantly being waged, everywhere, all the time."

"Of course. I just mean the battle here, between the Huntsman and the alpha male."

"Yeah, I guess."

His lack of enthusiasm puzzled her. Was he fearing the final battle? Had their encounter with Cadamus tonight given him a taste of what was to come? No. Nick wasn't afraid. His quick reflexes and cool thinking were what saved her.

"You're going to win, Nick."

"I am," he said with so much confidence Gillian's concerns fled. "It's not that."

"What then?"

"The Ancients don't do anything without a reason."

"Okay." She wasn't sure what he was getting at.

He leaned forward, his arms resting on the table. "If we've exterminated the creatures, why did the Ancients give me Stevie to train as the next Huntress?"

"Because they didn't know you'd succeed in eliminating the last female. No Huntsman ever has."

"I'd buy that except for one thing."

"Which is . . . ?"

"They haven't spoken to me and told me not to train Stevie."

"Do they always speak to you about everything?"

"Yes. Everything that matters."

"Give it time. Maybe they're waiting until after the final battle."

"You could be right." He finished his soda and gave her an encouraging, if obviously insincere, smile.

"I am right," Gillian said with what she hoped was enough commitment for the both of them. "Once you win the final battle, and you're going to, I have no doubt, the cycle will end once and for all."

Sanctuary.

It called to Cadamus, beckoning him to return and seek shelter in the cool, comforting darkness.

He was unsure whether he had the strength to make it.

He coasted along, dipping and rising in an uneven pattern. His feet brushed treetops and telephone wires as he limped past. With each flap of his wings, he fought the searing pain that all but immobilized his entire right side.

Too low. He must gain altitude if he were to elude the humans who stared at him with their myopic, single-lens eyes, convincing themselves they were mistaken about what they saw. Pushing himself to the limits of his endurance, he ascended one agonizing foot at a time, disappearing into the safety of the night shadows.

The hole in his right wing burned as if doused with acid. It was nothing compared to the anger consuming Cadamus, an anger matched only by the depths of his hatred.

The human bitch lived while his own mate, the last of the three, breathed no more. For that, the human female must die. She and the Huntsman both. Cadamus was now the last of his kind. He would see to it the same fate befell the Huntsman. But not before Cadamus gave him a taste of what it was like to see one's mate slaughtered before his eyes.

After the final battle, when those Cadamus served ruled the world, perhaps they would reward him with a new mate. They possessed extraordinary powers—anything was possible.

He ached with need for release. The females might have perished, but his body's drive to procreate did not die along with them.

A gust of wind no greater than a mild breeze whipped around the side of a building to strike him, and he nearly tumbled from the sky, somersaulting once before righting himself.

Rest, the Dark Ancients commanded him, *so that we might heal you.*

Cadamus was only too glad to obey. He was weak and growing weaker with each passing moment. Once the Dark Ancients restored him, he would return to his sanctuary and prepare for the final battle.

He must devise a plan. One that ensured his victory while exacting his revenge. Miguel could help. He was clever, loyal, and surprising resourceful for one so young and inexperienced.

Small balconies jutted out from the building before Cadamus. He often observed humans standing or sitting on the ledges, engaging in frivolous activities that made no sense to him. Such an inferior race. They were like insects, living in colonies and surviving only because of their vast numbers.

He scanned the ledges closest to him and nearest the roof, searching for one that was dark and deserted. His depleted condition didn't affect his ability to kill, but he'd rather not waste the energy when it wasn't necessary.

Retracting his wings, he dropped onto one of the ledges with a loud, clumsy thud.

"Hey, what was that?" a female voice from somewhere below called.

"I don't know," came another voice. "Must be the air-conditioning units acting up again."

Cadamus didn't bother reaching out to their minds. They weren't coming after him or alerting the police, that much was obvious. Stupid, stupid humans. They failed to detect danger even when it lurked right above their heads.

His senses told him no one was inside the dwelling unit behind the glass door. Sitting cross-legged on the floor of the balcony, Cadamus leaned against the building wall and folded his wings around him. Once he was comfortably in the resting position, he opened his mind to the Dark Ancients.

They came to him almost immediately, their soothing hands mending the torn flesh of his wing and taking away his pain. As he healed, he listened to their sweet song telling him that all was not lost. In fact, all was as it should be. When the time was right, Cadamus would know what to do.

He dozed briefly and woke a short while later, whole and strong and with a renewed sense of purpose. He stood and spread his wings, prepared to take flight. As had been his habit these last weeks, he lifted his face to the night sky and scented the air, detecting an odor that was familiar, yet different, just as the Dark Ancients had told him he would. Instantly, a powerful hunger overtook him.

It wasn't for food.

Cadamus soared into the air, once again strong and nimble, and went in search of the source of the odor. He didn't travel far.

On the other side of the building were more balconies. The odor grew stronger the higher he flew. And then he pinpointed it. On a ledge near the top.

He ascended to a position above the balcony, well out of sight of the single occupant. There, he hovered, silently watching, his eyes adjusting perfectly to the darkness. The odor was so strong now, he could taste it on his tongue, feel it on his skin. His heart drummed in response.

This odor was similar enough to the pheromones the female creatures emitted to inflame his senses and trigger a physiological response within him he was unable to stop. Not that he wanted to stop.

The human woman reclined on a chaise lounge, her eyes half closed. In her hand she clasped a half-empty wineglass. It was not her first drink. Cadamus reached into her mind and learned that it had been dulled by the effects of many alcoholic beverages consumed that night. Good. She would not put up much of a fight.

It was what the Dark Ancients wanted.

He swooped down onto the ledge, landing to stand directly in front of her. Looming over her, he advanced.

The human woman, fully alert now, looked up at him and released a startled shriek. She dropped the wineglass and scrambled backward, curling into a tight ball.

"Leave me alone," she screamed.

Only it wasn't a scream, and her mouth didn't move. Cadamus heard her voice inside his head as clearly as if she'd spoken out loud. Their psychic connection was complete.

"Quiet," he commanded.

"Go away!" Wild with fear, she pressed her back into the chaise and covered her face with her hands.

As if that would make him go away.

Cadamus bent and sniffed her hair, her ear, her neck. "You are ripe for fertilization," he said.

The human woman screamed.

Growling, he grabbed her arm and yanked her from the chaise. He was not one to question the Dark Ancients, but he couldn't help wondering if this sniveling, pitiful human female was worthy of bearing his offspring.

She is the one, the Dark Ancients whispered. *There can be no other.*

So be it.

Cadamus shoved open the door and carried the now-limp human woman into her dwelling. She made no protest, perhaps resigned to her fate. This mating was necessary but would hold no pleasure for either of them.

The wall inside her dwelling was covered with awards. There were also photographs of her and others. Many of the photographs included the Huntsman. Cadamus gleaned from her mind that she'd gathered the tributes to her many accomplishments and put them on display for all who entered her dwelling to see.

Egotistical, and something Cadamus might do in her place. Perhaps this human woman wasn't such a bad choice for a mate after all, he thought and took her right there beneath the shrine she'd constructed to herself.

CHAPTER NINETEEN

Nick stared down the length of the aisle, marveling at how it was he could come once a week to the grocery store and not notice there were so many varieties of cereal. He'd always been a bacon-and-eggs man himself.

"I like this kind." Stevie plucked a box off the lower shelf and placed it in the cart.

Nick picked the box up, examining the back, sides, and front. Tony the Tiger sat astride a purple horse and sported an absurd, openmouthed grin. "It doesn't look very healthy."

"It tastes good."

He started to tell her that taste wasn't as important as nutrition but bit back his words. One trip to the grocery store with Stevie and suddenly he was Mr. Healthy? What was with that?

"My mom used to buy that kind for me."

His niece—at least that's what the temporary guardianship papers Charlie had acquired for them

yesterday identified her to be—gazed up at him with
sorrowful eyes so brown they were almost black.

"Okay." Nick tossed the cereal back into the cart.
"I guess a few empty calories won't hurt you."

She gave him a tiny, sad smile. "Thanks."

"What's next on the list?"

"Ice cream?" Her smile, while still sad, turned
hopeful.

Stevie'd had good and bad days since her mother's
death nearly five days ago. This was apparently one of
her bad days. Gillian told him to be patient with his
new charge, that it would take months, possibly
years, for her to get over the trauma.

He wasn't sure anyone ever really recovered from
losing a parent. He hadn't. Neither had Gillian.

Ice cream, while not a cure, might help.

They'd stopped first at a discount department store
to buy Stevie some new clothes and other necessities
before heading to the grocery store. Nick didn't want
to risk anyone recognizing her, so they'd driven fifteen miles to another part of town.

"How soon until we move?" Stevie walked beside
Nick, her hand on the cart.

"I'll start looking at houses soon." With school
out, they had all summer to get situated.

"Can I come, too?"

"Of course."

Nick was postponing house hunting until after the
final battle. Until then, he couldn't bring himself to
move forward with his life. He and Gillian ventured
out every night, searching for Cadamus's sanctuary,
expecting him to appear at any moment and challenge Nick.

So far, they'd found no sign of the alpha male. Even

the string of unexplained murders had apparently come to an end.

Gillian was convinced that with the elimination of all three females, Cadamus had either perished or gone into hiding and was soon to perish. He'd been injured, perhaps unable to hunt. What purpose would there be in fighting Nick when his species was doomed to extinction?

Nick and Charlie believed no such thing. For one, Cadamus wouldn't give up so easily. He was born and bred to fight. The final battle was his destiny as much as Nick's.

For another, the Ancients hadn't spoken to Nick. Not since the night Cadamus attacked them and tried to fly off with Gillian. If the final battle were unnecessary, the Ancients would have told Nick. And the perpetual agitation gnawing at his belly would go away.

No, Cadamus was up to something. Nick just had to find out what it was before Cadamus had the chance to implement his plan.

When the hell would this infernal waiting come to an end? Nick gripped the handle of the shopping cart so tight his fingers cramped. He didn't think he could take much more.

"Is Gillian going to move in with us?" Stevie asked.

Nick strived to relax and speak normally. There was no cause to alarm Stevie, not when she was struggling with her own problems. "Would you mind if she did?"

"No. She's really nice. I like her."

"She likes you, too."

"What about Uncle Charlie?"

"Uncle Charlie will probably stay right where he is for as long as he can. He enjoys his independence."

Nick pulled items off the shelves as they walked by and flung them into the cart, no longer paying attention to nutrition or price or anything else.

"But he's old."

"Not so old he can't get around on his own. By motorcycle, in fact."

"Will he still babysit me?"

"Every chance he gets."

"And take me for motorcycle rides?"

"Not on your life."

Kids. Did they ever run out of questions?

Nick's cell phone rang. He assumed it was Gillian and didn't check the caller ID. She'd gone to Florence Prison to visit her father again and was probably on her way home.

He put the phone to his ear and said in a sexy voice, "Hello there."

"Hello to you, too, kitten."

"Max!" Nick cleared his throat.

His coworker laughed. "Just what kind of fishing are you doing there in Mexico?"

"I'll send you a postcard so you can see for yourself."

"I can't believe I got you. I figured your cell phone wouldn't reach across the border and I was just going to leave a voice mail message."

"I bought a booster antenna before I left," Nick lied. "What's up?" Max wouldn't have called him while he was on vacation unless it were important.

"I know it's pretty unlikely, but we were wondering . . ." Max's tone went from amused to serious. "Have you heard from Celeste at all?"

"No, why?"

"She didn't show up for work yesterday or today.

No one's been able to get hold of her and if she's home, she's not answering her door."

"Huh. You're kidding. That's not like her."

"No, it's not."

"Did you check with her family in Ohio?" Nick was pretty sure Celeste didn't have any local friends.

"This morning, and *nada*. Her personal assistant hasn't heard from her since Tuesday, and said she missed a manicure appointment yesterday, which, as you well know, is unheard of.

"Bradley's worried," Max went on.

"I don't blame him."

"He even had me call the local hospitals. Said if you hadn't heard from her, I'm to contact the police."

"I think you should."

Celeste rarely missed work and when she did, she called in without fail.

"Sorry to cut into your vacation," Max said. "How's it going?"

"Great." Nick winked at Stevie, who was watching him. "I'm having the time of my life."

"Excellent. Well, we'll see you when you get back. Everyone here says hi."

"Keep me posted on Celeste."

"I'll call you if we hear anything."

"*And* if you don't."

"Is something wrong?" Stevie asked when Nick disconnected from Max.

"Yeah." The agitation gnawing at him increased in intensity. Nick pressed a hand to his middle and rubbed. "I think one of my friends might be in trouble."

"Bad trouble?"

"Maybe. She's been missing since Tuesday."

The same day Nick and Gillian destroyed the last female creature and Gillian narrowly escaped Cadamus's clutches.

Coincidence?

Instinct told him there were no real coincidences, not where Cadamus was concerned.

Gillian stood at Nick's dining table, loading a video camera into her oversized fanny pack. She tucked the camera in beside a half-dozen plastic bags and a pair of latex gloves. There was little space remaining for the digital camera she also planned on taking with her.

"What are you doing?" Nick eyed her fanny pack and the digital camera in her hand. He wasn't smiling.

"Getting ready to go out tonight," she answered, her tone intentionally light. They were leaving in a few minutes on their nightly search for Cadamus's sanctuary. Nick had just finished putting Stevie to bed. Charlie was in the living room, busy running some new program on his laptop.

"Don't play games," Nick said. "You know what I'm talking about."

She didn't bristle at his borderline surly tone. Nick had been on edge for days. Learning about Celeste's mysterious absence that afternoon had only increased his edginess. While not exactly friends, they'd worked together for three years. Gillian could understand his worry.

"I thought if we found Cadamus's sanctuary tonight, I could take some pictures." She braced herself for his reaction.

"Why? By tomorrow the Ancients will have dissolved them."

"Not pictures of Cadamus. His sanctuary. When

we find it. Which we will." She refused to believe differently. "There's bound to be some evidence of him. I intend to photograph it and/or collect any samples. Hopefully, organic material that can be tested."

The painful burning in the back of her throat took her by surprise. She hadn't cried when her father broke his news to her earlier today. Nor had she cried on the drive home from Florence. Why now?

"I thought you'd given up searching for proof of the creatures' existence."

"No, you assumed I gave it up just because I haven't mentioned it lately."

Nick shook his head. "This isn't what we agreed to."

"Agreements can be renegotiated."

"You can't, Gillian. Revealing the existence of the creatures will shift the balance of pow—"

"It won't!" She reined in her soaring emotions before continuing in a calmer voice. "The female creatures are dead. Cadamus will die soon if he hasn't already. What harm can revealing their existence do now except solve a hundred unexplained murders and give grieving families and friends closure?"

And maybe free one man from prison so that he could live the rest of his life, however short that may or may not be, at home with his daughter.

Nick moved closer, bracing his hand on the back of a chair and blocking her escape. "Cadamus isn't dead."

She refused to be intimated. Squaring her shoulders, she said, "You can't be sure."

"I'm absolutely sure."

"Have the Ancients told you he's alive?"

"They haven't told me he's not. And they would."

"Well." Gillian shoved the digital camera into her fanny pack, her movements clumsy but defiant. "If

I'm not supposed to take pictures or collect evidence, the Ancients will stop me. Won't they?"

"Yes."

She hadn't been serious. Nick was.

"So, my taking the camera won't hurt anything." She swallowed a sob before it could escape.

"What's really wrong?" Some of the bite left his voice. "Why the sudden change?"

"Nothing's wrong. There is no change."

He touched her then, resting his hand on hers. Gillian's resolve to be strong and brave and in charge of her emotions went by the wayside, and she started to weep.

"Come on, sweetheart." He folded her into his arms and stroked her hair. "Tell me what's bothering you."

She was such a wimp. Even as she cursed her susceptibility to Nick, she poured her heart out to him.

"The doctors found two more lumps in my father's back. The cancer's returned."

"Do they know that for sure?"

If Nick were still angry at her, if he were still going crazy with waiting for Cadamus to appear, he hid all trace of it. His actions were strictly those of a lover and friend who was genuinely concerned about her and her father.

"No. He's scheduled for biopsy surgery early Friday morning."

"You should be there with him. I'll come, too."

"You don't have to."

He tipped her chin up and waited for her to meet his gaze. "I want to."

"Thank you." His support meant a lot to her. She withdrew from his embrace, more composed than she'd been a minute ago. "But I'm still taking the cameras with me." Not waiting for any potential backlash, she forged ahead. "I have to, Nick. My father's next parole hearing is six weeks away. If he winds up having a relapse of the cancer, I'm going to do everything in my power to get him released from prison. *Everything.* Including obtaining evidence of the creatures. The *extinct* creatures," she reiterated.

"There might be another way."

"What?"

"I know someone who can maybe help."

Though he wasn't one to string people along, she didn't totally trust him when it came to her father. "What kind of someone?"

"Let me make a phone call or two. Then we'll talk." He pushed an errant lock of hair from her face. "In the meantime, take your cameras and your plastic bags. I won't try to stop you."

"You won't?"

"No."

She got it then. "Because you think I'm wasting my time. The Ancients will destroy my film or cement my feet to the pavement."

"Something like that."

His assurance irked her. How could he be so sweet one minute and a first-class jerk the next?

She jammed the digital camera in the fanny pack and zipped it closed, forcing the zipper over the last two lumpy inches.

"Then you won't mind if I take my chances."

Not waiting for his answer, she trudged out of the kitchen, attaching her fanny pack to her waist as she went. An unexpected thought halted her in her tracks.

By "something like that" was Nick referring to him losing the final battle?

* * *

The cemetery was no less creepy with Nick walking beside her than it had been the night Gillian followed him from his apartment three weeks ago. More so, since she was inside the cemetery's fence and not just walking along beside it.

Granite headstones shone in the dark like silver beacons, reflecting the light from the nearby municipal buildings. Gillian tried not to read any of the epitaphs. She didn't want to know who was buried here or when they died.

"Where are you going?" she hollered to Nick.

He'd veered from the sidewalk to cut across the neatly manicured lawn. Gillian was loathe to follow him.

"The gardener's house."

Great. The place where Cadamus had murdered the elderly woman. "Why?"

"I have an idea." He turned around, finally realizing she wasn't following him, and motioned to her. "Come on."

Traipsing across the graves of dead people was not on her list of top ten things she most wanted to do. Gillian's skin crawled, and she rubbed her arms to ward off the sensation.

"How's the gardener's house going to help us find Cadamus's sanctuary?" she asked.

"Watch and learn."

They'd checked out all the buildings on every side of the cemetery the last four nights, with nothing to show for their efforts. When she'd broached the subject with Nick last night and suggested they expand their search, like, say, closer to the Hanson Building a few blocks over, he shot her down without so much as an I'll-think-about-it. According to him, they'd missed something their first go-around.

Whatever he had in mind for the gardener's house must be their second go-around.

"What's the matter?" He walked back toward her, his arm outstretched. "Scared?"

"No."

"This can't be any worse than crawling through the air ducts at Iglisia de San Pedro."

There were no graves filled with dead people at the church.

"I'll be right here the whole time." He clasped her hand firmly in his.

Gillian drew in a long breath. She knew her dislike—no, make that fear—of cemeteries was a holdover from her mother's funeral. So what? Identifying the cause of her problem didn't lessen her case of the willies one smidgeon.

Nick's fingers wrapped tightly around hers, however, did help. A fraction. It also helped that they walked in between the graves and not over them.

Soon, though not soon enough for Gillian, they left the headstones behind and made their way to the gardener's house, which was in an isolated corner of the cemetery.

At the door of the small building, Nick let go of her hand. She instinctively crowded in close to him, not to watch but to take comfort from his nearness. He pulled a small pick from his back pocket and set to work on the padlock securing the door.

"Let me guess," Gillian said. "Charlie taught you the art of breaking and entering, too."

"No. This is one skill I acquired myself."

"On the streets when you were growing up?"

"More like online." With a click, the padlock sprang, and Nick pushed open the door.

"What are we doing in here?"

"Looking for a ladder. I need it to get on the roof."

"Why?"

"Cadamus hatched from under that tree over there. After abducting the old woman, he came here. To the roof. From there, he flew off and found his sanctuary. I'm thinking, his sanctuary is someplace he could see from this roof."

"Let me get this straight. You think my idea that his sanctuary isn't right next to the cemetery is a good one."

"I think it's worth exploring."

"Would you mind repeating that?"

"Try to hold off on the gloating until we find his sanctuary, okay?"

"Come on. I want to hear you say it."

"Gillian." He heaved a tired sigh.

She stood her ground, refusing to budge.

"All right, all right. You're a good Synsär. The best."

"Thank you." She smiled smugly.

The gardener's house wasn't tall, only seven feet or so. But too tall for Nick to hoist himself up onto it without a boost.

There was no ladder inside. They did find two heavy-duty toolboxes, which they carried outside. Nick stacked them one on top of the other. It wasn't the steadiest of towers. Gillian acted as his spotter and, after one nearly disastrous attempt, Nick succeeded in dragging himself over the side of the building and onto the roof.

Gillian waited on the ground while he scanned the

surrounding skyline and commented on what he saw. Without Nick by her side, her case of the willies returned, and she continually cast furtive glances at the headstones just over the nearby knoll.

If not for her unreasonable fear, she might not have noticed a flash of movement by one of the trees. A shiver skittered up her spine as she stared into the darkness.

Nothing stared back at her.

As a precaution, she switched on the flashlight Nick had given her when they started out, and panned the area. When no boogeyman materialized, she told herself it must have been a small animal or a trick of the eye.

Nick made another comment from the roof.

She looked up. "What was that?"

"The old office building on Second Avenue. It's been abandoned for a few years now. You can just see it from here. I think we should check it out."

"Oh, okay." Gillian felt a strange tingle on the back of her head, like someone was watching her.

She turned around, aimed the flashlight, and saw it. No, not it. *Him.*

The young Hispanic boy. He stood half behind a tree, glaring at her, his expression challenging. How odd. Gillian forgot about her earlier fright.

"Nick," she said softly so as not to scare the boy away. She repeated his name a little louder when he didn't immediately respond.

Cadamus must be dead, she thought. Why else would the boy be here? Or, Cadamus wasn't dead and the boy had been sent to spy on them. But why then hadn't they seen any recent signs of the alpha male?

Suddenly, a jolt of excitement shot through Gillian.

What if they used the boy to lead them to Cadamus's sanctuary—and the proof she needed to free her father? This could be the break they'd—*she'd*—been waiting for.

Let the Ancients try to stop her.

"Nick," she said in a terse, singsong voice. "We have company."

She heard scuffling on the rooftop. "Who?"

Before she could answer, the boy took off, disappearing into the cluster of trees.

Gillian didn't stop to think. She chased after him, calling, "Wait! Come back."

He burst through the trees and ran in a straight line across the cemetery with Gillian in hot pursuit. She tried not to dwell on the graves or the dead people residing in them.

The boy was fast, having youth and agility on his side. Gillian fought to keep up. Soon, each breath became a struggle, and the muscles in her legs burned. She thought Nick might be behind her but couldn't be sure. The roaring in her ears blocked out all sound.

After another thirty seconds, she could take no more and slowed to a stop. Her chest heaving, her sides aching, she clutched her stomach and bent over, gasping for air.

And then she heard it. The unmistakable rustle of wings above her head. Large, leathery wings.

Cadamus!

Oh, God, no! It couldn't be.

Gillian raised her head and gazed skyward just as he swooped down on her, his arm outstretched.

"Nick!" she screamed and bolted.

She got no more than two steps before he grabbed her, his nails digging hard into her flesh. The ground abruptly fell away as Cadamus carried her high into the air.

"Nooooooo!"

He squeezed her chin and wrenched her head around, almost snapping her neck in half. "A mate for a mate," he hissed in her ear.

With sickening clarity, Gillian realized what she should have known all along.

Cadamus had set a trap, and she was to be his next victim.

Nick ran, keeping Cadamus and Gillian in constant sight—something he shouldn't have been able to do. Under normal circumstances, Cadamus could outfly him, even with the extra burden of Gillian's weight. Maybe the Dark Ancients he served had yet to heal his wing.

Wrong! The bastard was baiting him.

Nick wasn't the only one who witnessed Gillian being carried away or heard her screams. He doubted any of the individuals out on the street at that hour of the night understood what they saw or the implications.

Scaling the fence at the rear entrance of the cemetery, Nick raced down the service road. At the end, he paused to scour the sky, checking on Cadamus's location.

He was hovering, waiting for Nick to catch up. When he spotted Nick, he started flying again. East. Between buildings. Over rooftops. Darting in and out of shadows. One block. Two blocks.

Nick pushed himself as hard as he could, as fast as he could, as long as he could. His footsteps pounded on the concrete sidewalk, matching the thrumming in his temples. Gillian had stopped screaming, and her legs hung motionless. He couldn't tell if she was dead or possibly fainted.

Fainted. That was all. If she were dead, Nick's heart, unable to withstand the loss, would have stopped beating on the spot.

Suddenly, Cadamus ascended sharply and banked right, narrowly missing a flagpole atop the peaked roof of the historic Milford Hotel. Nick slowed his pace to a walk and stared, felt the pieces fall into place.

Yes, of course.

He knew Cadamus's destination then, should have known it all along.

The Hanson Building.

The place where he and Gillian had eliminated the first female. Where Carl Salvador was murdered. Where Nick and Cadamus would at last face their ultimate destiny.

Nick's blood was on fire, molten silver flowing through his veins. He ceased moving and stood in the middle of the mostly deserted street, his hand resting on the ritual dagger in his waistband. There was no need to hurry now.

Breathing deeply, he cleared his mind and forced himself to relax. The Ancients spoke to him then for the first time in days. They said only three words— the ones he'd been waiting twenty-five years to hear.

It is time.

CHAPTER TWENTY

Cadamus walked upright like a man. He had legs and arms, hands, feet, and a face, frightening though it was.

Gillian had never thought of him as possessing human qualities. She, like the dozens of people she'd interviewed, like Nick and Charlie, referred to the alpha males as creatures or monsters or beasts of the night.

The females were animals. Vicious, territorial predators. They crawled rather than walked, had brains the size of peas, and relied solely on instinct to survive.

But Cadamus was human-*ish*, at least in some ways. Physically, mentally, and emotionally.

He talked. He thought. His logic was admittedly skewed, and he had no morals whatsoever. But, unlike the females and contrary to what Nick had claimed, he possessed more than a rudimentary intelligence—as proven by his carefully orchestrated and successfully executed plan to abduct her.

He also felt.

At the moment, his range of emotions appeared limited to anger, frustration, and revenge—something that didn't bode well for Gillian.

She'd expected to be dead by now. Dismembered, her bones stripped of their flesh. Like her mother and the old woman from the cemetery and Carl Salvador. Instead, she was alive and huddled against the access door, watching Cadamus's every move with fearful anticipation and wondering what he was going to do next.

Why had he abducted her only to spare her? Did he intend to prolong her death? Torture her?

To bait Nick, of course. There could be no other answer.

Dear God in heaven. This was all her fault. If she hadn't chased after the boy, she wouldn't now be on the roof, the cheese in the trap Cadamus set to lure Nick.

He would come, too, Gillian had no doubt. To rescue her and to battle Cadamus. Possibly to die.

Cadamus was more than intelligent; he was cunning and calculating. Like an idiot, she'd played right into his hands. He'd used her desire to obtain proof of his existence against her. Against Nick. And she'd let him. *Her* fault. And there was nothing she could do to stop Nick from coming. Her cell phone was still attached to her belt. Even if she could call him and warn him about Cadamus's deception, he would still come.

The final battle. Nick and his goddamn destiny.

But hadn't she also embraced *her* destiny?

Looking back on her life, she realized Charlie was right. She'd been on the path leading to this moment

ever since the day she decided to make a career of researching the urban myths surrounding the creatures.
Maybe even since the night her mother was killed.

Guilt and despair welled up inside her, squeezing
the air from her lungs until she choked.

She let out a sob—which she bit back when
Cadamus wheeled around and scowled at her. Wings
partially unfurled, he stood at the edge of the roof
on a small ledge watching the street below. Watching
for Nick.

"He's here," Cadamus said and stared at her with
his cold, malevolent eyes. The red and yellow lights
mounted on the huge satellite dish behind him turned
his dark, scaly skin a strange shade of green. Not
human-*ish* at all. Not like anything on this earth.

Gillian chomped down on the inside of her mouth
to prevent herself from crying out.

Please Nick. Don't come for me. Stay far, far away.

She heard a click, and the door she leaned on suddenly opened. Letting out a small scream, she caught
herself before she tumbled forward.

The young Hispanic boy appeared. He pocketed a
key before stepping through the doorway, around her,
and out onto the roof. Sparing her no more than a
cursory look, he shut the door behind him but didn't
lock it.

"The Huntsman is on the stairs," he said.

Cadamus grunted—with satisfaction?—and returned to his vigil at the roof's edge.

If only there were something Gillian could do.
Some way she could alter the fate Nick and Cadamus
were both convinced waited for them.

Contacting Nick was pointless. But what about the
police? They had weapons that could destroy Cada-

mus. Long-range rifles. Helicopters to run him down. Gillian rested her hand on her cell phone. Her fingers toyed with the strap.

There can be no interference from outside sources.

Nick's warning, repeated to her over and over, rang in her ears. She let her hand slowly drop. What if it were true?

The boy scurried past Gillian to stand by a large air-conditioning unit. He was dirty, and he stank. His rumpled clothes were unwashed and his hair a tangled mess. If Cadamus were his protector, he didn't do a very good job of caring for the boy. Not like Nick cared for Stevie.

Gillian pressed a hand to her mouth, stifling another sob. If Nick died, what would happen to poor little Stevie?

To her?

Darkness crowded around the fringes of Gillian's mind, beckoning her to succumb. She resisted. She must not lose touch with reality. Not now. Nick might need her. Clasping her hands together and pressing them to her mouth, she willed herself to hang on.

A shadow crossed her line of vision.

She looked up to see Cadamus looming over her and started. Did he intend to devour her after all? Her heart beat so hard it slammed into her rib cage.

"It is time," he said and, grabbing her arm, hauled her to her feet. He dragged her away from the door, propped her up, and held her like a shield in front of him.

Terror seized her, spurring her into action. She screamed and kicked. Clawed at the arm he'd locked around her middle. Banged her heel into his shin.

"Let go of me!"

He groaned tiredly and whacked her on the side of the head.

Gillian yelped, slumped forward, and cradled her throbbing head with her free hand. Stars floated in front of her eyes.

Cadamus thrust his fingers into her hair and yanked, nearly ripping it out by the roots. He put his face next to hers. The stench of his putrid breath caused her to gag.

"Remember," he said in a low, guttural voice that sounded as if it came from inside her head and not his mouth.

An image of her parents' bedroom as it had been twenty-five years ago appeared to Gillian. She stood in the doorway, a teddy bear clutched in her arm, calling to her mommy. But her mommy didn't answer.

A monster, like the one in the cartoon she and her best friend Dorothy had watched the week before, stood by the foot of the bed, staring down at her mommy. Only this monster wasn't animated. It was real. And it had part of her mommy's leg in its hand.

"Leave her alone," Gillian had shouted.

The monster looked over at her, a grisly smile on its face, and said, "A mate for a mate," then threw her mommy's leg at her. It landed in the hallway.

"Remember well," Cadamus said from inside her head. "And know that the Huntsman will die as the one who bore you did."

In her mind's eye, Gillian walked toward her parents' bed, her legs moving of their own volition. Holding her breath, she looked down at the bloody remains of her mother. But it wasn't her mother's lifeless face that stared up at her.

It was Nick's.

The monster had grabbed for Gillian, and she'd begun to scream. She didn't stop until her father came running a few minutes later and gathered her in his arms. By then, the monster had flown out the window.

No! Not again. Don't let the creature kill someone I love.

The next thing Gillian knew, the access door burst open and banged into the wall with an earsplitting crash.

Nick stood in the doorway—very much alive, thank God—and filling it completely, his expression set in stone. In his hand he held the ritual dagger. Moonlight glinted off the blade.

His gaze went first to her, then Cadamus. "Let her go."

"As you wish."

Cadamus flung Gillian across the roof. She careened into the side of the metal air-conditioning unit, her back absorbing the brunt of the impact. Good thing. Had her head hit first, she might be dead.

Momentarily stunned, her legs buckled, and she slid to the floor like a marionette whose strings had been cut. Through a fog, she heard Nick.

"You'll pay for that."

Turning her head in his direction, she tried to focus. A golden light seemed to surround him. She didn't know if it was real or the result of the bashing her head had taken.

"When I'm through with you," Cadamus said, "I will feast on her over your lifeless body." He bared his teeth and unfurled his wings, which spanned at least fifteen feet tip to tip. The right one bore an ugly scar where Nick had pierced it with the ritual dagger.

Nick stepped away from the doorway out onto the roof. He seemed somehow taller, his shoulders broader, his muscles larger. The planes on his face were more defined, the ridges sharper, the shadows darker.

"You will rot in hell before you lay a hand on her or anyone else again."

Gillian stared at him, spellbound by this stranger with the harsh eyes and icy voice.

This wasn't the man she knew, the talented camera operator, doting new parent, sympathetic friend, exciting lover. He wasn't even the skilled warrior who had dispatched the three female creatures with relative ease.

No, this man was the Huntsman. The champion of good and, if he defeated Cadamus, the sole person responsible for saving the world.

Much as Nick wanted to lunge at his enemy and drive the dagger into his chest with all the strength he could muster, he refrained.

Cadamus had only one vulnerability—a soft spot in his armor-plated hide just above his waist. And Nick would have only one chance to strike. He must be swift and cunning and most of all, accurate. If he failed, it was all over. For him, for Gillian, and for the entire human race.

Circling right, then left, he waited for Cadamus, who possessed far less patience then Nick, to make the first move. He didn't have to wait long.

Cadamus flapped his wings and rose into the air. Six feet, twelve. Higher still.

Nick tensed, readying himself for the attack.

Like a seabird diving for prey in the ocean's wave,

Cadamus swooped, slashing at Nick with his long, sharp fingers.

Ducking sideways, Nick spun and jumped, dodging Cadamus's deadly reach with mere inches to spare. He hit the floor of the roof, rolled, and sprang to his feet.

Cadamus wasn't tall, barely reaching Nick's shoulders. But he was considerably stronger than Nick, and he could fly. In the air, he was invincible. On the ground, Cadamus's bulk worked against him, making him slow and ungainly.

To win the battle, Nick must ground Cadamus. Not by damaging his wing with the ritual dagger as he'd done before. Cadamus had proved his ability to fly even with a small hole in his wing. And Nick didn't want to risk losing the dagger by throwing it.

He had to find a way to completely—and permanently—incapacitate Cadamus.

Suddenly, a piercing pain penetrated Nick's skull. Holding the sides of his head, he looked up to see Cadamus suspended directly above him.

"Forget it, you bastard," Nick growled. "You're not reading my mind."

He blocked Cadamus's attempt to make a psychic connection with him by creating a mental shield, a technique Charlie had taught him. The pain instantly subsided, and Nick's vision cleared.

Cadamus let out an angry screech and dove at Nick once more. Again, Nick dodged his attack. Four more dives, four more near misses. Nick stumbled on the last attack. Cadamus caught hold of Nick's arm but lost his grasp. Gillian screamed.

They couldn't do this forever. Nick would tire before Cadamus. Already, Nick's lungs ached and sweat plastered his shirt to his back, while Cadamus looked ready to go another ten rounds.

Swift and cunning and most of all, accurate.

As he watched Cadamus hover overhead, an idea came to him. Arms by his sides, Nick left the safety of the wall and walked to the middle of the roof. Cadamus rose into the air and once he was in position, dove.

This time, Nick didn't duck.

Cadamus flew so close, Nick could see victory shining in his eyes. At the last possible second, when Cadamus's fingers were just about to close around his neck, Nick crouched and jumped.

He punched his fist through the scar in Cadamus's wing, grabbed onto the leathery skin, and pulled. Weakened from the previous wound, it gave easily. The sound of tearing skin was sickening. Cadamus screamed. Flapping his wings like a trapped moth, he tried to break free of Nick's grasp, wounding himself further.

Nick used his other hand, the one holding the dagger, to protect his face and neck from the blows Cadamus rained on him.

Cadamus tried to take the dagger from Nick. When he touched the blade, he screamed again and released the dagger. Puffs of smoke floated off his palm, and the foul scent of burning flesh filled Nick's nostrils.

It would be a hundred times worse when Nick plunged the dagger into Cadamus's chest.

Nick's arm ached, his muscles ready to snap. But still, he held on. Blood, both Cadamus's and his, covered his hands, making it harder to maintain his grip.

Cadamus thrashed, swinging at Nick's head. He gave another tug, separating more of Cadamus's skin from his bone until there was a hole the size of a basketball in the wing. But Nick knew he had yet to ground his opponent.

Using his slowly depleting strength, he curled his fingers around one of Cadamus's fragile wing bones and twisted. The bone splintered with a loud crack.

"Try to fly now," Nick grunted.

Cadamus went berserk with rage. His foot slammed into Nick's stomach, the force of it causing Nick to double over. Unable to stay in the air, Cadamus dropped to the roof. His right hand came from out of nowhere, smashing into Nick's ear.

It hurt like a son of a bitch but probably less than a broken wing.

Cadamus attempted to wrench Nick's hand from his wing, tearing the flesh on Nick's arm and leaving huge, bloody gashes. When Nick still didn't let go, Cadamus grabbed him by the rib cage, lifted him off his feet, and rammed him into the steel access door.

The intense shock to Nick's system temporarily numbed him from head to toe. His fingers useless, he released Cadamus's crippled wing. Collapsing in on himself, Nick slid slowly to the roof floor. The ritual dagger fell from his other hand, clattering as it skidded across the roof and out of his reach.

His enemy towered over him, preparing to wield the lethal blow. "You are finished, Huntsman."

Stand up.

The voice speaking to Nick was his own, not that of the Ancients. He wasn't going to fail, hadn't destroyed the three females, wiped out Cadamus's race, found love in Gillian's arms, only to be defeated.

"Nick! Over here."

He sat upright at the sound of Gillian's voice. To

his amazement, she'd crawled across the floor of the roof to his dagger. She quickly picked it up and tossed it to him.

Her aim was true.

Cadamus roared his anger. "She's mine to command, not yours."

"She will never be yours."

"You are wrong, Huntsman." He pointed to the boy. "Tend her."

Nick stood, the ritual dagger gripped firmly in his right hand. He faced Cadamus without fear.

Instead of striking him as he expected, Cadamus stepped back. His hearty chuckle rang through the night.

"It appears I no longer have a need to kill you, Huntsman, for I have already won."

"We're not finished. Not by a long shot."

"No?" Cadamus turned his head to the side.

Nick followed the direction of his gaze. Gillian crouched by the air-conditioning unit. She had her cell phone in her hands, frantically dialing. The young Hispanic boy leaned over her, speaking to her in a quiet voice. A second later, she put the phone to her ear.

"No, Gillian," he hollered. "Don't do it."

If she heard him, she didn't respond. Her glassy eyes stared at something only she could see. The boy nodded at Cadamus, then ducked behind the air-conditioning unit.

"Your mate betrays you," Cadamus said with a sneer, "and this world will soon belong to those I serve."

"Ma'am?" a young man's voice sounded in Gillian's ear. "Are you still there?"

"Yes." Gillian shook her head dazedly. When had she placed a phone call?

She'd been reliving her mother's death again and again and the awful moment when Nick's face and not her mother's stared up at her from the bed. She rubbed her eyes and the image disappeared.

Only to be replaced by an equally horrifying one, this one real. Nick slumped against the access door and Cadamus stood before him, laughing, looking over at her, his lipless mouth drawn back in a macabre grin.

"Ma'am?" the man asked.

"I'm still here," Gillian said weakly. Her brain was slow to function. "Who are you?"

"I'm the nine-one-one dispatcher. Can you tell me your location?"

She answered automatically. "The Hanson Building. Jefferson and Central. I don't have the exact address. It's the same place where Carl Salvador was murdered."

"Which apartment?"

"We're on the roof."

"You say you're being attacked?"

Had she said that? She couldn't recall. "Are the police on their way?"

"Yes, ma'am. I've sent a patrol unit to investigate. But I need to know. Is someone attacking you?"

Gillian must tell the man to stop the police from coming, but it was if someone else were moving her mouth.

"Yes, we're being attacked."

"By a man or a woman?"

"Neither." He wasn't even human.

Suddenly, a flash of lightning streaked across the

night sky directly above the buildings across the street. It was followed by a fierce clap of thunder, the echo of which Gillian felt inside her chest.

Rain? How could that be? The skies had been clear all day. *Were* clear now. She glanced up to see the moon shining brightly overhead. Then all at once, she couldn't see it. Something . . . a cloud maybe . . . blocked the moon's glow.

The fine hairs along her arms stood on end.

"Are you able to get away or hide? Hello? Hello?" the dispatcher said when she didn't answer right away.

"I . . . can't . . . get away. Hurry, please."

Hurry, please? That wasn't what she meant to say.

Gillian lowered her gaze. It landed on Cadamus. He was holding his belly and still laughing like a maniac. She'd been wrong, she thought. His range of emotions also included a warped sense of humor.

Then she understood. Cadamus was controlling her. His fingers had dialed the phone, his words emanated from her mouth.

"Stop," she said under her breath, concentrating on banishing him from her mind. "Stop now."

But it was too late.

The cloud covering the moon abruptly shrank, then just as quickly expanded into a whirling funnel that seemed to suck up the stars.

A second streak of lightning flashed and a third, then too many to count. More thunder rumbled. One minute the air was still. The next, a gust of wind blew across the roof, whipping Gillian's hair and clothes. She lowered her head and covered her face with her forearm.

"Ma'am, please answer me." The dispatcher sounded worried. "Are you all right?"

"Uh . . . no. I'm not." No one was.

A siren wailed, distant at first, but growing increasingly louder.

"The patrol unit just radioed in," the dispatcher said. "They should be arriving shortly."

Gillian wanted to tell the dispatcher to have the police turn around and go back. Her tongue, however, was glued to the top of her mouth. Damn Cadamus!

Above her, the funnel cloud danced across the sky. It left a huge tear in its wake from which poured liquid fire. At first Gillian thought it was her imagination.

She was wrong.

"Even now it begins," Cadamus roared and tipped his head back to take in the tumultuous sky. "The balance of power is shifting."

There can be no interference from outside sources.

The bottom fell out of Gillian's stomach. Her limp fingers were unable to hold the cell phone, and it dropped to her lap. The dispatcher's tinny voice floated up from the earpiece.

"Oh, God, oh God. What have I done?"

Exactly what Cadamus wanted. Once more he'd used her desire—this one to save Nick—against her. Without meaning to, without fully knowing what she was doing, she'd unleashed a destruction unlike any man had ever seen.

Cadamus staggered backwards, his remaining good wing extended, his arms raised to the sky as if to encompass it. With a shout of triumph to his masters, he turned, mounted the ledge, and looked down onto the street.

Arms still extended, he faced Nick, who crouched against the access door, and cried, "Your human soldiers come. I welcome them and their bullets. For the damage is already done. Your world belongs to my kind now."

Nick refused to back down. "Your race is extinct. I killed your females."

"You assume too much, Huntsman." Cadamus smiled scornfully. "As we speak, my seed lies in the womb of a female who will soon deliver my offspring."

No, thought Gillian, it couldn't be. There were only three female creatures. Always three. Cadamus was lying just to throw Nick off guard.

A pounding on the stairs heralded the arrival of the police.

"Go now," Cadamus shouted and pointed.

The young boy emerged from behind the air-conditioning unit.

Nick straightened to his full height, his chest expanding with each breath he took. No sooner did he move away from the access door than the young boy bolted past him and, wrenching the door open, escaped through it.

Nick didn't appear bothered by the boy's leaving. He reached calmly behind him and, after engaging the lock, shut the door, mere seconds ahead of the police.

When they encountered the locked barrier, they hammered on it with their batons and shouted, "Police. Open up."

"You think your pathetic attempts to stop your soldiers will save your world?" Cadamus hollered at Nick over the noise, his fist leveled in belligerent defiance. "Think again. It is too late."

"Now it is you who assumes too much, Cadamus."

Driven by a sudden and overwhelming fear she couldn't explain, Gillian hauled herself upright. Her instincts, or perhaps her ability to read Nick, told her something terrible was about to happen. Something that had nothing—or everything—to do with the approaching end of the world.

Nick took a step forward, then two. In his right hand, he gripped the ritual dagger. From his higher vantage point on the ledge, Cadamus eyed Nick and the dagger as if both were a grand joke.

"I don't fear you, Huntsman."

"You are a bigger fool than I imagined." Turning toward Gillian, Nick said, "You are my Synsär. Take care of Stevie. Raise her. Train her. Teach her everything you know. She, and you, are the only hope for this world."

"Nick!"

"I love you. Don't ever forget that."

"Noooooo!"

Time seemed to slow to half speed. Everything came at Gillian in tiny, disjointed fragments. Cadamus standing on the ledge, laughing. The police pounding on the door, then firing at it with their guns. The storm raging in the sky above them. Rain—when had that started?—pelting her face. Her legs weighed down by a hundred pounds of sand and unable to move.

And Nick, advancing on Cadamus, the ritual dagger raised.

Then suddenly, time sped up. So fast, Gillian couldn't take it all in.

She tripped and landed on her hands and knees, only a foot away from Nick. Lifting her arm, she reached for him. Her fingers grazed his pants leg.

"Don't," she cried.

Ignoring her, he lowered his head and charged Cadamus, colliding with him like runaway vehicle slamming into a tree trunk. For a single second that seemed to last forever, they teetered on the edge of the wall.

Gillian leapt to her feet and ran at them. She had no idea what she could or should do, only that she must act to save Nick and set the world right once more.

In the end, all she did was watch the man she loved and the creature responsible for his death topple over the side of the building.

"Nick!" His name, ripped from her throat, was carried away on the wind.

Bracing her hands on the ledge, she stared down into the swirling darkness and saw . . . absolutely nothing. No Nick. No Cadamus. Only another police car arriving on the street below and people gathering on the sidewalk to see what all the excitement was about.

Gillian buried her face in her hands, sank to her knees, and cried. She'd lost Nick forever and had no one to blame except herself.

Nick held on to Cadamus, his arms locked around the alpha male's waist. Cadamus's one good wing wasn't capable of keeping him and Nick from spiraling downward too fast to land safely. They would both be dead the instant they hit the pavement, which would be in another two or three seconds at the rate they were descending.

To be on the safe side, Nick plunged the ritual dagger deep into Cadamus's chest. Dead center of the soft spot.

His agonizing scream was the last thing Nick heard.

After that, there was only silence. Blissful, peaceful silence. And darkness. Not frightening at all but soothing and calming.

If this was death, Nick decided, it wasn't all bad.

A moment later, he heard voices and listened more intently. Yes, definitely voices. The Ancients were calling to him.

Then he felt their hands surround him, cradle him, and carry him away.

Those Cadamus served would take him, too, for there was never any evidence left of the battle for humankind to ponder.

All would be well, Nick thought. Gillian was safe and so was Stevie. They would fulfill their duty just as he had his and every Huntsman before him. He had faith in Gillian. More even than she had in herself.

Come, Nicholaus, the Ancients said. *It is time to go home.*

Closing his eyes, Nick sighed and went to sleep. The battle was over, and he'd won. He was only sorry he hadn't lived to see Gillian again.

CHAPTER TWENTY-ONE

Gillian walked out of the police station and into a bright, beautiful dawn.

After six long, miserable hours, four of which were spent waiting around and only two being questioned, she'd been released. She told the police nothing, nothing of value anyway. Certainly nothing about Nick and Cadamus.

When asked why she was on the roof of the Hanson Building, Gillian said she was researching her next book.

"How did you get on the roof? The access door was locked."

"It wasn't locked when I tried it." *A lie.*

"Were you alone?"

"Yes." *Another lie.*

"What happened to your attacker?"

"He went over the side of the building when he

heard the officers banging on the door." *The truth, sort of. Nick had pushed him.*

"Describe him."

"Very large, dark complexion, ugly, and mean." *Also the truth.*

"What was the boy doing on the roof?"

"I don't know. He was there when I arrived." *Yet another lie.*

"I thought you said you were alone."

"I *was* alone . . . I mean . . . I went alone to the Hanson Building. The boy was on the roof when I arrived. I don't know why he was there."

A entire pack of lies.

Gillian had asked about the boy, whether he was all right or not, but the police refused to give her any information. She knew only that he was in their custody. A far better fate, she was sure, than being in Cadamus's. From what she'd gathered, the boy had been as closemouthed as her.

Synsärs were loyal if nothing else.

The police must have believed part of her story, at least the part about her having been attacked. She sported a nasty gash on her forehead from when Cadamus threw her into the air-conditioning unit, cuts and bruises from when he'd mauled her during their flight to the roof, and a multitude of scrapes and scratches. The police just had trouble with the part of her story where her assailant went off the side of the building.

She could hardly blame them, since no one found a body splattered on the street below.

What had happened to Nick? She'd asked herself the same question a hundred times since the police loaded her in a squad car and brought her to the station. She suspected she was lucky they didn't charge her with calling in a false report.

Gillian stood on the sidewalk outside the police station debating what to do next. During the last six hours, she'd fought to keep her emotions under control and her grief at bay, determined not to let Nick down. He wouldn't want her to tell the police about the existence of the creatures. Neither would her father.

Finally, she understood their reasons. But it was too late for that understanding to do any good. Nick was dead. The only man she'd ever truly loved. And her father was still in prison—might soon die there if the cancer had its way.

With the ordeal over, her need to stay in control vanished, and the tears started flowing. Gillian couldn't stop them. No small wonder, she had a lot to cry about.

People passed her, giving her curious stares. She glanced around through blurry eyes, searching for a semiprivate place to sit until her crying jag ended and she could function normally. Eyes downcast, she headed toward a vacant bench beneath an awning.

"Gillian?" a familiar voice called.

She stopped and turned around to see Charlie and Stevie walking briskly toward her.

"I was monitoring the police radio last night and heard the call," Charlie said when he reached her. "We've been waiting for you to come out of the station since around two A.M. Are you okay?"

"No." She'd never be okay again. "Nick's dead." The tears flowed anew.

"I suspected as much when you both didn't come home and didn't answer your cell phones. I'm truly sorry," he said in a hoarse whisper.

"Me, too."

He opened his arms and she went into them. They stood for several moments, hugging. Gillian wasn't the only person to lose a loved one. Charlie had lost the second of his two sons.

"I'll call later today," he said when they broke apart, "try to find out where they took his body."

"There is no body."

"What?"

"It's true."

"I don't understand. Cadamus, yes. But the Ancients leave human remains alone."

"The police were adamant."

"What's going to happen to me?" Stevie asked. She looked almost as forlorn as Charlie did.

Gillian wiped her eyes and drew the little girl to her side. "I'm going to raise you and train you to be the next Huntress."

"Really?" Stevie gazed up at Gillian with huge, trusting eyes.

"That was Nick's final request to me, and I intend to see that it's carried out"

"I understand you wanting to raise Stevie," Charlie said, "but is it necessary to train her? You and Nick eliminated all three female creatures."

"Before he died, Cadamus claimed he found another female and mated with her."

"A fourth female?" Charlie shook his head. "Impossible."

"He could have been bluffing, but do we really want to take the chance?"

"No, we don't," Charlie said.

"Do the Ancients ever speak to you?"

"Sometimes. But they haven't lately and not about

this." He reached for Stevie's hand. "Why don't we go home?"

By home he meant Nick's apartment. As difficult as it would be for her, Gillian was determined to handle whatever tasks awaited her there before moving Stevie to her condo.

"We came in your car," Charlie said. "I hope you don't mind."

"Of course not." They'd have to arrange for Nick's car to be picked up. It was still parked outside the cemetery, if it hadn't been already towed. "Can you drive, please? I'm not up to it."

Gillian sat in the front passenger seat and stared out the window at morning rush-hour traffic. She tried not to dwell on the events of the last day and night but was unable to think of anything else.

She would do right by Stevie, make Nick proud of her. Of them both. He'd sacrificed his own life to save hers and the whole world. She owed him the next twenty-five years and much, much more.

I love you. Don't ever forget that.

"I love you, Nick," she said under her breath, too softly for anyone in the car to hear. "And I always will."

"You want to lie down and rest for a while?" Charlie asked Gillian shortly after they arrived at the apartment. "We could all use a nap."

They were in the living room, flipping through TV channels, looking for any relevant news items and finding none.

"In a little while." Gillian was tired but not yet ready to face sleeping alone or the unpleasant dreams she was sure were waiting for her. "I'll put Stevie to bed when she's done with breakfast. The poor kid's exhausted."

"I hated bringing her with me last night, but I didn't want to leave her alone either. I must have been making too much noise. She woke up and when she learned what had happened and where I was planning on going, she insisted on tagging along."

"She can be very determined." Gillian had turned down the sound on the TV so they could talk.

"You're going to have your hands full with her. I'll help you all I can. Though I don't know how much longer I'll be around."

"I appreciate that. I'm sure I'll need every bit of help I can get." She tried to smile at Charlie, but the corners of her mouth refused to turn up. "And speaking of Stevie, I'd better check on her."

Gillian found the girl sitting at the kitchen table, her cereal only half eaten, her head resting on the table beside the bowl. She was out like a light.

Gillian's heart, broken into a thousand pieces, hurt a tiny bit less. Stevie needed her, and she needed Stevie. Together, they might just make it.

"Come on, sweetie pie. Wake up."

She gently shook the girl's shoulder until Stevie roused enough to be led to the spare bedroom and the futon bed. Feeling she might already be failing as a parent, Gillian slipped off Stevie's shoes and socks and, leaving her in her clothes, covered her with a blanket. She hoped skipping a bath and teeth brushing this once wouldn't ruin the girl for life.

In the hall outside the spare bedroom, Gillian paused. A glance through the doorway into the living room assured her that Charlie was still on the couch, either watching TV or possibly snoozing.

Maybe now, when she was relatively alone, was the best time for Gillian to brave Nick's bedroom and confront her personal demons. Grieving was a long process. And while she had Charlie's and Stevie's support and comfort, she wanted to take this initial step alone—just her, Nick's memory, and no one else.

Her throat burning, her eyes watering, and her stomach tied in knots, Gillian slowly walked down the short hall, past the bathroom to Nick's bedroom. The door was shut except for a small crack. She placed her hand on the knob but didn't go in, needing another moment to muster her courage.

This, she said to herself, would be the most difficult part. If she could withstand being in Nick's bedroom, sit on the bed where'd they'd made love so often, and not fall apart, she could endure all the hardships ahead of her.

Pushing the door open, she stepped inside the room. Everything appeared exactly the same as before. The magazine Nick had been reading the other day lay on the nightstand. His digital alarm clock displayed the time in red numerals. The heel of one misplaced shoe peeked out from under the bed.

The ritual dagger was on the dresser.

"What . . . ?" Gillian stared. Where had that come from?

A sense of confusion overtook her, leaving her lightheaded. It didn't last. She was suddenly blinded by a bright, golden light emanating from the center of the bed. It wasn't altogether different from when the female creatures dissolved.

She shielded her eyes against the unbearable glow. "What the . . . oh, my God."

As the light dimmed, Gillian saw a form take shape on the bed. A human form. A man.

No, it couldn't be. She squinted, took a tentative step. "Nick!"

She flung herself toward the bed, falling onto the mattress beside him. With frantic hands, she touched his face and neck. His skin was warm. Gloriously, wonderfully warm. His pallor normal. She glanced down at his chest. It rose and fell, shallow but steady.

His eyes, however, were closed and though she repeated his name over and over, he didn't open them. What was wrong with him? Why didn't he wake up?

"Charlie," she screamed.

He came running as fast as his pushing-eighty legs could carry him. "What's wrong?"

"It's Nick. He's here."

"He's what?" Charlie burst into the bedroom only to come to an abrupt stop. His eyes went wide, and his face drained of color. "Well, I'll be damned."

"I came into the room, and he just appeared in this shower of golden light." Gillian spoke so fast, she babbled.

"Is he alive?" Charlie came closer.

"Yes. But not conscious. I think he's like Stevie was, communing with the Ancients."

"I don't believe it." He patted Nick's cheeks to confirm for himself Nick's live and—from all appearances—healthy state.

"How can this be? Do the Ancients bring back people from the dead?"

"Not that I've ever heard of. Unless . . ." Charlie frowned.

"Unless what?"

"Was he injured before he and Cadamus fell?"

"Yes, but I don't know how badly."

"If Nick killed Cadamus before they reached the ground, then technically Nick won the final battle."

"Why didn't the Ancients bring Jonathan back? He won his battle with Radlum."

"I don't know." Charlie shook his head in confusion. "Maybe because his wounds were fatal and Nick's weren't. Let's hope Nick can tell us when he wakes up."

"I wish he would soon." Gillian scooted over so that she sat right next to him. She kept touching him, assuring herself over and over that he was all right.

"It could be a while."

Gillian remembered back to when Stevie had her commune with the Ancients. It had lasted almost three hours. "I'll stay with him."

When Nick didn't wake up in the next fifteen minutes, Charlie left the bedroom. From his haggard expression and weary gait, Gillian figured he and the living room couch would soon be seeing eye to eye.

Once she was alone with Nick, she bent and kissed his forehead, cheek, and lips, which, while not responsive, were warm and soft and incredibly sweet.

"You scared me," she whispered. "When I saw you and Cadamus go over the side of the building, my heart stopped beating." She combed her fingers through his hair. "I'm so very glad you aren't dead."

Gillian wasn't sure if she should be talking to Nick or not while he was communing with the Ancients, but she didn't care. *Her* need to talk to him was too strong to go unrequited.

Just a short while ago she was convinced she'd never see him again and now, here he was. She sent a prayer of thanks heavenward, hoping it reached whoever was responsible for this miracle.

Eventually, Gillian's fatigue caught up with her. Attempting to disturb Nick as little as possible, she stretched out beside him, wrapped an arm protectively around his middle, and rested her head on his shoulder. Lying next to him, feeling every inch of him flush against her, was all her overtaxed mind and body needed to finally let go and relax. Within minutes, Gillian dozed off and spent the next hour drifting in and out of a fitful sleep.

At one point she dreamed—at least she thought it was a dream. Her mother appeared to her, her image as vivid as it had been that night in the parking garage when Gillian was attacked by the first female creature.

"You did well," her mother said in a voice gentle as a lullaby. "I'm proud of you."

Her praise filled Gillian with warmth. She put out her arms to embrace her mother, who floated just out of reach. "Come back."

"I can't stay." Her mother said, her image starting to fade. "Good-bye, Gillian. I love you."

"Don't go! Please."

"I have to. It's past time. And Nick is coming home. Be happy, darling."

Gillian came suddenly awake. Nick's face was the first thing she saw. He'd crawled on top of her, pinned her beneath him, and was pressing his very obvious erection into the junction of her legs.

"I couldn't ask for a better welcome home," he said, nuzzling her neck and rocking his hips.

"Nick. Oh, Nick! You're awake. I thought I'd lost you. When you and Cadamus went over the side of—"

He silenced her with a kiss.

Wrapping her arms around his neck and pulling

him close, Gillian poured all the emotions bottled up inside her into their kiss.

"Miss me?" He lifted his head and flashed her the sexy half grin she so adored.

"More than you can imagine." She cuffed him in the arm and scowled. "Don't ever do that again."

"You won't get rid of me that easy."

His hand snuck under the hem of her shirt to fondle her breast through her bra. His eyes glinted hungrily. "This makes everything worthwhile."

"Nick, Nick!"

Stevie came running into the room. Oblivious to what Nick and Gillian were up to, she dove onto the foot of the bed, her corkscrew curls in wild disarray. Gillian instantly sat up and rearranged her shirt.

Nick was a little slower to respond. He sighed with perfect parental patience and grumbled, "Kids. No respect for privacy."

Stevie promptly bombarded him. He hugged her tight and swung her around so that she stood on the floor in front of him.

"You're back." Her face was awash with joy.

He tugged on one of her curls until she giggled. "I couldn't leave you alone now, could I?"

"Gillian said she was going to raise me and train me to be a Huntress. The best one ever."

"She did?" Nick looked over at Gillian, his smile soft and for her alone. "Well, now we can do it together." He returned his gaze to Stevie.

"Cool."

"I see you finally decided to rejoin us." Charlie hobbled into the room. His joints were noticeably stiff from sleeping on the couch, but his smile was wide and exuberant. "Thought I was going to get stuck with training my third Huntsman."

"Nope. You can retire now, old man."

" 'Bout time."

Nick stood and went to his foster father and mentor. The two embraced fondly.

Gillian also stood and took Stevie's hand. They followed Nick and Charlie out into the living room.

"Are you hungry?" Gillian asked.

"More thirsty than hungry. I'll take a big glass of ice water if you're offering."

"I'm offering."

Gillian got everyone something to drink, then settled next to Nick on the couch. Stevie immediately snuggled beside her, and she automatically put her arm around the girl.

"What exactly happened after you fell off the building?" Charlie asked, sitting in the recliner. "Do you remember?"

"Some of it," Nick said after finishing half his water. "I remember the Ancients carrying me away. I thought I'd died."

"So did we," Gillian added, suppressing a shudder.

"Things are a little fuzzy after that. Then, I heard their voices telling me it was time to go home. I thought by home they meant the afterlife."

"Did they tell you why they brought you back?" Charlie asked.

Nick leaned forward and winked at Stevie, but the look he gave Gillian and Charlie was somber. "To train my successor. Cadamus wasn't bluffing. He did mate with a female. There will be a new generation of creatures in twenty-five years."

"How?" Gillian and Charlie said at the same time.

"The Ancients didn't explain. Evidently, there were four females and not three."

"But there are always three." Charlie's snow-white brows drew together in a puzzled frown.

"There have been a lot of differences this cycle. Cadamus had his own Synsär. And the females went from being timid to aggressive."

"That's true."

Well, thought Gillian, there went her theory about the eggs and destroying them before the larvae hatched, since they had no idea where the fourth female creature was hiding.

"You're going to have your work cut out for you, kiddo," Nick told Stevie. "Especially if the female creatures continue to become more aggressive."

"I'm ready." Her demeanor was that of someone considerably older than eight.

"Not yet. Though you will be one day, I have no doubt."

Neither did Gillian.

"So are you and Gillian getting married?" Stevie's glance went from Nick to Gillian and back to Nick.

Charlie coughed in an obvious attempt to disguise a laugh. Gillian felt her cheeks flush with embarrassment.

Nick grinned. "I've been contemplating it. What do you think?"

"I think yes and right away." Stevie beamed.

"I'm all for that." Nick chuckled. "But it's really up to Gillian." He reached over and brushed his knuckles along the line of her jaw. "She hasn't agreed to make an honest man of me yet."

"You're going to marry Nick, aren't you?" Stevie snuggled up closer to Gillian. "That way, we can be a real family."

Gillian tried to counter the unexpected rush of emotion with a light laugh.

"Maybe." She swallowed, which proved difficult because her throat had suddenly closed. "We'll have to see." She patted Stevie's knee, got up, and went to the kitchen, taking her and Stevie's glasses with her as an excuse.

Nick came up behind her while she stood at the sink, took her by the shoulders, and turned her around. "I'm sorry."

"For what?" She tried to pretend she wasn't upset.

"For botching my marriage proposal. Give me time, I'll do it right, I promise. Flowers, diamond ring, down on one knee. The whole nine yards."

"You didn't botch your proposal."

"You sure? Because you don't look like a gal who's just been swept off her feet. Is it the coming-back-from-the-dead part that's making you hesitant?"

"Not at all." This time her laugh was genuine, but short-lived. "I do want to marry you. And be a mom to Stevie. Even have one or two more kids if Huntsmen are allowed."

"We're allowed. Encouraged even." He tugged her into his arms and kissed the top of her head. "I promise you, Gillian, my hero days are over. The most dangerous work I'll do from now on will be as a camera operator for TV-7 News."

"Somehow, I'm not reassured. You embark on a lot of dangerous stunts in your job."

"Those days are also over. Now that I'll have a wife and kids to come home to every night, I'm planning on playing it safe."

She sighed into his chest.

He drew back to stare at her, his expression troubled. "What's wrong?"

"You're going to think I'm silly."

"Tell me," he coaxed.

"I want my father to walk me down the aisle." She sniffed back a tear. "But I don't know if that's possible."

"We'll make it possible."

"But the cancer. If it's come back, if he's terminal—"

"First of all, we don't know if the cancer's come back. We'll find out Friday after his biopsy surgery. Depending on the results, which could be negative," he reminded her, "and his treatment, we'll set a date for the wedding. And starting tomorrow, I'll go to work on getting him paroled."

"What can you do that I haven't already tried?"

"Like I said before, I have some connections. People of influence I've worked with over the years. In fact, I've already been laying the groundwork to see if they can help."

"What people?"

"A couple of state senators. The governor. The warden at Florence Prison."

"The warden?"

"My visits to Florence weren't always to see your dad. We did a story there last year about some new reforms that shed a positive light on the prison and particularly the warden."

The realization that her father hadn't been lying completely about Nick's visits made her glad. "Do you think they'll agree to help us?" For the first time in days, Gillian felt a ray of hope. She clung to it.

Nick hugged her to him and pressed a light kiss to her temple. "One way or another, my bride's father is going to give her away."

She held him tighter, deeply touched by his willingness to make her wedding day everything she'd ever imagined. "Oh, Nick. I love you so much."

"I know. I heard you," he said in her ear.

"When?"

"I'm not sure. I just remember your voice coming to me. It was soft and far away, but I could still hear it. You said, 'I love you, Nick. I always will.' "

"I did say that. In the car when Charlie was driving us home. But how could you hear me?"

He shrugged. "Some things defy explanation."

Gillian knew that to be true better than most. She'd seen enough examples during her lifetime, especially lately.

Standing on tiptoes, she wound her arms around Nick's neck. Just as their lips met, they were interrupted.

"I take it the wedding's on?" Charlie said from the doorway. Stevie stood beside him, her small hands clasped together in anticipation.

"It's on," Nick said, giving Gillian a lingering look that let her know exactly what was waiting for her the moment they were alone. "We just have to tie up a few loose ends before we set the date."

"Yippee," Stevie said.

Charlie strode forward and shook Nick's hand. "Congratulations."

"I'm hoping you'll be my best man."

"I'd be honored." His eyes misty, he bent to give Gillian's cheek a kiss. "This is a great day. I'm delighted for you both."

Stevie threw her arms around Gillian's waist. "Can I be your best lady?"

"You're a little young for that." She squeezed Stevie's shoulders. "How about flower girl?"

Stevie grinned up at her. "Awesome."

Awesome was a good word for it, Gillian decided, taking the hand Nick offered.

"You feel like going on a drive later today?" he asked.

"Where to?"

"Florence. I thought we might visit your dad. Check on his surgery Friday. Break the news to him that he's about to become a father-in-law and a grandfather."

If Nick's contacts paid off, he'd also become a free man.

"You sure you're feeling up to it?" she asked.

Even if the Ancients had healed Nick during his commune with them, he must still be exhausted. They all were.

"Tired and sore," he said. "But nothing a shower, nap, and something to eat won't fix."

A shower, nap, and something to eat. After everything they'd been through the last month, it sounded so mundane.

And wonderful!

Gillian was more than ready to trade her job of creature hunter for something routine and unexciting, like college professor, author, wife, and mother— which sounded anything but routine and unexciting now that she thought about it.

She gazed around the kitchen at the three people who'd recently come into her life, turned it upside down, then changed it into something new and incredible. Tears pricked her eyes.

"Hey. Are you okay?" Nick gazed at her with concern. He wasn't the only one. So did Charlie and Stevie.

"I'm fine." She smiled at them and then laughed. "Fantastic—actually."

"You think your dad'll be okay with us getting married?"

"Of course."

"Are you sure? I don't think he likes me much."

"Don't be ridiculous."

"I corrupted and nearly killed his daughter."

"There is that."

Nick pulled her into his arms. His mouth captured hers in a kiss that promised a long and joyous future together.

Gillian hadn't obtained the proof she'd been seeking to free her father. Instead, she found something else. Something better. Love with a man who completed her like no other and the family she'd always wanted. It had taken a long time, but she'd finally come full circle.

And with their destinies fulfilled, they were free to live their lives as they wished, happy and safe from the creatures.

At least for the next twenty-five years.